We hope you enjoy this book. Please return or
renew it by the due date.

You can renew it at www.norfolk.gov.uk/libraries or
by using our free library app.

Otherwise you can phone 0344 800 8020 -
please have your library card and PIN ready.

You can sign up for email reminders too.

NORFOLK ITEM

30129 086 097 392

NORFOLK COUNTY COUNCIL
LIBRARY AND INFORMATION SERVICE

'A quaint British cozy, complete with characters who are both
likeable and quirky'
Rosalee Richland

MURDER AFTER MIDNIGHT

LESLEY COOKMAN

ACCENT

First published in 2021 by Headline Accent
An imprint of HEADLINE PUBLISHING GROUP

1

Cataloguing in Publication Data is available from the British Library

ISBN 978 1 4722 7832 6

Typeset in 10.5/13pt Bembo Std by Jouve (UK), Milton Keynes

Printed and bound in Great Britain by Clays Ltd, Elcograf S.p.A.

MIX
Paper from
responsible sources
FSC® C104740

Headline's policy is to use papers that are natural, renewable and recyclable
products and made from wood grown in well-managed forests and other
controlled sources. The logging and manufacturing processes are expected
to conform to the environmental regulations of the country of origin.

HEADLINE PUBLISHING GROUP
An Hachette UK Company
Carmelite House
50 Victoria Embankment
London
EC4Y 0DZ

www.headline.co.uk
www.hachette.co.uk

Character List

Libby Sarjeant
Former actor and part-time artist, mother to Dominic, Belinda and Adam Sarjeant and owner of Sidney the cat. Resident of 17 Allhallow's Lane, Steeple Martin.

Fran Wolfe
Former actor and occasional psychic. Owner of Balzac the cat and resident of Coastguard Cottage, Nethergate.

Ben Wilde
Libby's significant other. Owner of The Manor Farm and the Oast House Theatre.

Guy Wolfe
Fran's husband and father to Sophie Wolfe. Artist and owner of a shop and gallery in Harbour Street, Nethergate.

Peter Parker
Freelance journalist and part-owner of The Pink Geranium restaurant. Ben's cousin and Harry Price's partner.

Harry Price
Chef and co-owner of The Pink Geranium. Peter Parker's partner.

DCI Ian Connell
Local policeman and friend. Fran's former suitor.

DS Rachel Trent
DCI Connell's colleague.

Hetty Wilde
Ben's mother. Lives at The Manor.

Flo Carpenter
Hetty's oldest friend.

Lenny Fisher
Hetty's brother. Lives with Flo Carpenter.

Jane Baker
Chief reporter for the Nethergate Mercury.

Reverend Patti Pearson
Vicar at St Aldeberge.

Anne Douglas
Librarian and Reverend Patti's friend and partner.

Edward Hall
Academic and historian.

Colin Hardcastle and Gerry Hall
Steeple Martin's newest residents.

Mike Farthing
Owner of Farthing's Plants and partner of Libby's cousin Cassandra.

Jemima Routledge
Landscape gardener.

Tim Stevens
Landlord of The Coach and Horses, Steeple Martin.

Sid
Landlord of The Poacher, Shott.

George
Landlord of The Red Lion, Heronsbourne.

Frank and Brenda
Landlords of The Fox, Creekmarsh.

Dame Amanda Knight
Doyenne of the theatrical world.

Lewis Osbourne-Walker
Owner of the Creekmarsh estate; assisted by his mother Edie.

Chapter One

'Did you hear about the murder over near Heronsbourne?' asked the
Reverend Patti Pearson one Wednesday evening in the pub.

'No!' Libby Sarjeant sat up straight. 'What murder?'

'I'm surprised, you knowing Lewis Osbourne-Walker so well.'
Patti grinned.

'What's he got to do with it?' asked Libby, alarmed.

'Well, his estate borders the golf course, doesn't it?'

Lewis owned the Creekmarsh estate and conference-cum-wedding
venue, and ran it with the help of his mother Edie.

'Golf course?' echoed Libby.

Libby's partner, Ben Wilde, groaned softly. 'Why did you mention murder?'

'You'll have to explain now,' said Patti's friend and partner Anne
Douglas, laughing.

'Come on, Patti.' Libby leant forward across the table. 'Explain!'

'You know the golf course, I suppose?'

'It leads off the road past Heronsbourne on the way to Creekmarsh,
doesn't it?' said Ben. 'Borders the shoreline.'

Patti nodded. 'Well, they found a body there the other day.'

'And it was – suspicious?'

'You're hanging this out, young Patti.' Peter Parker, tall and
ascetic, with fair hair flopping artistically over his brow, returned
from the bar with a tray of drinks. 'As far as was reported, Libby,
dear sleuth, it was believed to be connected to a rather wild New

1

Year's Eve party in the clubhouse. And this has revived all the ire of local protesters over the redevelopment.'

'Now you're doing it!' burst out Libby. 'I don't know anything about this! And why don't I?'

'Even I knew about the redevelopment row,' said Ben. 'What happened was—'

'Hello, dear hearts.' Harry Price, Peter's partner and chef-patron of The Pink Geranium restaurant, appeared among them. 'I'm gasping.'

'You're early,' said Libby.

'Very quiet. First week in January, ain't it? No one's got any money to go gadding about to restaurants. Now, what were you talking about?'

'Murder!' said everybody.

'Oh, gadzooks!' said Harry, leaning back in his chair. 'We've only just got over the last one!'

'I was just explaining,' said Ben, while Peter went to fetch Harry's drink. 'The Heronsbourne Golf Club was having a bit of a problem – oh, must be four years ago? Five? Falling numbers, that sort of thing; people don't want to join a club with ridiculous rules on clothing and women's membership, and a fairly tatty clubhouse.'

'I'll say,' said Harry gloomily. 'I did some catering there once.'

'So they decided – the committee did – to sell it off and close the club.'

'I bet that went down well,' said Anne.

Ben nodded. 'Exactly. So that was the first protest.'

'The first?' said Libby.

'Yes. The members revolted. So in the end the proposal was revised, and they sold off a corner of it next to the creek – you remember the creek? – and built three or four luxury houses, right opposite where the sailing club used to be on the edge of Lewis's land. Then they relaxed some of the rules – losing a few members in the process – and decided to build a new clubhouse in order to cash in on the thriving party and wedding reception market. And that was the second protest.'

'Why? Good idea, I'd have thought,' said Harry.

2

'Access is by a private drive leading off the Heronsbourne road, and there are a few very nice properties along there. The owners argued that there would be an increase in late-night drunken behaviour, bad parking – you know the sort of thing. And the residents of Heronsbourne felt much the same.'

Libby was staring at her beloved with her mouth open. 'How on earth do you know all this?'

Ben laughed. 'Don't forget I've been mixing with builders and decorators over at The Hop Pocket for the last six months! They get about.'

'OK – so what has this got to do with murder?' asked Harry.

'A body was found on the golf course last week,' said Patti.

'And apparently there are two schools of thought – one that it was after a rowdy New Year's Eve party in the new clubhouse, and another that it was something to do with the protesters,' said Anne.

'Doesn't seem likely to me,' said Peter. 'And please, my dear old trout,' he waved a forefinger at Libby, 'don't go poking your nose in.'

'No reason to, have I?' replied Libby, and returned to her drink.

The following morning Libby's phone rang.

'Morning, Lib!' came Lewis Osbourne-Walker's cheerful cockney voice.

'Lewis! How are you? Haven't heard from you since before Christmas.'

'Oh, I'm all right. How are you?'

'I'm fine. How's Edie?'

'Yeah, she's fine too. Listen, Lib—'

'Patti was telling us about the murder at the golf club near you the other day. What have you heard about it?''

'Ah.' Lewis's voice changed. 'Well . . . actually, that was why I was calling.' He sighed heavily.

'And?' said Libby, when he seemed to want a prompt.

'It's nothing, in a way, but . . .'

'Come on, Lewis! You wouldn't have called me if you weren't involved.'

'Not involved exactly, but . . . Well, I'm sort of on the edge, if you know what I mean.'

'Not really, no. What *do* you mean?'

There was a short pause.

'You remember the creek? Well, on the other side of the creek is the golf course. There's a sort of private drive that runs alongside the houses there. Big new ones.'

'Oh, yes. I've heard about them, and the protests.'

'That's what I got involved in. The protests.'

'You?' Libby was surprised. 'I didn't think you were into all that.'

'Not normally, no, but people kept asking me.' Lewis gave a nervous laugh, 'it was very awkward.'

'I can imagine,' Libby made a face. 'Which side were you on?'

'That was the trouble – neither. Look . . .' Lewis sighed. 'I don't suppose you could come over, could you?'

'Is it that urgent?' Now Libby was worried.

'Probably not. It's just – I just need to talk to someone.'

'What about Edie?' Lewis's mum was a down to earth Londoner.

'I don't want to worry her.'

'If she sees me there she'll worry straight away.'

Lewis laughed. 'Don't worry about Edie. Can you come?'

'When?'

'Er – soon as you like?'

Libby did a quick review of her day. 'After lunch?'

'You can come to lunch here if you like.'

'That would mean getting involved with Edie.'

'That's a point. OK, after lunch. Or – how about meeting at The Fox for a sandwich?'

'Are Frank and Bren still there?'

'Yeah – still plodding on. I think he's got a bit of an emotional attachment to the place.'

'OK – good idea. About one?'

After she hung up, Libby sat for a moment thinking, then called Fran.

4

'Hello,' said Fran warily. 'What's happened?'

'Why would you think anything's happened? Can't I phone for friendly chat?'

'Not at eleven o'clock on a Thursday morning, no. Friendly chats are at teatime.'

'Oh . . .'

'Come on, out with it.'

'Lewis just rang,' said Libby in a rush.

'That's nice. How is he?'

'No, listen – he wants our help. Well, mine anyway.'

'You're not making sense.' Fran sounded impatient. 'If you're getting us involved with something so soon after the last one . . .'

'Er—'

'You *are*! Oh, *Libby*!'

'Listen.' Libby took a deep breath. 'Patti came to the pub last night and asked if I'd heard about the murder at Heronsbourne Golf Club.'

'Don't think I remember a golf course at Heronsbourne.'

'I didn't either. Anyway, there is one and last week, New Year, I think, they found a body there. So this morning, just now, in fact, Lewis rang up and asked me over for a chat because he says he's involved in some way.'

'In the murder?' Fran was horrified.

'With the protests at the golf club, I think. It's quite complicated. So I've agreed to meet him at The Fox for lunch. Frank and Bren are still there.'

'I can't come,' said Fran instantly.

'I'm not asking you to,' said Libby with a sigh. 'I just thought you might be interested.'

'Ring me when you get back from seeing Lewis.'

'At teatime?' Libby grinned.

'At teatime,' confirmed Fran.

It was a typical grey and gloomy January day as Libby drove along the coast road towards Creekmarsh. She kept an eye out for the turning to the golf club, which was easy to spot as it sported a shiny new sign announcing itself. Funny she'd never noticed it before. Opposite the turning to Creekmarsh and the little church, she pulled in beside The Fox, a slightly lopsided, seventeenth-century building. She was the only one in the car park.

"'S all right! I'm here!' Lewis appeared in the doorway. 'I walked up. If Edie had heard the car, she'd have wanted to know where I was going.'

Libby allowed herself to be kissed on the cheek. 'So what's this all about then?'

'What d'you want to drink first? And eat? Bren does a great sausage bake.'

'Will she make me a cup of tea, do you think?' Libby sat down at a table near the fireplace. 'And OK, I'll have the sausage bake.'

Food and drink ordered, Lewis came and sat opposite her and looked into the fire.

'Come on, Lewis. Out with it.' Libby slipped out of her coat.

He frowned at her. 'What happened to your cape? You always wore your cape.'

'It got tatty. Don't change the subject.'

'Right.' Lewis sighed. 'Well, you've already heard about the protests about the golf club, you said.'

'Yes.'

'What, exactly?'

'First that they were going to close it, then they were going to build new houses and a new clubhouse. Apparently the local residents were worried there would be more noise. Is that right?'

'More or less,' said Lewis gloomily.

'And who wanted you involved?'

'The members of the club approached me, saying what a crying shame it would be to close them down, but I told 'em what I thought of their pettifogging rules. They didn't like that.' He smiled reminiscently.

'And the residents?'

6

'That was a bit later, after they'd sold off the little bit of land and had the houses built there. Then they wanted to rebuild the clubhouse and turn it into a venue. The residents didn't like that because of the increased noise—'

'And increase in drunken behaviour. Yes, I heard.'

'Well, I didn't mind them rebuilding the clubhouse, but we already have The Fox and my place, although Creekmarsh caters for a different sort, really.'

'Yes, weddings and conferences and stuff like that.' Libby nodded. 'So you joined that protest?'

'Not officially, especially when they started trying to stop lorries getting up the access road. It all got a bit – er – oh, I dunno.'

'Militant?' suggested Libby.

'S'pose so. But there was this other group. Residents who *did* want the venue. Like that girl.'

'What – the victim?'

'Yeah. Jackie something.'

Libby thought for a moment. 'How did you hear about all this?'

Lewis jerked his head towards the bar. 'Bren, mostly.'

'Bren didn't want the venue?'

'She wasn't that worried, although Frank was a bit annoyed. She said the sort of dos they have here are more family parties for regulars and not the same thing at all, although she was a bit worried about the noise – loud music and that sort of thing.'

Libby sat back and regarded him, head on one side. 'So where do you come in? Why did you want to talk to me?'

'That girl. Jackie, She tried to talk Bren round.'

'So?'

'And she had a go at me.' He looked uncomfortable. 'A right go.'

'When?'

'The night she was killed.'

Chapter Two

Libby stared. 'You're joking!'

Lewis gave a miserable little laugh. 'Wish I was.'

'So what happened? Where were you?'

Frank arrived just then with their sausage bakes, followed by Bren with Libby's cup of tea. When they had retreated to the bar, Lewis returned to his story.

'We had a sort of party, see, for all the employees, it being New Year. Nothing formal, just a jolly. And Jackie, well, she'd done a bit of casual waiting for me during the summer. So she came along with a couple of the other girls.'

'And had a go at you while enjoying your hospitality? What a bloody cheek!'

'She started off by saying we were too posh for this sort of thing. Me! Posh!'

Libby was amused. 'But you do provide a very upmarket venue and standard of catering.'

Lewis brightened. 'Do you think so?'

'Oh, Lewis! Of course you do.'

'Anyway, she went on and on, telling me I should be supporting ordinary people, not . . . well, she wasn't very nice about my clients.'

'I can imagine. Where does she live, this girl?'

'Not so much a girl, really. In her thirties maybe? Lives down the road a bit. Pedlar's Row in Heronsbourne. Near The Red Lion. Or lived . . .'

'I know it well,' said Libby. 'Fran and I got quite friendly with George at The Red Lion.'

Lewis sighed. 'Is there a publican you *don't* know in the area?'

'What happened next?' asked Libby, ignoring this sally.

'I asked her to leave. Well, she was upsetting everybody, not just me.'

'So not universally liked then?'

'Didn't seem to be. None of the others went with her. Mum was a bit put out.'

'Edie wouldn't approve of bad manners, would she?' said Libby.

'No,' said Lewis, smiling. 'Mum's old school.'

'I wonder where she went next.' Libby dug into her sausage bake. 'What time did she leave?'

'Oh, Gawd, I don't know. Nine-thirty? Ten-ish? I'm afraid we all forgot about her after that.'

'Have the police spoken to you yet?'

'No.' Lewis looked up nervously. 'D'you think I should tell 'em?'

'I would, before someone else does.'

'Who?'

'One of the other guests at the party. They'll have asked around to find out where she was. Did she live with anyone?'

'No idea. I don't even know if she was from round here. Wasn't from London, anyhow.'

'Well,' said Libby, 'I think you should talk to the police and I'll go to The Red Lion and see if George knows anything about her. He used to know everybody in Pedlar's Row.'

'Did he?' Lewis looked interested.

'It's a long story.' Libby grinned at him. 'One day, I'll write a book.'

'No one'd believe it.' Lewis grinned back. 'Who do I speak to in the police? Lovely Ian?'

'I don't know who's in charge of this, but probably no one we know. Do you know anyone at the golf club?'

'Couple of people.' Lewis pulled a face. 'I'm not their sort. Why?'

'They'd know who's in charge. They'll have been asked.'

9

Lewis sighed. 'All right, I'll ask.'

Frank appeared at the table.

'Everything all right?' he asked. 'You look a bit serious.'

'Oh, it's this murder,' said Lewis. 'I don't s'pose you've been questioned by the çops, have you?'

Frank beamed. ''Course we have! We came up in all the protests, so there we are – a couple with a motive.'

'You?' Libby was shocked. 'Why?'

'We were supposed to be against this venue business. We didn't think it would affect us, but there. The police have always been a bit suspicious of us since that other business.'

'Stupid buggers,' said Lewis.

'Why did you want to know anyway?' asked Frank.

'Lewis needs to speak to them. Do you know who he should speak to?'

'What for?' Frank was frowning.

Lewis explained.

'Not surprised you threw her out,' Frank continued. 'Silly mare. Anyway, I was told to ask for a DS Stone. They all work out of Canterbury these days, so it'll be that phone number. I reckon you need to look into it, young Libby, you and that Fran.' Frank looked curiously at Libby. 'Or is that what you're here for?'

'I asked her to come,' said Lewis. 'I was worried.'

'I can see that.' Frank nodded. 'So you think she ought to look into it, too.'

'Look,' Libby pushed her empty plate away, 'I am *not* a detective. I've got involved in some of these things entirely by accident! And it's the police who've solved the crimes.'

'Not without help from you,' said Frank.

Libby sighed. 'I've said I'll ask some questions, but I don't know any of the people involved, so I won't be much help.'

'You didn't know us,' said Lewis and Frank together.

Libby laughed. 'I met you, Lewis, through my son, and I met you, Frank, through Lewis. So not quite the same.'

10

'Anyway, you're going to look into it, aren't you?' said Lewis hopefully.

'I told you, I'll ask some questions.'

Frank gave her a knowing look and returned to the bar.

'Right, is there anything else you can tell me about the situation?' Libby leant back and surveyed Lewis.

'Like what?'

'I don't know — when exactly she was found? Where?'

'New Year's Day and on the golf course. Don't know any more.'

'Oh, well, I'll ask some questions, as I said.' Libby stood up. 'Give my love to Edie.'

'You're going?' Lewis looked startled.

'Yes, I need to get back.' Libby smiled at him. 'Thanks for the lunch. I'll ring you.'

Libby turned right out of the car park and drove back towards Heronsbourne reflecting on what she'd been told. It certainly didn't seem as though there was anything for Lewis to worry about, or, indeed, much for Libby to look into. But, following her promise, she drew into the familiar car park next to The Red Lion. As usual, George the landlord was sitting at the end of the bar with a newspaper.

'Well, look who's here!' he said, standing up with a broad grin. 'And I bet I know why.'

'Oh?' Libby returned the grin, hoisting herself on to a bar stool.

George brandished the newspaper. 'This!'

Libby glanced at the headline displayed. 'Now why would you think that?'

'Body on the golf course? Soon as there's a local murder, you turn up.'

Libby sighed. 'What an indictment. Yes, all right. I was told she lived here, in Pedlar's Row.'

'She did that. Just down from your mate's house, March Cottage.'

'Not so much a mate, George. Haven't heard of her for years.'

'Suppose not,' said George, looking sombre. 'Sold ages ago, March Cottage.'

Libby and her best friend, Fran, had first come across March Cottage, Pedlar's Row, and indeed George himself, during a previous adventure, which had had one happy result in that Fran had adopted Balzac the cat.

'So, you knew this girl?'

'Jackie? Yes. Part of a crowd, she was. They come in here regular. Not that I've seen her much recently. Want a coffee?'

'No, thanks, I've just had tea up at The Fox.'

George raised his eyebrows. 'I've got competition, have I?'

'I met Lewis there for lunch.'

'Lewis from Creekmarsh? Hmm. He will have been asked about the golf club business, won't he?'

'If you mean the protests, yes. Were you?'

George nodded. 'Not that it's anything to do with me. I'm a bit far away for it to cause me any trouble and I don't do functions, as such. Some of them were all for it, some of young Jackie's crowd, f'r instance.'

'Were they?' Libby leant her elbows on the bar.

'Stands to reason. Not much to do for youngsters round here. Not that they're that young, Jackie's crowd. Thirties and forties mostly.'

'You know them well, then?'

George put his head on one side, considering. 'As well as I know most regulars, some better than others. Not real mates, though.'

'Anyone I could talk to?'

He narrowed his eyes at her. 'Investigation, is it, then?'

Libby shrugged. 'Lewis wanted my advice. She worked for him sometimes.'

'Ah. Bit of a handful was she?'

'We-ell . . .' said Libby.

'Ah.' George nodded. 'She did like stirring.'

'That wouldn't be enough to get her killed, though, would it?'

'Wouldn't have thought so,' said George. 'But I wouldn't know. Only thing I can suggest is you come by for a drink one evening, and if any of her mates are in, I'll introduce you.'

'Better than nothing, I suppose.' Libby slid off her stool. 'Which house in Pedlar's Row was hers? Do you know?'

'Not sure. There's only eight in that row.'

'I suppose it doesn't matter. Thanks, George. You've been a great help.'

George raised his eyebrows again. 'I have?'

'Oh, yes.' Libby grinned. 'You always are.'

Marjorie Sutcliffe stared at the uninspiring lumps of stone which were all that was left of St Cuthbert's Church. Screwing her eyes up against the intrusive January wind, she transferred her gaze to the majestic, gnarled, multi-trunked yew that stood alongside the ruins, then to the wide stretch of tussocked grass between her and the sea.

Far to her right, she was aware of three buildings which presented their grey fronts to the world. She turned her back on them and began to trudge away from St Cuthbert's and towards the road. The wind now teased her ears and she pulled up her coat collar. No need to keep her vigil now. Not for a while.

Libby called Fran as soon as she reached home.

'It's teatime,' she said.

Fran laughed. 'All right – go on.'

Libby told her what she'd learnt from Lewis, Frank and Bren, and George.

'I think I know something about those protests,' said Fran slowly. 'But not what you said earlier.'

'Oh? What, then?'

'It was about destruction of the environment. When the golf club first decided to sell off the site.'

'Oh, I bet I know! They found it was the habitat of some almost extinct beetle!'

'Not quite, but close.' Fran was silent for a moment. 'Apparently, the golf course has some particularly venerable trees, oak and yew mainly, I gather.'

'Yew? I thought they grew in churchyards. There's the one next to the ruins of St Cuthbert's church.'

'They were planted in churchyards. Or near religious sites. To keep off the evil eye, at least, I think so. And apart from them, a lot of the locals were just angry about the area being dug up.'

'That's happening everywhere,' said Libby, 'and I agree it shouldn't happen unless it's absolutely necessary. If it was for low-cost housing, for instance—'

'But it wasn't,' said Fran. 'That blew over, anyway, although they did still get some new housing.'

'Yes,' said Libby darkly. 'Luxury housing.'

'Is it that intrusive?'

'I don't know, I didn't see it.'

'So it's really just a lot of stick-in-the-muds disapproving of noise?' said Fran.

'If you like to put it like that,' said Libby, 'but I do see their point. It's a very quiet, residential country area, not a major town centre ready for Saturday night frolics.'

'No, I see that. If that girl – what's her name?'

'Jackie.'

'If Jackie wanted that sort of fun, why didn't she go off to Canterbury or Maidstone? Why stay here?'

'Even worse than here,' said Libby, 'if you mean Nethergate.'

'Oh, you know what I mean. The area. All the way from St Aldeberge right past Creekmarsh – it's just rural. Not a hen party in sight.'

'Yes, I suppose it is odd.' Libby thought for a moment. 'I don't suppose you fancy popping over to George's for a drink one evening?'

'I can't think of a good reason. Why would we go? We'd stand out like a couple of sore thumbs. It's not even as if we'd be going to meet Lewis.'

'We could!' said Libby. 'That's a great excuse.'

'Oh, come on, Libby! You've been and given Lewis advice – as long as he takes it – what else are you supposed to do?'

14

'I don't know,' said Libby. 'Nothing, I suppose.'
'Exactly,' said Fran. 'You are *not* involved.'
'No, you're right, I'm not,' said Libby.

It was very nearly seven o'clock when her mobile rang.
'Hello, Libby,' said a familiar voice.
'Hello, Ian,' said Libby.

Chapter Three

Ben appeared at the bottom of the stairs looking vaguely concerned.

'Surprised to hear from me?' Detective Chief Inspector Ian Connell went on. 'You shouldn't be, considering a murder has been committed in the area.'

'But it isn't anything to do with me!' protested Libby.

'Well, no, I didn't think it was either, until your name came up this afternoon.'

Libby's breath caught in her throat. 'How?'

'When Lewis Osbourne-Walker gave a voluntary statement to DS Stone, he mentioned that it was on your advice. DS Stone, who has her head screwed on, recognised your name and decided to tell me. Being a stickler, she did of course report it to DI Winters, who is technically SIO.'

'I see,' said Libby whose heart was still beating erratically, 'is it a problem?'

'Could you just tell me how it came about?' asked Ian.

Libby cast an agonised look at Ben and swallowed hard.

'Lewis called me this morning wanting advice. So I told him to tell the police. I thought I was doing the right thing.'

'Admirable,' said Ian. 'And then you proceeded to talk to Frank at The Fox and George at The Red Lion.'

'Yes.'

'Hmm.' Ian was silent for what seemed like minutes. 'And did you find anything out? About the victim, for instance?'

Libby repeated what she had been told.

'And I assume you are now eaten up with curiosity?'

'Er, well, I – um. Well, of course—'

'Of course you are. Would it do any good if I told you to keep out of it?'

Libby felt herself going red. She heard Ian sigh.

'As I'm driving past your pub this evening to pick up Edward, would you like to meet me there for a drink?'

'Really?'

'Yes, really.' Ian laughed. 'I might as well give you an outline. You'll only ferret it out on your own otherwise.'

'Oh.'

'Yes. I'll see you about eight, shall I?'

'Yes. Thank you,' said Libby and heard silence.

'Are you in trouble?' asked Ben as she put down the phone.

'He wants us to have a drink this evening.' Libby shook her head. 'I'm not sure what he wants.'

'Are we going?'

'Oh, yes.' Libby gave him a crooked smile. 'Might as well find out.'

When they arrived at the pub, they found Edward and Ian deep in conversation with one of the regulars.

'Hi!' Edward flashed his broad white grin at them. 'You know Philip, don't you?'

Philip Jacobs, every inch the country solicitor, beamed. 'Certainly they do. And as I was just trying to persuade Edward to join our newly formed quiz team, could I persuade any of you?'

Ian and Ben both jabbed Libby in the ribs and spoke together quickly. Libby looked indignant.

'I can never guarantee being free,' said Ian.

'Sounds like a good idea,' said Ben. 'When is it?'

'I'll get the drinks,' muttered Ian and Libby scowled.

'Very ad hoc, so far,' said Philip. 'Like the chess club. But Tim liked the idea. We can play your pub, Ben, when it's open.'

Ben sighed. 'I'm not sure it'll ever be open,' he said. 'Everything's taking more time than I thought.'

'Really?' Philip looked concerned. 'Oh, that is a shame.'

'Well, we'll see,' said Ben. 'Anyway, yes, the quiz sounds a good idea. Is it just teams from here?'

'So far – but it would be good to have inter-pub nights, wouldn't it?' Philip looked over at Tim, who had just finished serving Ian's order.

Tim grinned. 'Ask Libby! She knows all the local pubs!'

Philip sent Libby an eager glance. 'Really?'

'Yes,' said Libby, and sighed.

Ian dispensed the drinks and they retired to a table in the corner, while Philip remained at the bar.

'Now, are you going to tell me what this is all about?' asked Libby.

'You know most of it,' said Ian. 'The victim was found early on New Year's Day in a shallow bunker on the Heronsbourne Golf Course.'

'New Year golfers?' suggested Ben.

'No, the ubiquitous dog walker,' said Ian. 'They aren't supposed to, but they walk along the shoreline. The dog, as dogs do, sniffed out the victim.'

'You'd think murderers would find rather better hiding places, wouldn't you?' said Libby with a shudder. 'After all, the golfers would have found her soon enough.'

'Perhaps he didn't care,' said Ian.

'Oh, it was a he, then?'

'We don't know yet, but it was vicious enough.' Ian frowned. 'Anyway, what did you glean from Lewis and George about her?'

'Only that she worked occasionally for Lewis, as I've told you, she kicked up a rumpus at his staff party, and George didn't seem enamoured, despite the fact that she was more or less a regular. Oh, and she lived in a cottage in the same row as March Cottage.'

'Yes, we knew that. Jackie Stapleton, her name was. Day job in a café in Nethergate.'

'So why did you want to see me?' asked Libby.

Ian regarded her thoughtfully. 'Because you frequently winkle out information we don't get.'

Libby and Ben looked at one another.

'And?' said Libby.

'You might be able to find out a few things we can't.'

'You're asking her to help again?' Ben sounded incredulous.

'Yes.' Ian looked vaguely uncomfortable. 'And Fran.'

'Well,' said Libby, after a fraught silence, 'George did suggest going along there one evening when her crowd were in.'

'And just start asking questions?' said Ben. 'How to look suspicious in one easy lesson . . .'

'Oh, I think we could come up with an excuse,' said Ian. 'Don't you, Libby?'

'I expect so,' said Libby, sending Ben a wary look. 'And you could always come too, Ben.'

Ben sighed.

'So far,' said Ian, 'all our investigations have come up with is that she lived alone – mostly – and had a temper. She doesn't seem to have had many friends, except one or two we've uncovered, but perhaps this crowd George mentioned were close to her.'

Ben sighed again.

'Sorry, Ben.' Ian sent him an apologetic smile. 'But you have to admit, this idea of a pub quiz is a good one!'

'Well, I knew what was coming,' Libby said, as she and Ben walked home later. 'All a bit of a set-up if you ask me.'

'It did rather fall into Ian's lap,' said Ben with a grin. 'So you'll call George in the morning, will you?'

'Yes!' said Libby irritably. 'And Frank and Bren for verisimilitude.'

'Good idea,' said Ben, smirking. 'See! You're getting into it, now.'

Libby made a noise like an expiring balloon and stalked ahead.

She was still suffering from a sense of ill usage the following morning when she called Fran.

'I don't know what you're annoyed about,' said Fran. 'It's a brilliant idea. And perfect for finding stuff out. Can I be on the team?'

'I suppose so,' grumbled Libby. 'But then we'll have to ask The Sloop, as well.'

'What's wrong with that?' asked Fran.

'We could end up having to do quiz nights every week at this rate!'

'I repeat – what's wrong with that?'

'Oh, all right!' Libby gave in with a sigh. 'And actually, Tim's getting in touch with George today. Apparently he and Ian arranged it after Ben and I left last night. I'll let you know how it turns out.'

'I know what's wrong with you,' said Fran. 'You're annoyed because you didn't think this up yourself.'

'I'm not!' protested Libby, albeit a little guiltily.

A little later that morning, she was surprised to receive a phone call from someone else.

'Hi! Remember me?'

'Jemima!' Libby beamed. She had met Jemima Routledge during the recent investigation in which she and Fran had been involved. 'Nice to hear from you. Is it too late to say Happy New Year?'

'Of course not. Anyway, by an extraordinary coincidence, I think we're going to meet again.'

'Oh?'

'Well, if it's true you're bringing a quiz team to The Red Lion?'

Silence fell.

'Libby?' Jemima sounded worried.

Libby sighed. 'Yes, it's true. How did you hear about it? If it's The Red Lion at Heronsbourne?'

'Yes. And I heard about it because that's where I meet up with friends now and then.'

'The Red Lion?' Libby almost squeaked.

'Yes . . . Anything wrong?'

20

'No.' Libby paused. 'Did George say anything else?'

'Like what? I went in today to pick up my veg box—'

'Veg box?'

'Yes. George gets his veg from a local farm shop and offered to add my order on to his. First week we've done it.'

'Oh, right. And?'

'And what? Oh, did he say anything else? Well, yes – he said he thought you'd organised it and did I want to be involved.'

'Is that all?'

'Yes – what else could he have said?'

Libby thought for a moment.

'Listen – do you fancy meeting up for a drink? I'll come over to The Red Lion if you like?'

'Just what I was going to suggest!' Jemima sounded happy. 'Unless you'd like me to come over to Steeple Martin?'

'Well – perhaps that might be better. Today?' suggested Libby rashly.

'About an hour?'

'Great. See you then.' Libby ended the call, reflecting on the imponderable workings of providence.

However, she thought, it wasn't that much of a coincidence. They both lived in the same area, and, as Jemima had said when they first met, they had many links via their respective occupations, if Libby could be said to have an occupation. Jemima was a landscape gardener, while Libby's son Adam worked with a garden designer and her cousin's partner was a nurseryman, not to mention the fact that her local farm shop owner had known Jemima and her father for years. And Libby's penchant for falling headfirst into local mysteries meant that she had built up a network of contacts of all types throughout the area.

And, Libby continued to herself, it was unreasonable to be annoyed that Jemima hadn't mentioned having other local friends before.

Tim looked surprised when she walked into the pub an hour later

21

and ordered a snack, but merely raised his eyebrows, nodding knowingly when Jemima followed five minutes afterwards.

'How often do you go over to Heronsbourne?' Libby asked when they were settled at the table by the fireplace. 'I didn't know you had friends in that neck of the woods.'

Jemima laughed. 'Oh, I'm a bit like you! Friends all over the place! I first met John and Sue when I did their garden years ago.'

'Oh, I see.' Libby bit into her sandwich, not knowing what to say next. She didn't need to.

'And George tells me there's been a murder and you're looking into it.' Jemima cocked her head on one side.

'Mmm.' Libby nodded. So did Jemima, who grinned.

'And,' she said, 'it's one of John and Sue's neighbours.'

Chapter Four

Libby was too startled to speak.

'I thought that would surprise you,' said Jemima, still grinning. 'That's really why George mentioned it. They aren't neighbours in the next-door kind, they live sort of behind Pedlar's Row. Do you know where the victim lived?'

'Er – yes. I used to know someone who lived in the same row of cottages.'

'Pretty, aren't they?' said Jemima. 'Anyway, George said that your landlord here had been in touch about this quiz thing and would I be on your team or his. Not that I live in either place.'

'Oh!' Libby cast a slightly annoyed glance over at Tim. 'I thought he was going to let me speak to George.'

'I don't know about that,' said Jemima, finishing the last of her sandwich. 'So what about this quiz team, then?'

'I don't know. I don't know how many we're supposed to have for a start. We've got me, Ben, Edward, Fran – I don't know about Guy – and a chap called Philip Jacobs, who's a solicitor or something.' Libby sat back in her chair. 'I suppose I ought to find out. It looks as though the whole thing's on, doesn't it?' She grinned. 'I'll go and ask Tim.'

'I thought,' she said, approaching the bar with what she hoped was a forbidding stare, 'you wanted me to talk to George.'

Tim smiled. 'You didn't look too happy last night, so I thought I'd do it. We've got George, and Frank at The Fox – oh, and Sid at The Poacher over in Shott already.'

23

'We haven't got to go to all of them, have we?' asked Libby nervously.'

'Eventually, but Frank's coming here, so's Sid. At first, at least. We're going to George though. How would Monday suit you?'

'*This* Monday?'

'You want it to be soon, don't you?'

'I suppose so.' Libby glanced over to Jemima. 'And how many in the team?'

'Maximum of eight.' Tim nodded over to the fireside table. 'Your friend joining in?'

'Is that all right? She doesn't live here. In fact, she lives near Shott. And it was George who told her about the quiz.'

'Oh, come on! We're too new to be precious about ringers!' laughed Tim. 'Anyway, I've signed up for the questions – there's a website you can join, you see—'

'Yes, well, I'll leave it to you,' said Libby hastily. 'I'll tell Jemima.'

Jemima was delighted. 'And I'll stay with John and Sue so I can have a drink.'

'You might want to join your home team, though,' said Libby. 'Tim's signed up Sid at The Poacher.'

'But I hardly ever go there, so I'd rather be on your team.' Jemima settled back and smiled. 'So, now, tell me about the murder.'

The first Monday Night Quiz League quiz turned out to be quite an occasion. All the landlords of the pubs signed up so far were present to cheer on their teams, or, as Tim said, to see how it all worked. George, with a not-so-subtle wink at Libby, had talked a few of the murder victim's friends into being on his team, although one of the women confided to Libby that she felt a bit awkward.

'It feels a bit disrespectful,' she said.

'Oh, why is that?' Libby asked.

'One of our friends was murdered on New Year's Day,' said her informant. 'Did you not hear about it?'

'Yes, of course, Jackie Stapleton,' said Libby. 'She was a friend of yours, was she?'

'Well, yes. In a way. She was nearly always with us when we met up in here.' She pulled a face.

'That doesn't look as if you were pleased about it,' said Libby, with a short laugh.

The woman looked guilty. 'I didn't like her much.'

'Ah.' Libby smiled. 'I won't say a word.'

And I'm a terrible liar, she thought.

The first few rounds of the quiz seemed to go well, although team members did have to be reminded not to shout out the answers several times. When George, acting as quiz master, called half-time, there was a general rush for the bar. That was when Libby's previous acquaintance buttonholed her again.

'I know who you are, now,' she said. 'You're the woman who does the murders.'

Fran, sitting beside Libby, snorted with laughter.

'With my friend here,' said Libby, fixing Fran with a baleful stare. 'Who told you?'

'My friend over there.' The woman nodded at her table. 'He lived in Pedlar's Row when that woman from March Cottage—'

'Yes, yes,' Libby interrupted. 'That was ages ago.'

'Oh, yes. Jackie didn't live there then. I'm Chrissie, by the way.'

'Libby, and this is Fran. So your friend knew Jackie, as well?'

'We all did,' said Chrissie. 'Dan remembers you took that black and white cat away. He was worried about it.'

Fran laughed. 'Tell him to stop worrying! I adopted him and he now lives in a seafront cottage in Nethergate.'

Chrissie grinned. 'I'll tell Dan. So – are you here because of Jackie?'

'Not really.' Libby crossed her fingers under the table. 'We're all regulars at the pub in Steeple Martin and were there when this idea came up.'

To her relief, at this point, George called for the start of the second half.

An hour later and Sid's team from The Poacher were announced the winners with the Steeple Martin team a respectable second. George stood by the bar, mopping his brow and beaming, as a steady flow of drinks accrued for him.

'I'll never manage all those,' he confided to Libby, when she went to congratulate him. 'Charities'll do all right this week!'

'It worked well,' said Libby, and lowering her voice, 'and I've had a chat with Chrissie.'

George nodded in the direction of Libby's table. 'On her way to talk to you again, by the looks of things,' he said.

Libby returned to her table. Tim was busy congratulating the men, while Jemima and Fran talked to Chrissie. She turned to Libby.

'Dan reckons you're helping the police again,' she said abruptly. 'And we think you ought to know about Jackie.'

Jemima pushed her chair back and stood. 'I'll go and speak to my friends,' she said. 'Can't ignore them, as they're being nice enough to give me a bed for the night!'

Chrissie, looking worried, watched her go. 'I didn't mean—' she began.

'Jemima knows the score,' said Libby, patting her arm. 'So what does Dan think we ought to know?'

'What she was like,' said a voice behind her.

Libby and Fran turned to find a burly, greying, middle-aged man beaming at them.

'Me and the others all reckon she pushed someone too far.'

'Only a matter of time,' nodded a smaller, dark man, looking wise.

Libby realised that they were now surrounded by the whole team from The Red Lion, all of whom were making sounds of agreement. She sat down and looked around the group.

'Tell us, then,' she said. 'Only bear in mind that if it's relevant the police will have to hear about it.'

26

Dan had obviously been voted spokesperson, and pulled Edward's abandoned chair round to face Libby. 'Well, see,' he said, 'she was a stirrer.'

'We've heard that,' said Fran.

Dan nodded. 'And she was always going on about the golf club.'

'Yes, we heard that too,' said Libby, 'but what did she want to happen? We can't work out quite what was going on there.'

A chorus of voices now tried to tell them exactly what was going on, until Chrissie shouted 'Stop!' She turned back to Libby. 'She was all for the golf club doing all those club night sort of things. Got right pissed off with all the locals who didn't want that.'

'Threw bricks,' added another girl.

'Attacked one woman,' said another.

'Are you sure?' asked Fran. 'This isn't just hearsay?'

'True as I'm standing here,' said Chrissie.

Fran and Libby looked at one another.

'What would she have been doing on the golf course on New Year's Eve?' asked Libby.

'Fu . . . Gawd knows,' pronounced another man gloomily. 'Couldn't work out what she wanted most of the time.'

'Liked being the centre of attention, it sounds like,' said Jemima, who had returned to the table, piping up for the first time.

There were murmurs of assent throughout the group.

'She tried to get us on her side,' said Chrissie. 'Couldn't understand why we didn't want hen nights or stag nights or club nights—'

'Hen nights are the worst,' said one of the men, prompting a gale of laughter.

'Whatever,' said Chrissie with a shrug.

'Who *was* on her side?' asked Fran.

'A few kids,' said George, suddenly appearing at Libby's side, 'some of the golf club members – mostly from out of the area.'

'Oh, of course,' said Libby. 'They wouldn't be upset by the – er – goings-on, would they?'

'Or have to clear up after it,' said the gloomy contributor.

'If it's not a silly question,' said Jemima carefully, 'what was she trying to stir up now? I understood the row was all over?'

'Well, now,' said George. 'It is and it isn't.'

'You didn't tell me any of this,' said Libby, turning to George accusingly.

'I told you some of Jackie's crowd were all for the club thing.'

'Some of them were,' said Dan. 'The younger ones.'

'So, as Jemima said, what was she going on about *now*?' asked Fran.

'It was still the golf club,' another woman piped up from the back of the crowd. 'She wanted to be able to drink there.'

'It wasn't actually that,' said Chrissie. 'She wanted the clubhouse to be a venue sort of place, and one of the things they told her was that she wouldn't be able to use it because she wasn't a member.'

'But if it became a venue,' butted in someone else, 'anyone could go in.'

'And she was still angry because she couldn't drink in there,' continued Chrissie. 'They have extended drinking hours, see.'

George snorted his disapproval and asked if anyone else wanted a drink before closing time.

'Were you her neighbour?' Libby asked Dan as the drinks were ordered.

'Me?' Dan looked startled. 'No!'

'Oh – I thought Chrissie said you lived down Pedlar's Row.'

'Not any more! Wife and I live round the corner from here. Used to, though. That's how I remembered you.' He gave Fran a friendly grin. 'And you rescued that cat? Had a funny name, didn't he?'

'Balzac,' said Fran. 'He's doing very well, thank you.'

George called Libby to the bar and handed her a large scotch.

'Did the takings a bit of good, this did,' he said. 'Good crowd for a Monday night.' He nodded at the drink. 'On the house. Get any information?'

'A bit. Very useful, in my opinion,' said Libby. 'Whether the police will think so's another matter.'

The evening finished with a general round of congratulations as

28

the participants began to drift out of the pub. Libby went over to Jemima to say goodbye and was introduced to her friends.

'John and Sue Cantripp,' said Jemima. 'They knew Jackie!'

The comfortably middle-aged couple beamed and held out their hands.

'Only vaguely,' said Sue.

'Not actually *knew*,' said John.

'No,' said Sue. 'We just live behind Pedlar's Row. We used to see her quite often though.'

'She used to cut through by us from her back gate,' said John. 'We could never work out where she was going. It wasn't exactly a short cut.'

'She always seemed a bit – well – furtive, if you know what I mean.' Sue frowned. 'But maybe that was just me taking too much notice of what I'd heard about her.'

'About her tendency to stir up trouble?' asked Libby.

'Especially with all the golf club business,' said John. 'We didn't fancy the idea of turning it into a nightclub.'

'But of course, we know Hannah Barton quite well,' said Sue, as if that explained everything.

Jemima and Libby looked at each other in puzzlement.

'Oh, didn't you know? Jackie pinched Hannah's fella,' said John.

'Go on, look,' said Jemima. 'Ben's getting agitated. Come over and see them tomorrow. I'll still be there.'

'What was that about?' asked Fran, who was waiting by her car. Libby told her.

'I'll come with you – ring me.' Fran got into the car.

Ben, apart from a dark look, asked no questions, and the drive home was enlivened by discussions about the quiz.

Declining Tim's offer of a nightcap when they arrived in Steeple Martin – after all, it was a Monday – they went home.

'So?' asked Ben, as soon as they were on their own.

'I think we've found out a bit more about our victim,' said Libby.

'What's all this "we" and "our"?' Ben grinned at her.

29

'Ian did ask me to find out about her.' Libby opened the door of number seventeen Allhallow's Lane. 'Would you like a nightcap after all?'

Ben made an exasperated face. 'So that you can tell me all about it?'

'Well, yes,' said Libby with a shamefaced grin.

Ben sighed.

'Those people I was talking to . . .' began Libby when they were seated either side of the fireplace.

'George's team,' said Ben.

'Yes, them. Well, they knew Jackie. And they didn't much like her. And they weren't as dead set on this golf club as a nightclub idea as she was. But the interesting part was Jemima's friends.'

'Is that who you were talking to at the end?'

'Yes. They live right behind Pedlar's Row.'

'Where this woman lived?'

'Yes. And they told me she pinched someone else's boyfriend.'

'That happens all the time though,' said Ben. 'It doesn't usually lead to murder.'

'No, but she *has* been murdered. So worth looking into, don't you think? And it strikes me that all this kerfuffle about the golf club isn't quite what it seems.'

Ben frowned. 'Why? Seems fairly straightforward to me.'

'I could bear to know a bit more about it,' said Libby. 'I shall go and see Jemima's friends, anyway. She suggested it.'

Ben sighed again. 'I just hope they don't turn out to be mad axemen.'

Chapter Five

The following morning, Libby wasn't surprised, on opening her laptop, to find an email from Jemima containing John and Sue's joint email address, along with her suggestion that Fran should accompany the visit. Libby grinned, and typed in the address, forwarding copies of her acceptance to Fran and Jemima.

Within an hour, a meeting had been set up for early afternoon. Fran reported that Guy had expressed similar doubts to Ben's, but had nevertheless accepted the inevitable.

Libby followed Jemima's directions down Pedlar's Row to where a gravel track led off to the left. A band of trees on her right appeared to form the boundary of the golf club, and what looked like a narrow dyke crept alongside it towards the sea. To her surprise, she saw three or four pretty Jersey cows and a few sheep grazing the tussocked ground.

Hobson's, as Jemima had told her John and Sue's house was called, stood alone apart from a couple of small outbuildings. A two-storey brick and timber building, its south-facing windows reflected the grey light. Jemima stood on the gravel driveway, where Fran's car was already parked.

'Come in,' she said. 'The kettle's on.'

In the long, low sitting room, John was settled in a large wingback chair by the fireplace, but rose as they entered and waved at the equally large sofa.

'So this is one of your famous investigations, is it?' asked John. 'Sue's very excited.'

'Not really,' said Libby. 'We were just asked to find out a bit about Jackie Stapleton.'

'I hear you're quite good at it, though,' said John, standing up to take a tray from his wife.

'Good at what, dear?' asked Sue.

'Investigations.' John put the tray down on a coffee table he had pushed forward. 'Eh, Jem?'

Jemima passed mugs to Libby and Fran. 'I think so. I've only been involved in one – and you know all about that.'

Sue sat down opposite John and tucked her feet under herself. 'So – how can we help?'

'You obviously know something about Jackie Stapleton,' said Libby. 'You said something about her stealing someone's boyfriend?'

John and Sue looked at each other. John nodded.

'I hope we're not speaking out of turn,' said Sue. 'But Hannah Barton's a friend of ours.'

'We know her through the amateur dramatic society,' said John. 'And you've got something to do with that, haven't you?'

'Yes.' Libby frowned. 'You don't mean to say you belong to the Oast Theatre group?'

'Oh, no!' Sue laughed. 'Nothing so grand. We've got a little one here in the village.'

'In Heronsbourne?' said Fran, looking surprised.

'George never told us!' said Libby. 'I wonder why?'

'I expect he thought it would be a bit beneath you.' John grinned.

'Honestly!' Libby was indignant. 'I'm not a snob!'

'Anyway,' said Sue, 'we were all members. We only do a silly little pantomime every February. Nothing as grand as yours, of course. Jackie used to join in as long as she could be the princess, or whatever, and kick up a fuss if she couldn't. Hannah was always backstage, or doing teas or something. And Gary was always involved one way or another.'

'And were thcy all involved this year?' asked Fran.

'Hannah is. Or was. We're probably going to cancel, now. But Jackie and Gary weren't. Jackie got him away from Hannah at one of our socials.' Sue looked across at her husband. 'Whitsun, was it?'

'So there are opportunities for – I don't know – fun?' said Libby. 'Why was she so keen on the nightclub idea?'

'Oh, our idea of fun was too old fogeyish for Jackie,' said John.

'But she still always barged in,' said Sue. 'Even at this year's party, although she must have known she wouldn't be welcome.'

'When was that?' asked Fran.

'Our New Year's party on the beach,' said Sue, sounding surprised. 'She turned up late. Didn't you know?'

Libby and Fran stared. Libby became aware that her mouth was hanging open and shut it with a snap.

'No,' she said. 'Did you tell the police?'

'No one's asked us,' said John, also looking surprised. 'We assumed they knew.'

'Perhaps they do,' said Fran, looking across at Libby. 'You'll have to ask.'

'I shall.' Libby shifted in her seat. 'Will you give them a statement if they ask?'

'Of course,' said John. 'Perfectly ordinary party – you know, bonfire, fireworks. Lots of people from the village join in. Everyone brings bottles, fireworks, and something to eat.'

'Only she didn't bring anything,' said Sue, grumpily.

'She'd been at the staff party at Creekmarsh,' said Libby, 'only Lewis had to ask her to leave because she more or less started a fight there.'

'Bloody hell, she was a nightmare,' said John, shaking his head.

'So this Gary, was he at the party?' Libby sipped her rapidly cooling tea.

'No. He split up with Jackie after a few months, but he's been avoiding Hannah ever since. They were practically engaged when Jackie broke them up.' Sue shook her head sadly. 'He's ashamed of himself now, of course. I told him to talk to her – Hannah, not Jackie – but I think he's scared to.'

Libby opened her mouth and Fran butted in hastily.

'Perhaps we'd better not talk to him,' she said. 'You can tell the police, and maybe they can.'

'You can talk to Hannah, though, can't you?' said Sue. 'We usually meet up at the pub on Thursdays. Hannah lives in the village.'

'And she was at the New Year's party on the beach?' queried Fran.

'Yes.' Sue scowled. 'Very difficult. We all tried to keep them apart, but Jackie was determined to get at Hannah.'

'How do you mean, "get at"?' asked Libby.

'She barged in to every conversation Hannah was in, even when it was obvious no one wanted her,' said John. 'I tried to ask her to leave at one point.' He flushed. 'I won't repeat what she said.'

They all murmured appreciation of this.

'Anyway, come down to the pub on Thursday with us,' said Sue. 'Gary and Hannah might be there. At least, one of them might be.'

After this, conversation became more general, although it mostly consisted of John and Sue asking about previous cases in which Libby and Fran had been involved, especially those in St Aldeberge and Felling. As they left, seen off by all three of their hosts, Jemima said she would come on Thursday too.

'I'll follow you to Nethergate,' said Libby to Fran as they reached their cars. 'Is that all right?'

Fran rolled her eyes to the sky, grinned, and got into her car.

'Party on the beach, eh?' said Libby, as soon as she got inside Coastguard Cottage. 'And Jackie gatecrashed it, before being found in a bunker just a little way away. The police *must* know about it, surely?'

Fran switched on her kettle and shrugged out of her coat. 'Ian didn't mention it?' she said.

'No. Seems very odd, doesn't it?' Libby scowled down at Balzac the cat, who had jumped up on to the window seat, waving an insistent paw.

'You've got to tell him what you've found out about Jackie, so you can mention it then. I expect he knows, anyway.'

Libby settled on the window seat. Balzac crawled on to her lap. 'I suppose so. She does seem to have been rather generally disliked, doesn't she?'

'Somebody must have liked her.' Fran poured water into mugs. 'That Gary, for instance.'

'But they split up,' said Libby. 'I wonder why she was like she was?'

'Something in her childhood?' said Fran, bringing the mugs into the sitting room. 'That's what they say, isn't it?'

'Mmm.' Libby took her mug. 'I suppose we'll never know. And I suppose it doesn't matter. Poor girl.'

'She wasn't exactly a girl,' said Fran. 'Sounds as if she was at least in her thirties.'

'Lewis is the one to ask,' said Libby. 'I'm sure he told me that when I met him.'

'Give him a ring then.' Fran sat back in her armchair.

Libby fished out her phone and found Lewis's number.

'Hello, Lib.' Lewis's voice crackled over the line.

'Are you outside?' asked Libby.

'Yes. Hang on – going into the kitchen.' The voice sounded clearer. 'What's up?'

Libby told him what she and Fran had found out about their victim. 'And we want to know what she was really like. We thought you would know. And she was in her thirties, wasn't she?'

'I thought so. Well, I didn't really *know* what she was like. I told you she was a stirrer. Just not very nice. Even Frank said so, didn't he?'

'He called her a silly mare,' said Libby. 'Oh, well, nothing new, then. Everyone seems to have the same opinion. *Someone* must have liked her.'

'Good luck with that,' said Lewis. 'Let me know if you find anything out.'

Libby ended the call and looked across at Fran. 'Nothing new. I'll send Ian a text. Shall we talk about something else?'

★

35

Libby was at home preparing dinner when Ian rang.

'You said you had a report.'

'Nothing much,' said Libby, and told him what she'd found out. 'And you know she'd been at the New Year's party on the beach, don't you.'

'Yes, Lib. So no startling motives jumped out?'

'Only this business with Gary – don't know his surname – and Hannah Barton. Any help?'

'Might be.' He paused. 'But feel free to keep asking.'

'Who will you ask, though?' said Ben when Libby related the conversation.

'Well, we thought we'd go over on Thursday and see if anyone felt like talking.' Libby pushed her plate away. 'And I thought I might go over and have a walk across the marsh. It joins up with the golf club. I might get an idea why people were so stirred up about it.'

'It's marsland, is it?'

'Yes. So is Lewis's land really. That whole sticky-out lump of land is marsh. Must have been drained back at some time. It's not as big as some of the Kent marshes, but it's good agricultural land.'

'Not with a golf course on it, it isn't,' said Ben. 'Or Lewis's ground.'

'No, but it was. I expect Creekmarsh had its land long before it became farmland, and certainly before the golf club. And before the whole area was built up.'

'Lewis's land doesn't look like drained marshland, does it?' said Ben.

Libby glared at him. 'I don't know, do I? But the lump behind Pedlar's Row at Heronsbourne does, so I expect the golf club does too.'

'OK, but what has that got to do with the murder? Or the arguments about the golf club, come to that.' Ben sat back in his chair and looked triumphant.

Libby let out a hiss of impatience.

'I don't know that, either, but I'm sure it does.'

Ben grinned. 'And you're going to find out whatever anyone says. Go on, then. Have a field day.'

The sun came out on Wednesday morning. Libby parked in the car park of The Red Lion, pulled her coat tight up to her neck, and set off down Pedlar's Row. At the bottom, where it petered out, a footpath was signposted leading seaward. Libby took it.

Chapter Six

The ground was slightly bumpy. Tussocked grass spread as far as the eye could see, towards a faint, shadowy line that Libby presumed was the sea. A wavy line of reeds indicated a dyke, and small white dots of sheep moved slowly to and fro. The occasional tree provided punctuation, and over to her left she could see John and Sue's house. To her right, she saw what appeared to be lumps of masonry together with a bigger evergreen tree.

It was far less featureless than she had imagined, and she assumed that a fair bit of landscaping must have been done to the golf course in order to provide fairways and greens. But there was nothing here that added to her knowledge of anything that might have contributed to Jackie Stapleton's murder.

'I don't know why I thought it might,' she muttered to herself, slowly pivoting on the spot.

'Sorry, what?'

Libby nearly jumped out of her skin.

The woman standing behind her gave a tentative smile.

'Oh!' Libby's hand flew to her mouth. 'I didn't see – oh. I'm sorry, I was talking to myself.'

The woman nodded. 'I do it all the time. Are you lost?'

'No.' Libby's heart rate returned to normal. 'I was just – exploring.'

'I've seen you before.' The woman cocked her head to one side. Her curly grey hair was moving slightly in the breeze. 'In the pub.'

'Oh, have you?' Now, where do you go from here, Libby wondered.

'Yes. You're a friend of George's, aren't you?'

'Yes. Are you a regular at The Red Lion?'

The woman hunched her shoulders inside her rather battered-looking padded jacket. 'I go in there now and then.' She narrowed her eyes. 'You were asking questions.'

Here we go, thought Libby.

'I was?'

'About the murder.'

'You were there for the quiz, then, were you?'

'Not for the quiz, but yes, I was there on Monday.'

Now Libby was stumped. What did she say now?

'What did you think of it?' she eventually asked brightly.

The woman shrugged. 'All right, I suppose. I don't go in for that sort of thing myself.' She stepped a little closer. 'But you weren't there for that, were you?'

'Er . . .' said Libby.

'You wanted to know about that Jackie.'

'Um . . .' said Libby.

The woman turned and surveyed the landscape. 'She used to live here, you know.'

'Used to?' repeated Libby.

'Before she was murdered.'

'Oh, I see. Yes, I know.'

'But she didn't care about it.'

'Didn't –? Oh, the land, you mean?'

The woman turned an indignant face back to Libby.

'Of course. It all used to be marsh, you know.'

'This and the golf course? Yes, I thought so. It was all drained, wasn't it?'

'Salt marshes.' The woman nodded, thrusting her hands harder into her pockets. 'Heronsbourne Flats, these used to be known as.' She gestured towards the golf course. 'That's quite new, you know.'

'The golf course?' Libby was mystified.

'Yes. Only just before the war.'

'The war?' Libby found herself stupidly repeating. She realised she knew very little about the history of golf clubs.

'Yes. Had to close then, of course. We were on the front line here, you know. Although the history books ignore us.' The woman sniffed.

'Ah.' Libby nodded wisely.

'But at least they left the land alone.' The woman squinted at Libby. 'The wildlife, you know. And the rare plants.'

'Yes.' Libby backed up a pace. 'Are the birds disturbed by the golf club? Marsh harriers, I presume?' she added, taking a wild stab.

'Yes. And just think what would have happened if they'd built all over it!'

'But that didn't happen, thank goodness,' said Libby.

'No thanks to that Jackie.' The woman turned towards the sea. 'Mud flats down there, now. Good for the birds.'

Libby wondered whether to risk dredging up a little more wild-fowl knowledge, but the woman turned back, pulling herself up decisively.

'Well, I hope you catch whoever did it,' she said, to Libby's sur-prise, 'although not many here will miss her.'

Libby wondered whether to question the assumption of her detective powers or the general attitude to the victim.

'Oh, yes.' The woman's smile was faintly sinister. 'We all know what you're here for. Police ask you in?'

Libby's denial stuck in her throat.

'And the people at Creekmarsh,' she confessed.

'That Lewis Osbourne-Whatsit? Friend of his, too, aren't you?'

'Er – yes.'

The woman nodded. 'At lease he's kept the ground how it was.' She shrugged. 'Gardens put down hundreds of years ago. Don't mind them.'

Libby decided not to mention her son's involvement in the restor-ation of Lewis's gardens.

40

'Don't let 'em get near the yews. Or the oaks.' The woman turned to go.

'Sorry – but can you tell me – is that a yew over there?' Libby put a hand out to stop her.

'St Cuthbert's yew.' The woman nodded. 'Did you know there's no law against digging up a yew tree?'

'Isn't there?' Libby was surprised. 'But—'

'I know. You'd think, wouldn't you. We protect it.' The woman's face turned suddenly thunderous. 'And the church.'

'The church?'

'You can see it. By the yew.' The woman sank her chin into the collar of her jacket. 'Good luck.'

Libby watched her walk away towards the sea, and decided not to follow. She hesitated until the woman was out of sight, then began to make her way towards the yew.

St Cuthbert's Church. As she got nearer, Libby could see that the walls were still partly standing. Thirteenth century, perhaps, she guessed. Maybe twelfth, or even older if there had been a wooden Saxon church here first. There were even a few battered-looking gravestones, with interesting carvings. The yew tree was splendid. Not quite as ancient as some – the trunk was still more or less in one piece – but it loomed protectively over the gravestones and the remaining church walls. Libby could see why the strange woman wanted to protect it.

But why, she wondered, had the woman suddenly appeared and begun talking about Jackie?

A gust of wind brought her attention back to the marsh. Turning away, she pulled her coat collar even further up round her ears and began to walk. Well, of course, she told herself, the woman had seen her at The Red Lion, and was obviously part of a group of campaigners, but why mention Jackie?

She frowned. Jackie hadn't threatened to do anything to this little area of marsh, had she? As far as Libby knew, all she'd done was try and persuade the golf club to turn themselves over to the pursuits of pleasure. Although selling all the land for housing wasn't exactly that, was it? And, of course, everyone said she was a 'stirrer'. Did that mean she just *liked* stirring up trouble, or that there was always a purpose behind it?

Then there was the business of the boyfriend theft. That was the sort of thing that went on in every society, though. Nothing particularly out of the ordinary, however unpleasant. Libby peered out towards the sea, but could no longer see anyone.

When she arrived back at The Red Lion, George was just preparing for the first influx of customers: 'Well, one or two of the old lags, anyway,' he said, retiring to his corner of the bar. 'Do you want coffee?'

'Oh, I suppose I might as well,' said Libby, hauling herself up on to a stool. 'How did you think it went on Monday? Have you had any feedback?'

'Everyone thought it went very well.' George placed a cup into the maw of his new coffee machine and prepared to demonstrate its abilities. 'Especially,' he said, with a grin over his shoulder, 'my lot who had the third degree!'

'Oh, George, I didn't!' Libby was shocked.

'Nah, 'course you didn't. It was them, wasn't it? All wanting to get in on the act.' He put her coffee in front of her.

'Something funny this morning, though.' Libby looked out of the window down Pedlar's Row. 'I went down there this morning, onto the marsh. I didn't realise it actually *was* marsh.'

George nodded. 'Heronsbourne Flats, that is. Used to be salt marsh.'

'Yes. I met this woman.' Libby frowned at him. 'She seemed a bit odd. Said she – well – *they* – were trying to protect the trees? Said she was here Monday.'

'Oh, ah.' George perched on his own stool. 'Marjorie, that'll be. Marjorie Sutcliffe.'

'Right. Well, she didn't seem overkeen on Jackie, either. In fact she didn't strike me as being keen on anyone. She was talking about the yew tree.'

'St Cuthbert's yew.' George grinned. 'Should be protected, by rights. I dunno why they aren't, yew trees. Other trees are.' He got comfortable on his stool. 'Oh, yes, Marjorie's dead set against anyone doing anything to our bit of marsh. She'd have the golf club dug up completely if she could.'

'She said it was new – the golf club?'

'New to her's anytime in the last two hundred years.' George grinned. 'But it is quite new, compared with some. Nineteen-thirties or thereabouts.'

'Hmm.' Libby sipped her coffee, carefully licking froth off her top lip. 'What's it got to do with Jackie, though? She was only concerned with turning the clubhouse into a nightclub, surely? Not even turning it all over to housing – or was she?'

'She made such a noise about it all, everybody sort of connected her with everything.' He shrugged. 'I dunno why she got so het up about it. Why didn't she just go and move to Canterbury, or Maidstone or somewhere, if she wanted more life?'

'Yes, it does seem odd.' Libby took another sip. 'But so was that woman. What did you say her name was? Marjorie?'

'Like I said, she's against everything. Young Jackie just – what's the word? – everything Marjorie hates.'

'Personified?'

'Yeah, that. Marjorie doesn't even much like Lewis and Creekmarsh, and that's been there hundreds of years.'

'She said she didn't mind Creekmarsh *because* it's been there hundreds of years.' Libby sighed. 'So it's not really worth taking any notice of her, then?'

'Well, there's quite a few of the locals who agree with her, more or less. They've got a Save the Yew gang up, and they've applied to some "save old churches" group.'

'It's derelict, though. They won't be able to save that.'

George shrugged. 'Oh, I dunno. She'll have a go about anything.'

'But it's not personal.'

'Shouldn't think so.' He leant forward on the bar. 'D'you find anything out on Monday?'

'Just that she wasn't much liked.' Libby decided not to say anything about the boyfriend-snatching. 'I think I'd better go and investigate the golf club next.'

'Will they let you in?'

'No idea. But I can walk round the edges, can't I?'

'Bloody long walk!' said George. 'You could go along to Creekmarsh and walk down by the side of the creek to the shore, then walk along that edge. There's a couple of cuts through the dunes you can get through. Not supposed to, though.'

'Still sounds like a long way,' said Libby doubtfully. 'Nowhere I can drive down?'

'There's the drive that leads to the new houses.' Now, George looked doubtful. 'But it's supposed to be private.'

'The golf club road only goes as far as the clubhouse, then?'

'And that's private too. It was the residents along there that made the loudest fuss!'

'Didn't someone tell me Jackie's murder was supposed to be at a rowdy party at the golf club itself?' Libby leant her elbows on the bar and looked hopeful.

'That was a rumour that went round at first,' said George. 'But it couldn't have been. No way she'd have been allowed in.'

'Oh,' said Libby despondently. 'I suppose I'll have to go and look round, then. Not much point in trying to find things out without knowing the territory, is there? Pity it isn't summer.'

George grinned. 'Yeah – now a Midsummer Party would have been much nicer!'

Chapter Seven

Libby returned to her car and sat for a moment. Go home? Go to Nethergate and see Fran? Go to The Fox? Or go to Creekmarsh and see Lewis?

Plumping for the last option as being the most likely to allow her to investigate access to the golf course, she turned left out of the car park. Approaching the golf club, a few upper-income-bracket houses screened the view. Slowing to peer down the drive itself, Libby could see several more. These, then, were the residents who objected to the up- – or possibly down- – grading of the clubhouse. And the giving over of the whole course to housing? It would certainly stop the area being regarded as exclusive.

She turned left to go to Creekmarsh, past the little church and on to the area cleared for the parking of large cars that arrived laden with brides, grooms, guests, and conference-goers. The side door was opened immediately.

'Hello, love!' Edie Osbourne-Walker appeared, beaming broadly. 'Come in, come in! Does Lewis know you're here?'

By the time Libby was settled at the kitchen table with tea and a plate of biscuits, Lewis had been located.

'Are you on the trail?' he asked, his arm round his mother. 'She knows now, so we can talk about it.'

Edie jabbed him in the ribs. 'I knew that Jackie was a bad lot before she was killed.' She nodded portentously. 'Come to a bad end, she would.'

'What makes you say that, Edie?' Libby grinned at Lewis. 'I bet she knows more about her than you do.'

Edie pulled out a chair and sat down. 'You hear a lot when people don't take much notice of you. All the girls had something to say about her. 'Specially on New Year's.'

'Really?' Libby and Lewis exchanged surprised looks.

'She'd been messin' about with someone else's bloke.' Edie nodded. 'Deliberate, like. Just because she could. And she'd been gettin' right up the noses of them Save the Marshes people.'

'Had she? I didn't know that.' Lewis pulled up his own chair.

'I met one of them this morning,' said Libby. 'George said her name was Marjorie Sutcliffe.'

'Oh, her!' Edie sniffed.

'Who's she?' asked Lewis.

'Lives in Heronsbourne,' said Edie. 'Save the Whales and all that.' Libby snorted.

'She'd have a job round here,' laughed Lewis.

'Actually, it's Save the Oaks and Yews. I think the golf club must have been going to dig up the trees on the course.' Libby frowned at her tea. 'But I don't know who's trying to do it to the marshes.'

'So what was Jackie trying to do to annoy them?' said Lewis.

'Dunno.' Edie shrugged. 'Just turned up when they was holding meetin's and such. Laughed at 'em, I think.'

'I wonder,' said Libby slowly. 'Suppose someone is trying to dig up Heronsbourne Flats?'

'Where?' said Lewis and Edie simultaneously.

'That's what the marsh is called; you know, behind Pedlar's Row and next to the golf course.'

Lewis was staring into space. 'What was the builder called?'

'Builder? What builder?' said Libby.

'The one who was going to build houses on the golf course.'

'Oh, had they actually got that far?' Libby was surprised.

'Oh, yes. On the quiet, you know. The offer was in. Word was that all the plans had been drawn up.'

'And how many were low-cost housing?'

Lewis made a face. 'Not many, I wouldn't think.'

'So Jackie could have been poking round there, too,' said Libby thoughtfully. 'And if they're after the marshes . . .'

'Goin' to find out, gal?' Edie gave her a wink.

'I might ask Ian,' said Libby.

'Your pet copper? How is 'e? Nice bloke.'

'He's fine. Lives near us now. He's moved.'

'Got a girlfriend now, then, has 'e?'

Libby shook her head. 'Not yet. I wish he would, though.'

'Oh no you don't,' said Lewis with a grin. 'He wouldn't be so available then, would he?'

'Anyway,' said Libby, disregarding that remark, 'I thought I might have a look round the golf course.'

Lewis and Edie looked at her in surprise.

'How?' asked Lewis. 'They won't let you in.'

'I thought along the beach. George said there are a couple of cuts where you can get in.'

'And how are you going to get to the beach?' Lewis leant forward and stared at her.

'Well,' said Libby, thinking rapidly, 'how did all the people having the beach party get there?'

'Got you there, boy!' said Edie.

Lewis frowned. 'Along from Nethergate?'

'All that way? Could they have got there from here? Across the creek?'

Lewis shook his head. 'They'd have to have asked permission.'

'But the turning past the church is public.'

'But once you get here, you're blocked. There used to be access to the sailing club, but not now.'

'New houses.' Edie looked smug.

Lewis looked at his mother dubiously. 'That's a private road too.'

'Footpath to the beach,' said Edie. 'They all had to say yes.'

'What, the new owners?' said Libby.

''Course. In the deeds, it was.'

'And how do you know, missus?' Lewis jabbed his mother in the ribs.

Edie cackled. 'I got friends, you know! And Dotty Barlowe joined our group.'

'Group?' said Libby.

'Dotty Barlowe?' said Lewis.

'Group of us meet at the pub. Bren does a pensioners' lunch on a Friday. Dotty Barlowe and her hubby bought one o' them houses and she come along.' Edie shrugged. 'All right, she is.'

'Well!' said Libby, sitting back in her chair.

'And now you want to talk to her,' said Lewis.

'Of course!' Libby grinned at him. 'So do you think it'll be OK if I go down the footpath, Edie?'

'Yeah, 'course it will. Only keep on the path. Their drive runs alongside.'

'I can't drive down there, then?'

'No. That *is* private. Mind, if you was visitin' . . .'

'Oh, Mum!' Lewis groaned. 'Now she'll want an introduction.'

Edie shrugged. 'Why not? Dotty'd be pleased. She's a Londoner like us. Gets a bit bored round here.'

'Hmmm,' said Libby. 'Did you know I was originally a Londoner, too?'

'Were you?' said Lewis. 'I knew Fran was . . .'

'I lived in South London when I was a child.'

'Well, well!' Edie sat back looking satisfied. 'So you'd 'ave something in common.'

'Just about,' said Libby with another grin.

'Tell you what,' Edie sat forward again. 'I'll give 'er a ring, and say can we come and visit. What about that?'

'She'll want to know why,' said Lewis.

'Oh, that's all right. Told you, she's bored.'

'Lunch first,' said Lewis firmly. 'Libby?'

'If you've got enough,' agreed Libby.

Edie produced bread, cheese, and soup.

'Now I'm goin' in to my room to phone Dotty,' she said.

'Borrow mine,' said Lewis.

'Nah. Number's in my room.' Edie got up and trotted out of the kitchen.

'Hetty's the same,' said Libby. 'Ben bought her a smartphone last Christmas, but she can't get to grips with it. All her friends have got them, even Flo and Lenny, but she's adamant.'

'What about online shopping?' said Lewis. 'Edie gives me a list and I order it.'

Libby nodded. 'Yes, Ben does the same, although I go into Canterbury once a week and get whatever she wants at the same time, but usually she says she can get what she wants in the village.'

Edie reappeared. 'After lunch all right?' she asked. 'Told you she'd be pleased.'

To Libby's surprise, Edie directed her down the golf club drive.

'Turns off here, see.'

Sure enough, the familiar wooden footpath signpost appeared on their right, with a tarmacked drive leading on from that. Both the footpath and the drive were shielded from the golf course by a line of shrubs, and eventually, the drive widened out into a flat area in front of three modern houses. All of them had first floor balconies which must have looked out over the course and the sea. Ideal for watching the New Year party on the beach, Libby reflected.

'Come on,' said Edie, climbing out of the car. 'Dotty's the middle one.'

As they approached the front door of the middle house, whimsically announcing itself on a wooden plaque as 'Spindrift', opened to reveal a middle-sized woman with grey hair, wearing jogging bottoms and a sweater.

'Edie!' she said. 'Come in! And this is your friend?'

Edie waved a proprietary hand towards Libby. 'Yeah, this is Libby. Libby, this is Dotty, who I was telling you about.'

'Oh, dear – what was she telling you?' Dotty grinned and held out a hand. 'Lovely to meet you. Come upstairs.'

Upstairs, she led them into a large sitting room which opened out to the balcony.

'What a lovely room!' said Libby, going straight to the French windows. 'And what a view!'

'What sold it to us, really,' said Dotty, coming up beside her. 'We bought it when it was only half-finished, see, and this was the only one left. We would have liked the end one, really, but Godfrey got in first.' She laughed. 'Not that he likes being called Godfrey. *Mr Godfrey Peterson*, he is.' She turned away. 'Anyway, come and sit down. Edie said you had something to ask me?'

Libby made a face at Edie. 'Only if you'd allow me to park here while I explored the beach, really.'

''Course! No probs.' Dotty perched on the edge of one of the large sofas, waving a hand towards the rest of her collection of sofas and armchairs. Edie was already comfortably ensconced in a large, squashy armchair.

'Libby lived in London too,' she said now.

'You said.' Dotty beamed at Libby. 'Where was that?'

'Wandsworth. Outer London, then, but inner London now.

'Oh, we were the other side of the river. Crouch End. Do you know it?'

'Not very well, I'm afraid,' said Libby. 'I was only a child, then.'

'So what did you want to talk to me about?' Dotty fixed Libby with sharp blue eyes. 'Not just parking, I bet.'

Edie shifted uncomfortably and Libby frowned at her.

'Oh, don't blame Edie. You're good for a gossip on a Friday in the pub.' Dotty tucked her feet up under her.

'Oh, Edie!' sighed Libby. 'What have you been saying?'

'We know all about your cases.' Dotty nodded. ''Specially the ones at Edie's place.'

Libby laughed. 'Oh, well, all in the public domain now, I suppose. And yes, I did want to ask you a couple of questions. Although I expect the police have already asked you.'

'We did have a couple round on New Year's Day.' She shrugged. 'Couldn't tell 'em anything, though.'

'You saw the party, I expect?'

'Well, we watched the fireworks. But then we came in and closed the blinds. Triple-glazed, those windows, so we didn't hear much noise. Don't think it went on much past twelve, though.'

'Oh, well, I expect if you'd seen anything the police would know already,' said Libby.

'We knew who she was, though,' said Dotty, settling herself more comfortably. 'We talked about her on Friday, didn't we, Edie?'

'Really?'

'Yes, but look! I haven't offered you anything! Tea? Coffee?' Dotty sprang up.

'Cuppa'd do me nicely,' said Edie.

'Yes, thank you, tea,' said Libby, who really wanted to get on with the questions now it was getting interesting. But she contained her soul in patience and joined Edie in praising the house and the view, while Dotty pottered in the open-plan kitchen at the back of the room.

At last, with large mugs of tea on the table in front of them, Dotty returned to the subject of Jackie Stapleton.

'Yes – first time we came up against her was at the golf club.'

'*At* the golf club?'

'A meeting, see. We'd only just moved in, and they wanted to talk about the plans for the new clubhouse.'

'Oh!' said Libby. 'I thought the new clubhouse was built at the same time as the houses?'

'No, well, not exactly,' said Dotty. 'The building was there, but it was what was going inside they were talking about. And blimey! Did she make herself heard! No one else hardly got a word in edge-ways. And when they weren't saying what she wanted, she was yelling at them. Had to be chucked out in the end.'

'Goodness!'

'Oh, yes.' Dotty nodded forcefully. 'Threatened to make sure it never happened, she did. Never heard such a fuss.'

51

Chapter Eight

There was a short silence

'So she upset the golf club members as well as everyone else,' Libby said eventually.

Dotty nodded.

'And did you know Edie knew her?'

'Not 'til we talked about her on Friday,' said Edie. 'I didn't know it was her what got killed 'til then, either.'

'Did you all speculate about the killer?'

'We didn't know enough about 'er,' said Edie. 'Just what we knew personal, like.'

'And that wasn't much?' said Libby.

'Not really,' Dotty and Edie said together.

'Right.' Libby heaved a sigh.

'See,' said Dotty, 'she was one of those people everyone talked about. Whether you knew her or not, everyone knew *about* her. I mean, the police are going to have a right job finding out who killed her. Is that why they've asked you? Oh!' Dotty's hand flew to her mouth. 'I'm not supposed to say that, am I?'

'Silly cow,' said Edie comfortably.

Libby laughed. 'Looks as if you talk about me as much as you talk about her!'

Edie grinned. 'Sometimes.'

Libby drank some of her quickly cooling tea. 'Yes, in fact I was asked to see if I could dig up any gossip. Mainly because I'd advised

Lewis to tell the police about Jackie being at Creekmarsh on New Year's Eve, and he told the police I had. Advised him, I mean.'

'So you're official?' Dotty sounded excited.

'We-ell, sort of. Helping the police with their inquiries in the best sense.'

'She can go where they can't,' said Edie. 'And people talk to her.'

'But you mustn't say that,' said Libby, 'or people won't talk to me at all!'

'No, I can see that.' Dotty put on a wise expression. 'Have you talked to many people round here? Not that I know many yet.'

'No – I don't know many, either. I talked to some people in the pub when they had the quiz.'

Dotty looked as though she would go on asking questions all afternoon, so Libby finished her tea and put her mug down. 'It was really nice to talk to you, Dotty, but we'd better be going.'

Dotty and Edie both looked surprised.

'Don't you want to go to the beach?' said Edie.

'Not now, Edie, it's getting a bit too late. I've got to drop you off and get back home.'

'Well, come and park here anytime,' said Dotty. 'I'd love to see you.'

'Thank you, much appreciated.'

'I can drop Edie home,' Dotty went on. 'If you want to hang on for a bit, Edie?'

'Lovely.' Edie beamed. 'You don't mind, do you, Lib?'

Libby finally extricated herself from the two ladies, turned the car, and made her way back to the coast road. The sky was a sulphurous yellowy-grey, and the lights were on in the self-satisfied looking houses she passed on the way. Just as well she'd left when she did, or she would have got home later than Ben.

It was, in fact, dark by the time she got home. Sidney was sitting close to the empty fireplace looking as grumpy as only a cat can, so after putting on the kettle for even more tea, Libby lit the fire, fetched her mug, and settled down on the sofa with the laptop.

And then the phone rang.

'It's me,' said Fran. 'Guy and I thought we'd come up this evening.'

'Oh, lovely. Any particular reason?'

'To see how you're getting on with your investigations, of course. Is Ian coming?'

'Don't know. He doesn't seem to be actively involved in the murder, so he might not be too busy.'

'How about seeing if Harry can fit us in at the caff with Patti and Anne?'

'Great idea,' said Libby. 'Will you ring him, or shall I?'

Harry was only too pleased to fit them in along with Patti and Anne's regular Wednesday dinner, as January was proving rather slow in the restaurant business, so Libby and Ben duly arrived at The Pink Geranium at seven-thirty.

Patti and Anne were already in place at the big round table in the window, and Harry arrived promptly with a bottle of Libby's current favourite red wine to join Anne's preferred Sancerre.

'Is this a murder conference?' asked Anne.

'Not really,' said Libby, sending Ben a swift glance.

'Harry said Fran and Guy are coming over,' said Patti, a quizzical look in her eye.

'They often do,' said Libby.

Ben dug her in the ribs. 'Tell the truth, Lib. That's a priest.'

Patti and Anne laughed and Libby went pink.

'Oh, all right, sort of.'

'I heard about your quiz night,' said Patti. 'George told me.'

'George? Oh yes, Heronsbourne's one of your parishes, isn't it?'

Patti smiled. 'I'm even a courtesy member of the Save the Yew group.'

'Really?' Libby's eyes widened. 'And St Cuthbert's?'

'Of course. They've applied to the Friendless Churches people, but I don't think they'll get very far.'

'Friendless Churches?' echoed her audience.

'But they don't save ruins,' Patti added, 'and St Cuthbert's is a ruin, isn't it?'

54

'You know Marjorie Sutcliffe, then?' asked Libby, sipping the wine Ben had just poured.

'Oh, yes. She's the leading light.'

'I won't tell you any more,' said Libby. 'Here's Fran and Guy. I'll wait for them.'

In fact, Libby had to wait until after everyone was settled and had ordered.

'Why didn't you stay with us?' Ben asked, as his bottle hovered over Guy's glass.

'As I'd invited us over, I didn't think we should ask,' said Fran.

'That's daft,' said Libby. 'Spare room's made up and we can lend anything you want. Balzac won't starve overnight, will he?'

'His bowl is overflowing with expensive dry food,' said Guy. 'Well, if you don't mind . . .'

''Course not,' said Libby, and Fran grinned sheepishly.

'Now perhaps she'll tell us what she's been doing for the last week,' said Anne. 'We gather there's an investigation under way.'

'I've got to catch up, too,' said Fran.

Libby launched into the story of the past week, helped out by Ben and Fran when it came to the quiz night. By the time she'd reached the end of the current day, they were all mid-way through their main courses.

'Shame I don't know any of the Heronsbourne people,' said Patti. 'Or only a few of them, anyhow.'

'Isn't there a church in Heronsbourne?' asked Guy.

'Oh yes, or it wouldn't be mine,' said Patti. 'But only half a dozen turn up for services.'

'No golf club members, then?' said Anne.

'No.' Patti shook her head. 'I did think we might get one of the new houses—'

Ben and Guy tittered.

'You know what I mean.' Patti frowned at them. 'One of the new residents is supposed to be a member of the clergy, but I haven't seen hide nor hair of him.'

'I told you, I met one of the others today,' said Libby. 'Nice woman. Ex-Londoner, friend of Edie's.'

'And no one had much to say about Jackie Stapleton?' asked Fran, neatly placing her knife and fork together.

'Only what I've told you,' said Libby with a sigh. 'Looks pretty hopeless to me.'

'She was obviously not a very nice person,' said Anne. 'Pinching boyfriends and stirring up trouble.'

'Sounds troubled herself,' said Patti. 'I feel rather sorry for her.'

They all looked at her in surprise.

'It sounds as though she was trying to hit back at something. Or someone.' Patti took a thoughtful sip of wine. 'Didn't anyone try and make friends with her?'

'It doesn't sound like it,' said Libby, pushing her plate away. 'I don't know about where she worked.'

'I've got a feeling it was a café,' said Patti with a frown. 'Not sure why, though.'

'There aren't any cafés in Heronsbourne. Perhaps it was in Nethergate?' suggested Fran.

'It was,' said Libby. 'Ian said – a job in Nethergate. But frankly, I can't see what else I can do. Jemima asked me to go over to the pub with her friends, John and Sue, tomorrow, as the slighted girlfriend will be there. But what can I say? I'll just come over as a nosy old cow.' She held up a hand. 'Don't say it!'

Ben snorted and the others laughed.

Harry arrived to offer desserts, which only Ben and Guy ordered.

'Quiet, isn't it?' he said.

'It'll pick up in a few weeks,' said Fran.

'Hope so. I'll go and get the puds, then I'll come and join you.' He wandered off kitchenwards, and in a few moments came back with the orders and a fresh bottle of red wine.

'So you're all trying to help Madam here work out her investigation strategy?' he asked, turning a chair round and straddling it.

'I haven't got one,' said Libby. 'I'm going to tell Ian if he comes in tonight. I can't go on – I haven't got an excuse.'

Ben looked puzzled and Fran doubtful. The others just shook their heads.

'I'll believe it when I see it,' said Harry, pouring himself a glass of red wine and topping up Libby's.

By unspoken agreement, the subject turned to other matters, in particular Ben's renovation of The Hop Pocket pub, about which he was having doubts.

'I've talked to Tim about it,' he said, 'and we're both now wondering if there's enough business in the village to support two pubs.'

'But you were going to be appealing to two different markets,' said Guy.

Ben shook his head. 'Not sure . . .'

'But you've invested so much money!' said Fran.

Libby wisely kept her mouth shut.

Dinner over, they were all ensconced at their favourite table in the pub when Ian and Edward entered. Ben and Guy stood up and went to the bar to order more drinks, and Ian pulled a chair up and squeezed in next to Libby. Everyone else looked at him hopefully. He looked round quizzically.

'What?' he said.

'Libby says she's going to back out of the investigation,' said Anne. 'What do you say?'

Ian turned to Libby. 'Well?'

'I don't know how I can ask any more questions,' she said. 'I haven't got any sort of "in" with anybody. And I don't know anything about the victim's private life.'

A chorus of protest arose.

Ian's mouth lifted into a smile. 'Apparently your friends disagree.' He looked up to accept a drink from Guy. 'And now tell me what you've been up to since we last spoke.'

57

Libby sighed and launched into her story, frequently interrupted by her friends when she left out a vital detail. Anne was particularly vocal.

Towards the end of the story, Harry and Peter arrived to enlarge the group. Harry demanded to hear everything all over again and was shouted down.

Ian stood up. 'Come on, Libby. Let's see if we can find a corner on our own.'

Libby, looking sheepish, followed him to the corner beside the huge fireplace. Ian pulled out two chairs and gestured her to sit.

'Now, Mrs S,' he said. 'What's the problem?'

'I just don't think I can poke my nose in any more.' Libby swirled her beer around in her glass. 'It's all right if it's people I know, or something that affects me, but this is nothing to do with me. And I don't know any of the people involved – though half of them seem to know who I am!'

'You've met several so far, it seems to me,' said Ian.

'But none of them are friends. And I couldn't care less about the golf club, frankly.'

'What's something that *would* interest you?' asked Ian. 'The pub?'

'If that was threatened with closure, you mean? Yes, I'd turn out to help George, I suppose.'

Ian sat back in his chair and regarded her with his head on one side.

'And what else?'

'Eh?' Libby looked startled.

'What else gets you wound up?'

Libby frowned. 'I don't know what you mean.'

'Come on, Lib. Yes, you do. Wildlife.'

Libby stared at him. 'If you mean the Save the Yew group—'

'That's exactly what I mean.' Ian sat forward. 'It's actually a Save the Marshes group. You'd be all for that, wouldn't you?'

Chapter Nine

'I thought it was just saving the yew and the ruined church,' said Libby, after a long pause.

'It's an offshoot of the Save the Marshes group,' said Ian.

'That Marjorie woman I met didn't say that. Neither did George.'

'Well, it is.' Ian stood up. 'Another drink?'

'Oh – er, yes. Please.' Libby looked down at her hands.

'Don't worry Ian,' said Ben behind her. 'I'll get them.'

Ian sat down again.

'No. Something you obviously haven't picked up. Unlike you.' Libby glared at him.

'The objections to the sale of the golf club. What about that?' Ian tapped a finger on a beer mat.

'The members didn't want to lose their club,' said Libby.

'Right. And?'

'They won?' suggested Libby hesitantly.

Ian made an exasperated sound. 'What else were people cross about? Not just the members?'

'I don't know, do I?' It was Libby's turn to be exasperated.

'You actually mentioned it while you were telling me all about your adventures.'

Libby scowled at the table. Ben leant over her shoulder and placed a glass in front of her. 'Builders,' he whispered.

'Oh!' Libby sat up with a jerk.

Ian grinned. 'You're not supposed to be listening,' he said to Ben.

'Was that it?' said Libby. 'We wondered if the builders were planning to build on Heronsbourne Flats as they'd been cheated out of the golf course?'

'Exactly.' Ian sat back again, looking triumphant. 'Thanks, Ben.'

'And are they?'

'That's what the word is,' said Ian. 'Your Marjorie Sutcliffe might be more invested in the yew and the church, but the group was actually set up to try and protect the marsh against development.'

Libby took a sip of lager. 'I didn't hear very much about it. Who are they? And who is going to sell them the marsh?'

'The council, of course.'

'But isn't it an SSSI, or something?'

'Site of Scientific Interest? Yes, it is. But as you know, local planning is very concerned about building so many houses within the next year or so.'

'How do they get away with it?' Libby was aghast.

'Money, of course.' Ian smiled at her. '*Now* are you interested?'

'Well, yes. But I still don't see what I can do.'

'Join the group.'

'Oh.' Libby looked over her shoulder to where the rest of their friends were deep in conversation. Ben looked up and winked.

'Are you going to join Lewis's mother and her friends tomorrow?'

'It was Jemima's friends, actually,' said Libby. 'To meet the dumped girlfriend.'

'Who may well be part of the group.'

'Who are the builders?'

'Rochester and Brown.' Ian picked up his glass.

'If you know, what else is there for me to find out?' said Libby.

'As much as you can about Jackie Stapleton, of course.'

Libby stared at him. 'Should you be doing this? I mean, I was told there was a DI and a DS in charge down there.'

'DI Winters and DS Stone, yes. But I'm still involved. Just desk-bound.'

'Or supposed to be.' Libby gave him a grin.

'Which is why I really didn't want a promotion.' He stood up. 'So, yes. I'd like you to poke around – unofficially, of course.'

'Of course.' Libby got to her feet. 'And Fran?'

'I wouldn't expect otherwise,' said Ian

They rejoined their friends and Libby murmured in Fran's ear. Fran's eyes widened.

'I'll ring you in the morning,' said Libby.

Everyone else looked questioningly.

'They're just going to do a little investigation for me,' said Ian. 'Nothing to worry about.'

'Famous last words,' muttered Ben.

As promised, Libby called Fran the following morning.

'I assume we're going to investigate this Save the Marshes group?' said Fran.

'That's what Ian suggested.'

'Hmm.' Fran was quiet for a moment.

'What?' said Libby.

'Couple of things I don't understand,' said Fran slowly.

'Yes? What?' said Libby again.

'Well, first, Jackie Stapleton is hardly likely to have been mixed up in the Save the Marshes group, is she? And second, why is Ian so intent on getting us, and particularly you, involved in all this?'

'Eh?' Libby was temporarily stunned. She pulled herself together. 'Well . . . he's asked us before . . .'

'And now he's sending us off on something that apparently has nothing to do with the case.'

A long silence ensued.

'Do you think,' said Libby hesitantly after a minute, 'He's trying to head us – me – off?'

'It did occur to me,' said Fran, the suspicion of a chuckle in her voice.

'Oh.'

'Think about it. According to him, there's a DI and a DS on the

61

case, not to mention a team of DCs, I expect. They'll have found out all about the boyfriend and the wronged girlfriend, and the rows at the golf club, won't they? And her workmates in the café at Nethergate, no doubt.'

Libby scowled at her feet. "Course they bloody well would.' She took a breath. 'But *why*?'

'To keep us out of their way, I expect. After all, he's not around to provide us with a buffer, is he?'

'So what do we do?' asked Libby, feeling distinctly put out.

'Back out? I seem to remember you saying it was nothing to do with you, as you always do.'

'Did I say that to you?'

'I bet you said it to somebody,' said Fran.

'Well, yes . . .' muttered Libby.

'We can still go over and meet Jemima and her friends this evening. And play it down, perhaps. Find out if the police have been questioning everyone.'

'Yes.' Libby brightened up. 'We might find an angle.'

'Don't let's try too hard, though,' said Fran. 'Remember, I said we've only just come out of one investigation, which, let's face it, wasn't exactly pleasant.'

'All right.' Libby crossed her fingers. 'We won't try.'

Libby thought about this all morning, and at lunchtime, went up to The Manor, where Ben was attending to estate business in his office.

'It sounds as though Fran could be right,' he said, when Libby had relayed the phone call.

'He's never minded me being there before,' protested Libby.

'Think about it,' said Ben.

Libby thought. 'Oh. Well. Not much, anyway.'

'He's provided you with something to look into, hasn't he? And I bet you get interested in that, even if it isn't the actual murder.'

'Mmm.' Libby played with a piece of paper on Ben's desk until he took it away from her. She stood up. 'I'll go and see Hetty.'

'She's down at Flo's. They're having one of their old girls' meetings.'

'Oh.' Libby sat down again. 'Have you had lunch?'

Ben grinned. 'No. I'll come back home with you, and you can pamper me.'

Libby laughed. 'That'll be the day.'

All through their lunch of soup made from odds and ends in the bottom of the vegetable basket, Libby pondered about the new scenario suggested by Fran.

'When you think about it,' she said to Ben, as they loaded plates into the dishwasher, 'it is a rather unlikely situation.'

'Which bit?' asked Ben.

'Middle-aged civilian women investigating rural crime.'

'Not in fiction,' said Ben.

'No – well, that's what I mean. Harry used to call me Miss Marple, didn't he? People take the mick.'

Ben leant back against the Rayburn and folded his arms. 'You have actually got to the bottom of quite a lot of mysteries.'

'More or less at the same time as the police,' said Libby ruefully.

'And Ian has relied on you to ferret out background stuff, hasn't he?'

'But I'm usually involved somehow or other.'

'And this time you're not. But, Lewis did ask your advice. You didn't just butt in.'

Libby gave a rueful laugh. 'And then Ian barrelled in with his suggestions because I might get above myself.'

'If you like to put it like that.'

'Proof if proof were needed that I am just a nosy old bag.'

Ben threw his head back and laughed. 'But you're *my* nosy old bag,' he said when he'd recovered. 'I wouldn't have you any other way.'

'Hmm,' said Libby. 'Sometimes you would. Every time something comes up, you complain.'

'And you don't take any notice.' Ben pushed himself upright. 'So

63

this time, do what you suggested yourself. Look into the situation on the periphery. Plenty to go on, I would have thought.'

Libby continued to reflect on this for the rest of the afternoon, then called Fran again to make arrangements to meet her that evening at The Red Lion.

'And we're going to ask questions?' said Fran.

'We'll see,' was Libby's gnomic reply.

When Libby arrived at The Red Lion, she found Fran already seated in a group with John and Sue Cantripp, Jemima, and three other men, as well as, to her surprise, Dotty Barlowe.

'Hi!' said Dotty brightly. 'This is my husband, Eddy. Eddy, this is Libby.'

'Hello.' Libby held out her hand to the short, burly man.

A chair was found for Libby, and Jemima sprang up to fetch her a drink.

'Tonic water for me, please. I'm driving,' said Libby.

'So you've come along to find out about Jackie Stapleton?' said one of the other men, not looking too happy about it.

Libby shot a look at Fran, who gave a slight shrug. 'Not exactly.' She took a deep breath. 'Actually, I think the police have finished with me, now, so we won't be nosing around.'

Sue Cantripp looked disappointed. 'Don't you want to meet Hannah, then?'

Put on the spot, Libby struggled to find an answer. 'Not for that reason,' she said finally, grasping the glass Jemima held out.

'We're here for a social reason,' said Fran.

The assembled company looked from Fran to Libby in obvious puzzlement.

Libby sighed. 'Well, the police have asked all the questions already, haven't they? And I don't think there's anything we can find out that they don't know.'

There was a resigned sigh and shifting in seats.

'She's right,' said John. 'After all, we don't know much about

Jackie, do we? We told her about Hannah and Gary, and to be honest, there isn't anything else we know – not for a fact.'

'What about the golf club?' said the man who had spoken before.

'The police know all about that, Ray,' said Sue.

'Although there's one thing I don't understand,' said Fran, and everyone turned to look at her. 'Nothing to do with Jackie, but Libby and I have heard about the Save the Marshes group, and something about building on the land? The same as they wanted to do with the golf course?'

This provoked a chorus of response. In the end, it was Dotty who made herself heard.

'We've heard all about that,' she said. 'I meet some friends in The Fox on a Friday and they know all about it.'

'Oh, we know all about that, too,' said John heavily. 'If the builders get their way, we'll be turfed off the marsh.'

'But yours is a listed building!' said Libby, shocked. 'And anyway, I thought the marsh was an SSSI?'

All her listeners voiced agreement.

'Shocking, it is,' said the man who hadn't yet spoken. 'It was part of what stopped the golf club, although they put it about it was because of what the members wanted. So they just moved over to the Flats. And then Ma Sutcliffe got involved. Stuck her sticky beak in.'

'Good job she did, this time,' said the man known as Ray.

'She's more concerned about her precious yew tree,' said Sue, 'but at least she's motivated people to try and oppose the sale.'

'Do you belong to the group?' asked Fran.

'Of course!' Sue grinned. 'But we're up against money. And the council going on and on about all the homes they're supposed to build.'

'For rich people,' said Libby.

'Exactly,' said John. 'Nothing for all the poor buggers desperate for a council house.'

'And homelessness on the rise,' added Ray.

'Hello – you talking about the fight for the flats?' said a new voice, and Libby looked up to see a pretty young woman smiling at the group.

Chapter Ten

'Hello, young Hannah,' said John, and stood up. 'Here, have my seat. I'll grab another one.'

Hannah exchanged greetings around the table and finally smiled hesitantly at Libby and Fran.

'I don't know you, do I?' she said.

'Friends of ours,' said Sue, clearing her throat.

'And mine,' beamed Dotty. 'This is Libby and this is Fran. This is Hannah.' She waved an introductory hand.

'Hi,' said all three together.

'Yes,' said the so-far unnamed man. 'Save the Marshes and all that.'

'Well, I'm all for it,' said Hannah, putting her glass on the table.

'We've only just heard about it,' said Libby. 'How come it hasn't made the papers?'

'There aren't any papers!' laughed Eddy Barlowe.

There was a rumbling chorus of disapproval for the lack of local newspapers.

'They're online,' said Jemima hesitantly.

'Not the same,' said Ray.

'No, it isn't,' agreed Fran. 'Tell you what, Lib, why don't we ask Jane?'

Libby turned to the rest of the group. 'Jane's a friend of ours. She used to be editor of the *Mercury*, but now she's a sort of group editor working online. But she usually knows what's going on. I'm surprised she hasn't told us about this. She knows we've got friends in the area.'

'We know quite a bit about it,' said Hannah. 'Those builders are after the Flats.'

'Are you a member of the group?' asked Libby. 'The Save the Marshes group?'

'I go to some of the meetings,' said Hannah. 'But they seem to want to start – well, more *direct* action, if you know what I mean. I don't.'

'Like that Jackie,' rumbled the unnamed man. The atmosphere tensed.

'Oh, she'd never be involved in saving the marshes,' said Sue breezily. 'She'd have wanted to build a nightclub on them!'

There was a tentative giggle. Everyone seemed to be avoiding looking at Hannah, who sighed.

'I take it you know about Jackie Stapleton being murdered,' she said directly to Libby. 'And probably about my . . .' she paused. '*Relationship* with her.'

Libby, on the spot, simply nodded.

Hannah sighed again. 'I thought so.' She looked round at the group of friends, who looked either sheepish or uncomfortable. 'In that case, I think we ought to have a chat.' She stood up. 'Come on. I'll find us a corner.'

Libby opened her mouth, closed it, and stood up.

Hannah led the way to a small table by the door, avoided by the regulars because of the intermittent draughts. Libby, followed by Fran, joined her.

Hannah grinned up at them. 'I heard you came as a pair.'

Libby felt the colour seeping up her neck, and noticed a matching colour staining Fran's porcelain cheeks.

'I'm sorry,' she said simply.

'Oh, not your fault,' said Hannah with another sigh. 'I know I'm the subject of a lot of gleeful gossip, and poor Jackie's death has just made it worse.'

'If it's any use,' said Fran, 'we came here today to tell them we weren't looking into it any more.'

'Oh?' Hannah looked surprised. 'Why not?'

'The police only ask us – well, Libby – if there's some background information that she might learn that they wouldn't.'

'And wasn't there?' Hannah looked at Libby.

'Just that Jackie worked occasionally for Lewis at Creekmarsh and had a row there on New Year's Eve. Everything else they knew,' said Libby.

'But you carried on asking?' Hannah's face had taken on a steely look.

'Actually,' said Fran, 'all these people just kept wanting to tell her things. And not just about you.'

'Is that true?' Hannah fixed a gimlet eye on Libby.

'Yes.' Now Libby was getting annoyed. 'In fact, I'm now far more interested in Heronsbourne Flats.'

Hannah frowned and picked up her glass.

'And are you going to look into that?'

'Does it need looking into?' Libby was equally steely.

Hannah stared back and then grinned again. 'Yes, I'd say so.'

'Before we go into that,' said Fran hastily, 'let's just get Jackie out of the way.'

'Oh, all right.' Hannah settled back in her chair. 'I expect you know it already. I was going out with Gary Turner and Jackie pinched him. That's about it, really.'

'We heard she tried to wind you up recently,' said Libby.

Hannah laughed. 'Not just recently. She always has.' She leant forward. 'I'll tell you the whole sorry story, but first, would you like another drink?'

They both refused, but Fran volunteered to fetch Hannah another half-pint.

'Jackie lived nearby, you know that?' Hannah began. 'She started coming in here for a drink and George introduced her to some of us, as she didn't seem to know anyone. She was fine then.' Hannah gazed into space for a moment. 'We got quite friendly, you know, used to meet for a drink, or occasionally go into Canterbury to the pictures. Not often. I think she had friends in Nethergate. But then she began to get restless. Started wanting to go clubbing – that sort of thing. Not my idea, at all. And she seemed to get – oh, I don't know – prickly. Started thinking people were against her, somehow. Talking behind her back.'

'And were they?' asked Libby.

'Not then. But she started sort of throwing her weight around. Joined the am-dram society and wanted all the best parts.'

'Yes, John and Sue told us that.'

Hannah nodded. 'Then she got worse. Always stirring up trouble. I tried to calm her down, but she wasn't having any. She was trying to prove something.'

'And you had no idea what?' asked Fran.

Hannah shook her head. 'None. And then she started on Gary. And he, the worm, fell for it. It wasn't actually until after all the golf club trouble that it happened. By that time, because of all the problems she'd caused there, we were barely speaking. She was just so – unpleasant. And yet . . .'

'And yet?' prompted Libby.

'I always felt she was unhappy, somehow. I even made excuses for her. Said she'd had an unhappy childhood, although I have no idea if that was true. She never even said where she'd moved from, although I don't think it was far. She knew the area too well.'

'She worked in Nethergate, didn't she?' asked Fran. 'That's where I live.'

'Yes, in a café. I know she'd worked somewhere else before that, but she never talked about it.'

'That's a bit odd, isn't it?' said Libby. 'You usually know at least vaguely what people do, don't you? Even if it's only, builder, shop assistant, waiter.'

Hannah looked amused. 'What do you two do, then?'

'I help my husband in our shop,' said Fran, 'and Libby looks after holiday lets and the Oast Theatre.'

'And I'm a secretary in a firm of solicitors,' said Hannah. 'Very boring.'

'And Jackie knew about your job?' said Libby.

'Of course – everyone round here knows. They aren't above asking me for free advice. And I knew where she worked – we all did. We all shop in Nethergate.'

'But she wasn't forthcoming about anything else?' said Fran.

Hannah shook her head. 'Except trying to drum up support for turning the golf club into some kind of nightclub. And there wasn't much support, believe me.'

'So we gathered. So did she stay out of your way after she'd – er – got off with Gary?' asked Libby.

'Not really. Especially after they split up. She came looking for me. You heard about New Year's Eve on the beach?'

'A bit,' said Libby.

'Which was why the police came after me.' Hannah shrugged. 'Can't blame them.' She looked up and smiled. 'So that's me.'

They both smiled back. 'Well, I'm more interested in this Save the Marsh group now I've heard about it,' said Libby. 'I bumped into Marjorie Sutcliffe the other day.'

'Ah.' Hannah laughed. 'She's more interested in the yew and the ruined church.'

'So we heard,' said Fran. 'Did she fight off the builders when they were trying to build on the golf course?'

'No, there were more than enough members and residents to do that.' Hannah stretched. 'Including me and Gary.'

'You're members of the golf club?' said Libby, surprised.

'No – residents. Gary's parents live in one of the houses on the drive up to the golf club, although he doesn't. We've both got flats in St Mary's.'

'St Mary's?' echoed Fran and Libby.

'Have you not come across it? Just behind here, more or less. Used to be St Mary's Convent.'

There were several questions Libby wanted to ask, but decided they were far too intrusive. Instead, she shook her head and sighed.

'Well, I'm pretty sure the police know everything you've told us about Jackie. That's why we decided not to poke around any further.'

'But we both got interested in the Save the Marshes campaign,' said Fran. 'Nothing to do with the murder investigation.'

'You'd be welcome to join,' said Hannah, 'except that you might find Marjorie's leadership a bit – what? Draconian?'

Libby surveyed the young woman with interest. Obviously well educated, she didn't, to Libby's prejudiced eyes, seem quite the same type as her friends.

'Do you come from round here?' she asked. 'I mean, when you were a child?'

Hannah laughed. 'I don't seem the type, you mean?'

Libby, once again, felt colour creeping up her neck.

'Actually, I'm from just the other side of Canterbury. I went to Askews.'

'Ah!' said Libby.

'Askews?' said Fran.

'A rather posh girls' school,' said Hannah.

'Girls who didn't get into Askews tended to go to Foxgrove, according to my researches,' said Libby.

Fran's eyebrows rose.

'You know about Foxgrove, then?' said Hannah.

They both nodded.

'And it's all but closed down now, hasn't it?' said Fran.

'It has.' Hannah looked mournful. 'And Askews is being pressured into taking boys.'

'Not from Foxgrove!' said Libby, horrified.

'No. I gather the authorities are having a few problems, there.' Hannah looked thoughtful. 'I'm friendly with a couple of the mistresses at Askews, they keep me up to date. Frankly, I'm surprised it took them so long to shut the place down. It was only when—' She stopped abruptly, her eyes widening. 'Oh, wait a minute! It was you, wasn't it?'

Libby wriggled uncomfortably.

71

'We did get rather involved in that business, yes,' said Fran calmly. 'It happens.'

'But you're proper detectives!' said Hannah.

'No, we're not!' said Libby and Fran together.

'But you help the police!'

'Sometimes. It's all a bit unfortunate, really,' said Libby.

'Well, in that case,' said Hannah firmly, ignoring Libby, 'I think you should look into Jackie's murder.'

Libby and Fran exchanged glances.

'Why?' said Fran. 'Libby feels, and so do I, that we could be rather intrusive.'

'How did you get involved?' asked Hannah. 'Did the police just come and ask you?'

'Er – no. I gave Lewis Osbourne-Walker some advice – to go to the police, as a matter of fact. Then they asked me – us – in.'

'You know Lewis?'

'Very well,' said Libby. 'My son worked with him.'

'Really?' Hannah looked delighted. 'I've always wanted to have a look at that house – and the gardens.'

'It is open to the public,' said Fran.

'Only if you're going to a conference or a wedding,' said Hannah.

'Oh, we'll take you over there,' said Libby. 'Jackie did some work for Lewis occasionally.'

'Did she? I wouldn't have thought she would . . .' Hannah trailed off.

'She didn't.' Libby grinned. 'Lewis threw her out on New Year's Eve.'

Chapter Eleven

Hannah whooped with laughter. 'Oh, she wouldn't have liked that!'

'She didn't,' said Libby. 'And she marched straight over to the party on the beach. Where we gather she set about making more mayhem.'

'And that's where the trouble started.' Hannah sighed. 'Actually, I felt sorry for her. I often did. No one seemed to want her.'

'She didn't try very hard to be liked,' said Fran. 'According to what we've heard.'

'No.' Hannah was thoughtful. 'And yet she seemed to want to prove something. That she was better than other people? Or that she knew something they didn't?'

'Like what?' asked Libby.

'Oh, I don't know. It was just the way she was.'

'Well, now we've had our chat,' said Fran, 'don't you think we ought to go back to the others? After all, it was John and Sue and Jemima who asked us over.'

Libby and Hannah obediently stood up and followed Fran back to the others, who looked up, but carried on talking.

'Are you going to join the Marshes group?' asked Sue.

'Maybe. We're a bit wary of Marjorie Sutcliffe.' Libby sat down.

'That's why all her support dwindles,' said Ray. 'If she wasn't so . . . so . . .'

'I think we've got the picture.' Libby grinned at him. 'By all accounts, it was a good job Jackie didn't join the group. There would have been some right royal battles.'

'Oh, there were,' said Dotty. The others nodded.

'There were?' repeated Fran.

'With the golf club. They were on opposite sides, of course, but that made it worse.'

'Poor girl,' said Libby.

A mild outcry arose.

'She was nothing of the sort!'

'Poor girl? Bad girl, more like.'

'Troublemaker.'

'I know what Libby means,' said Hannah. 'I can't help feeling there was something that made her like that.

'I agree,' said Fran, 'and I didn't even know her.'

'Yes.' Libby looked down into the remains of her drink. 'What made her like that?'

The others round the table looked slightly abashed.

'Whatever it was,' said Dotty, 'it's not going to help the police find out who killed her.'

Libby raised an eyebrow at Fran, who nodded.

The conversation became general and, after refusing two more drinks, Libby decided it was time to go.

'Come and join us again,' said Sue, as the two women stood to leave.

'We will,' said Fran. 'It's been a nice change.'

They were silent as the walked to their cars.

'What do you think?' asked Libby, as she unlocked hers.

'Despite what they said, I'd like to find out more about Jackie's background.' Fran aimed her key fob at her car.

'I agree. And I'm not sure it wouldn't help find her killer.' Libby opened her door.

'You think it might be someone from her past?'

'It wouldn't hurt to look,' said Libby. 'Tell you what – I'll report to Ian that we're backing out, but ask if they've found out anything about where she came from. I'll ring you tomorrow.'

As she drove home, she reviewed the investigations she'd blundered into over the years. So many of them had, in fact, been rooted in the past lives of the victims. Far more than those almost incidental crimes that seemed to happen every day in the streets of the big cities. But then, whatever had happened in each case, it was almost always a reaction to a previous action. Unless it was an accident, and this was most certainly *not* an accident.

The following morning, after Ben, not looking cheerful, had left for a meeting at The Hop Pocket with his builders, Libby called Ian's office at police headquarters in Canterbury. To her surprise, he answered.

'You didn't expect me to be here?' he said, sounding amused. 'Going to leave a message, were you?'

'No! I wanted to ask you a question.'

'Oh?'

'Well, mainly, I wanted to say Fran and I don't think we can dig out any more information that you haven't got yourselves.' Libby paused, waiting for Ian to comment. When he didn't, she went on. 'And we just wondered if you'd found out about her background. You know, where she came from.'

'Do you think her killer came from her childhood, perhaps?' Ian still sounded amused.

'Well, they have done in the past,' blustered Libby.

He laughed. 'Absolutely right, but the truth is, we can't find anything out about her. She seems to have turned up in a bedsit in Nethergate about eleven or twelve years ago with no history. No National Insurance nor tax number – nothing.'

'Oh.' Libby frowned. 'I suppose it does happen.'

'It does,' said Ian, 'and there are mechanisms which allow you to provide yourself with all the necessary documentation. And that's as far as we've got with young Ms Stapleton. We don't even know how old she is. She said she was thirty-four, but who knows?'

'How awful, though. To have no family – nothing.'

'But, quite possibly, she felt better without?'

'I suppose so,' said Libby slowly. 'Perhaps she wouldn't have wanted anyone to ferret out her background?'

'Perhaps not, but it opens up all sort of questions. Could someone have recognised her and needed to silence her? Did she maybe recognise someone else and try a spot of blackmail?'

'The people we've been talking to – at least, some of them – felt there was something in her past that made her the way she was. She needed to prove something, one of them said.'

'That fits,' said Ian. 'If she had a terrible childhood or adolescence, and she's trying to blend in with society . . .'

'Exactly,' said Libby. 'Did you not even try to find out where she originally came from?'

'How?' said Ian reasonably. 'Look, you're not going to give this up, are you?'

'We were,' mumbled Libby. 'We thought you'd asked me to look into stuff to keep me out of the way.'

Ian laughed. 'Not far wrong, but more to keep you out of the main line of inquiry.' His voiced became brisk. 'I think you could probably find out a lot more, although it will be difficult. I'll put you down as – um – Social Investigators! That's it. And I'll tell you what we've got so far – as far as I'm allowed to. Not everything, obviously. What do you think?'

'Are you sure?' said Libby doubtfully. 'We might make a total hash of it.'

'No, you won't. And I won't keep hounding you, I promise.'

'But how?' asked Libby, with the suspicion of a whine in her voice.

'Talk to people. You're good at that.'

'But suppose she came from the other side of the county? Or London?'

'Cross that bridge when you come to it,' said Ian. 'Look, I must go. I'll be in touch over the weekend.'

When he'd gone, Libby sat looking at the phone for a long time. So this was it – the first proper, official investigation. And with no real hope of finding anything out.

Eventually, she called Fran, only to find she was tied up with a customer in Guy's gallery-cum-shop.

'I'll call you at lunchtime,' she said, before ending the call.

Now Libby didn't know what to do. She wandered into the kitchen, peered at the Rayburn, the dishwasher, and the washing machine, made an annoyed sound, turned on her heel and went back to the sitting room.

Luckily for her sanity, Ben called with an urgent request to bring some paperwork he'd forgotten to The Hop Pocket. Throwing on her coat, she collected it from the table in the window and set off, avoiding Sidney, for the high street.

It was still grey and cold.

'January must be the most miserable month,' she said to herself, as she pulled her coat more firmly round her and crossed the road opposite the pub. When would she stop calling it 'the Pub', she wondered? As soon as The Hop Pocket opened, it would stop being the Pub, it would be One of the Pubs. Although Ben no longer seemed confident about that. She looked back at the gold lettering ranged above the door and windows. The Coach and Horses, she read. So it would soon become simply 'the Coach', she predicted.

She walked on through the village to The Hop Pocket. Inside, Ben was seated at one of his new round tables with a group of men. They all looked up, but only Ben smiled. Libby handed over the paperwork and beat a hasty retreat.

Now what to do? Peering across the high street, she settled on The Pink Geranium and decided she would treat herself to lunch and possibly a mind-settling chat with Harry.

A few ladies of the village were already in the restaurant, but it wasn't particularly busy. Harry appeared almost as soon as she did, and ushered her to the table in the window.

'Soup?' he asked. 'And we've baked some rolls to go with it.'

'Yes, please.' Libby shrugged off her coat.

Harry put his head on one side. 'And a chat with management, by the look of you.'

Libby smiled ruefully. 'You know me so well.'

Ten minutes later, Libby had a large bowl of experimentally-flavoured soup in front of her, plus a basket of rolls, and Harry opposite, pouring two substantial glasses of red wine.

'Now, what's the trouble? Is this something to do with Ian's little job?'

'How did you guess? Ow! This is hot!'

'Comes from a hot place,' said Harry. 'Like it? It's new.'

'Very spicy,' said Libby.

'So, come on. Tell Uncle Harry.'

Libby related what she and Fran had learnt at Heronsbourne the previous night.

'And Ian thinks we should go on looking into Jackie's past. Except I can't see how, if no one knows where she came from in the first place.'

Harry stared at the ceiling.

'Bedsit in Nethergate, you said?'

'That's what Ian said.'

'So go and ask there. And at the café she worked in. If she's been there some time, they're bound to have some kind of records – or at least knowledge.'

'But they might have taken her on cash-in-hand,' said Libby.

'And she stayed there all this time? Not likely. If I take on casuals I want to know everything, that is, if they're here after a few sessions.' He sat forward in his chair, bringing the front legs down with a thump. 'I could ask them, if you like? Fellow caff owner?'

Libby squinted at him. 'That's not a bad idea.'

Harry beamed. 'OK, you let me have the name of the place as soon as you have it, and I'll give them a ring. If they're a bit cagey on the phone, we can always run down there. Mondays are good.'

'As I know to my cost,' said Libby.

Harry threw a roll at her. 'Cheeky.'

Libby finished her soup. 'Come on, what would make a young woman, a teenager, perhaps, run away from home? Any ideas?'

'Abuse,' said Harry firmly. 'You know that.'

Libby did.

'And peer pressure?' she suggested.

'Only if it was gang-related, and that's more boys than girls.'

'So was she in a home?' Libby sipped her wine.

'Don't ask me – I don't know.' Harry twirled the stem of his wine glass. 'Homes are – or used to be – the worst places. Think about the mother and baby homes back in the fifties and sixties. Even when everywhere else had been more or less cleaned up, they were still appalling.' His face was grim, and Libby knew he was reliving his own youth.

'You would come out of that feeling worthless, wouldn't you?' said Libby hesitantly.

'Oh, yes. I did.' Harry shut his mouth like a trap. Libby subsided into her chair. Then he looked across at her under his brows. 'Come on, poppet. Cheer up. I got out of it, didn't I? No reason this Jackie shouldn't have.' He reached across to top up her wine glass.

'No, but she wasn't lucky,' said Libby, and sighed. 'OK, when I get the stuff Ian's promised me, I'll let you know.'

'Good.' Harry raised his glass. 'Cheers.'

Chapter Twelve

Ben had arrived home looking glum not long after Libby had settled in.

'What's the matter?' Libby got to her feet after lighting the fire. 'The pub looked ready to go to me.'

'It turns out I haven't got all the right licences in place.' Ben, unfamiliar in his going-to-the-office suit, flung himself on to the sofa. 'I don't know how we missed them.'

'Surely that's down to your solicitor, isn't it?' Libby sat down beside him.

'Should have been, but it turns out they have a separate department for dealing with that sort of thing, and somehow it all got missed. I've already put a rocket under them, and apparently they "just can't understand it!" They found all the documentation I sent them, so it isn't down to me.'

'So . . .' Libby began, and then didn't know what to say. Ben turned a tired face towards her and smiled.

'Oh, don't worry. I'll survive, even if I have to sell it off. Annoying, though. I think I'll pop down and see Tim later. See what he says.'

'Well, if you don't open, he won't have the competition,' said Libby.

'But he was rather relying on me in order to get his gastropub with rooms off the ground,' said Ben.

'He's already got that!' said Libby.

'But he's still providing a "local",' said Ben. 'Makes it difficult.'

Libby wasn't sure about that, but just at that moment there was a loud knock on the door.

'Oh!' said Libby, seeing a large police officer standing outside and grinning, holding out a large brown box.

'Compliments of Mr Connell,' said the officer. 'Are you all right with this?'

Ben appeared behind Libby, cast his eyes to heaven, and said, 'Yes, I'll take it.'

'All right with that, Mrs Sarjeant?' asked the officer. Libby nodded, smiling at him.

Ben and the officer effected the changeover, Libby said goodbye, and turned to look at her beloved.

'Well? What is it?' he asked. 'And where shall I put it?'

They decided on the conservatory and Libby went to put on the kettle.

'Ian sent it,' she explained, when they were settled back in the sitting room. 'It's all the stuff on Jackie Stapleton.'

'So you're not backing out after all?' said Ben. 'I might have known.'

Libby sighed and tried to explain.

'Well, it'll keep you occupied, I suppose,' said Ben. 'And at least you're official.'

'But I won't be able to help you,' said Libby, a little tremulously.

Ben patted her hand. 'Nothing you can do at the moment. And at least I won't be going on at you all the time.'

'That's what Ian said – oh, not about you, about him.' Libby stood up. 'I'd better call Fran.'

Much later, after dinner, when Ben had gone off to the pub to try and talk to Tim between his Friday night customers, Libby went into the conservatory to start going through the material Ian had sent. After half an hour, she wasn't entirely sure what, exactly, she was looking at. She called Fran.

'Look,' she began, 'I'm really sorry to disturb you, but I can't make head nor tail of all this stuff.'

'Hold on a minute,' said Fran, and Libby heard the muffled sound of a conversation. Then, 'Guy has let me off Saturday duty, so if it suits you, I could come over tomorrow and we can spend the day going through it. How about that?'

'Oh, yes!' Libby let out a long breath of relief. 'And why doesn't Guy come over in the evening and he and Ben can go into a huddle about The Hop Pocket? I'll cook.'

Fran passed this on to Guy, and Libby came off the phone in a much happier frame of mind.

She still wasn't sure about getting further involved with the investigation and wondered if this was a side effect of getting old. After all, she was old enough to be a grandmother now. Fran already was one, even if neither of them, in their own opinions, either looked or behaved like it. It just showed, she thought, turning out the conservatory light, how attitudes had changed since she was a child, when ladies in their – let's say Middle Years – wore Crimplene and had rigidly set hair.

Fran arrived shortly after ten the next morning while Libby was still wearing her dressing gown and tidying the kitchen.

'Go on,' she said with a sigh. 'You go and get dressed – I'll make a start on this stuff. And bring a coffee with you when you come back.'

Chastened, Libby fled up the stairs to have a shower in record time. By the time she arrived in the conservatory, bearing two large mugs of coffee, Fran already had an impressive pile of paperwork beside her.

'There isn't much to go on,' she said. 'The first mention of Jackie is when she rented the bedsit in King Edward Street.'

'Is there a tenancy agreement?' asked Libby, settling down opposite Fran.

'No. The police asked the landlord, but it turns out that he wasn't the landlord then. He bought the property from the original owner as an investment with the sitting tenants.'

'What about the original owner?'

'Dead.'

'Oh.' They both stared at the paper. 'So what about the café?'

Fran rummaged among the other papers. 'Here we are. "Hal and Sal's Place".' She made a face. 'It's in Wellington Street at the back of the town, near the station. But apparently, Jackie came to them from somewhere else – with references.'

'Really?' Libby was surprised. 'Then why haven't the police checked with the references?'

'Because it was a retirement home which is no longer in existence.'

They sat and looked at each other.

'We could,' said Libby slowly, 'see if we could find someone who remembered the retirement home?'

'It's a long time ago,' said Fran dubiously.

'Fifteen years?' Libby rustled among the papers again. 'Look – Jackie went to the café fourteen years ago, so if she was telling the truth about her age, that would have made her twenty, and if she left the home because it was closing, that's not really that long ago. There'll be people in Nethergate who remember it.'

Fran stared at her, lost in thought. 'Patti,' she said eventually. 'She'd know.'

Libby brightened. 'Yes! Even if she doesn't – personally – people in her congregation will. Think of all those old ladies we met . . .'

'Who probably won't want to have anything to do with us after last time,' said Fran, recalling the unpleasant memories she and Libby had unearthed during their last investigation.

'Worth a try, though,' said Libby. 'Drink your coffee.'

They spent the rest of the morning going through the other documentation Ian had sent and finding nothing. Jackie appeared to have had no life before arriving at her bedsit in Nethergate, and very little since, apart from her interference into the lives of the residents of Heronsbourne.

'She must have had boyfriends,' said Libby, as she cut bread for sandwiches at lunchtime. 'She was attractive, wasn't she?'

'If she pinched someone else's boyfriend, she must have been,' said Fran.

'Hannah would know,' said Libby.

'Bit unkind to ask her,' said Fran. 'The crowd in the pub would know.'

'It didn't sound as though they did,' said Libby, passing a plate across to Fran. 'Surely someone would have let something slip.'

'Ask George?' suggested Fran.

'Or John and Sue,' said Libby. 'Sue, anyway.'

'You know,' said Fran, finishing a mouthful of sandwich, 'this isn't official documentation of the murder investigation.'

'He did say he'd tell us what he was allowed to.'

'Which frankly isn't much. All the official interviews, and grubbing around in records and CCTV – he'd never be allowed to let us see that. I think he's still trying to keep you – us – out of the way. Any other officer would throw up his hands in horror.'

Libby sat and stared at her. 'So what do we do?' she asked eventually.

'If you want to go on looking into Jackie's background, we can. But bear in mind we haven't got anything like the full story.'

'He wouldn't lie to us!'

'No – just not tell us everything. He's not only trying to keep us safe, but trying to keep us from messing up his inquiry.'

'Oh.' Libby chewed thoughtfully at a sandwich. 'We might as well give up then.'

However, they were to receive a helping hand from a most unexpected source later in the afternoon.

Just as Libby had lit the fire and made large mugs of tea, her phone rang.

'Hello, Libby?' said a hesitant voice. 'I'm sorry to bother you, but I – er – I've got – well, there's someone who'd like to – or I think ought to—'

'What?' Libby was half-laughing. 'Come on, Hannah! Spit it out.'

Fran looked up quickly.

'Gary,' said Hannah quickly. 'I think he ought to speak to you.'

Libby made a surprised face at Fran. 'Gary Turner? More to the point, does *he* think he ought to speak to us?'

'I told him he should,' mumbled Hannah.

'Ah.' Libby was grinning.

'Could we come and see you?' Hannah's voice was stronger. 'Tomorrow morning, perhaps?'

'We're out from about twelve,' said Libby, 'but perhaps at about ten-thirty? Would that be convenient?'

'That's fine. Could I have your address?'

Libby gave her the address and rang off.

'So she and Gary are back together again?' asked Fran.

'I didn't like to ask, but it sounds like it. We'll see tomorrow. Are you staying tonight? Will you still be here in the morning?'

'I'll make sure I am,' said Fran.

In fact, before Guy left for Steeple Martin that evening, he had filled Balzac's bowl with more of the expensive dry cat food and treats in anticipation of not only staying overnight with Libby and Ben, but also being invited to Hetty's for Sunday lunch the following day.

So on Sunday morning, after breakfast, the men were sent off to inspect The Hop Pocket, while Libby and Fran waited for Hannah and Gary, who turned up just after ten-thirty.

Hannah looked bright and bouncy while, slightly behind her, Gary was tall, slim, and rather mournful-looking, 'face like a sad elephant', muttered Libby.

After offering coffee and having it refused, the four of them sat down in the sitting room, displacing a disgruntled Sidney, who took up a seat on the table the window. Hannah opened the proceedings.

'This is Gary,' she said unnecessarily. 'We decided to make friends again.' Both she and Gary turned slightly pink. Gary cleared his throat. 'And we got talking about Jackie.'

'Have the police been to see you?' asked Libby.

Gary nodded. 'I couldn't help them.' He a deep, rather husky voice.

85

'At least,' amended Hannah, 'he thought he couldn't. But then I told him you were looking into it, and we talked about what we knew about her. And we realised Gary probably knew more than he thought.'

'And what was that?' asked Fran.

'Little bits, really,' said Gary. 'She talked about her job in Nethergate.'

'And the people there?' asked Libby.

'A bit.' Gary looked uncomfortable. 'She didn't seem to like them.'

'Did she seem to feel she was better than they were?' said Fran.

Gary's eyes widened. 'Well, yes, she did a bit. How did you know?'

'It was the impression we got from talking to everyone else,' said Libby.

'She – well – she was always going on about how the job she had before was much better.' Gary looked at Hannah. 'Didn't she mention it to you?'

'Only once or twice. Wasn't it a care home?'

'She said it was a private hotel,' said Gary.

'Hmm.' Libby frowned. 'Did she say what it was called?'

'Yes – it always stuck in my mind. Apparently it closed down. It was called The Nightingales.'

'That's really helpful,' said Fran. 'We might be able to find someone who remembers it.'

'That wasn't all, though,' said Hannah. 'Was it, Gary?'

Gary looked even more uncomfortable. 'Er – no.'

'Come on, Gary, it might help to find her murderer,' said Libby. 'It can't hurt her now.'

He took a deep breath. Fran stood up. 'Would you like that coffee now?'

Gary looked up gratefully. 'Could I possibly have tea?'

Libby stood up, too. 'I'll do it, Fran,' she said, recognising that Fran's gentler touch was probably going to obtain better results.

Ten minutes later, all settled with tea and a plate of ginger biscuits on the table in front of them, they began again.

'Well,' said Gary, looking more relaxed, 'it was about her background. Her childhood, I supposed.'

'Oh?' Libby sat forward. 'Did she imply she'd been ill-treated?'

'It was very difficult to say.' Gary frowned. 'It was almost as though she couldn't help bringing it into conversation, but she didn't want to.'

'Go on,' said Hannah, when Gary seemed to dry up.

He took another deep breath. 'Well, it seemed to me as though she resented someone. As though they had actually allowed her to be abused, and she wouldn't ever allow it to happen again.'

Chapter Thirteen

'I know it's a bit of a leap,' Gary continued with a deprecating smile, 'but I've thought a lot about it in the past week or so.'

'It makes sense,' said Fran, 'but I don't know how we'd prove it.'

'It all sounds a bit too much like the last business,' said Libby.

'What last business?' asked Hannah.

'Oh, the last police investigation we were involved in,' said Fran, sending Libby a warning look.

'There are always things that seem similar,' said Libby hastily. 'Just nasty things people do to each other.'

'I wonder if we could find someone who remembers The Nightingales?' said Fran.

'I don't know.' Gary shrugged. 'I don't know Nethergate.'

'Tell them the rest,' prompted Hannah.

'As I said, it was only bits and pieces.' Gary went back to looking uncomfortable.

Hannah made a sound of exasperation. 'It was all about the people she particularly didn't like. Like Marjorie Sutcliffe. And the people who bought the new houses on the golf course.'

'Why didn't she like them? Didn't they want to turn the golf club into a venue?' asked Fran.

'Not according to Dotty,' said Libby. 'I think they all bought the houses for the peace and quiet.'

'And the view,' said Hannah.

'So not Jackie's cup of tea,' said Libby. 'Did she like *anybody*?'

'Some of the crowd at the pub,' said Gary. 'And a couple of the girls she met at Creekmarsh.'

'Really?' Fran looked at Libby. 'But I thought . . .'

'Lewis had to throw her out of his New Year's party because she was causing a disturbance.' Libby nodded. 'I'll see if he'll let me question his girls.'

'Or if Edie will!' said Fran with a smile.

'Who's Edie?' asked Hannah.

'Lewis Osbourne-Walker's mother. Old school Londoner,' said Libby. 'Anything else, Gary?'

He shook his head.

'It was more about her background, really,' said Hannah. 'It made such an impression on him.'

'I felt sorry for her,' Gary burst out suddenly. 'I know she was . . .'

'A cow,' Hannah finished for him.

'Well. But I did. No one liked her and I felt sorry for her.' He hung his head and stared at the floor.

Shortly after this, Hannah bore Gary off, apologising for disturbing their Sunday morning.

'Honestly, it's no trouble,' said Libby. 'Just glad to see you're friends again.'

'Well, it'll take a bit of time, but so am I.' Hannah looked over her shoulder to where Gary was unlocking the car. 'But he's really bothered about Jackie.' She frowned. 'I wanted to make you see that, but I'm not sure . . .'

'Oh, yes,' said Fran. 'We saw.'

'Did we?' murmured Libby, as their guests drove away.

'Oh, yes. We were right. She was a very troubled soul.' Fran went back into the sitting room and sat down. 'We need to call Patti.'

'Not today we don't – it's Sunday.'

'Tomorrow, then. I'm sure she'll provide us with a link.'

'Meanwhile,' said Libby, 'I'm going to google The Nightingales. And was it a retirement home – or a private hotel, as she called it – or a care home? There's a difference.'

However, nothing came up under that name, and Libby was forced to abandon her search when Ben and Guy came back from The Hop Pocket and they left to walk up to The Manor.

Hetty had a full house this morning; not only Libby, Ben, Fran, and Guy, but also Peter and Harry, who, as they had no bookings, had decided to close The Pink Geranium, plus Flo and Lenny, and Edward.

'Did you want me to call that caff?' Harry asked.

'Not at the moment,' said Libby. 'Tell you later.'

'Ian working?' she asked Edward, as they all ranged themselves round the table.

'Well, he hadn't appeared this morning, so I assume so,' said Edward. 'I thought you'd know better than me. I'm only a neighbour.'

Peter and Ben were dispatched to fetch wine to augment Flo's contribution. Both she and Hetty were notable wine connoisseurs thanks to their late husbands. Libby went to help Hetty at the Aga but was shooed away.

'Flo,' she said, sitting down beside Hetty's best friend. 'What do you know about care homes in Nethergate?'

'Me?' Flo looked outraged. 'Nothin'! Why should I?'

'Because you know a lot of people in the area and I don't know who to ask.' Libby crossed her fingers beneath the table.

'Not thinkin' of puttin' Het in one, are you?' Flo cackled mightily.

'No, the one I'm thinking of closed down sometime ago,' said Libby.

'Not much bloody use, then is it?'

'What's it called?' asked Lenny. 'I looked at some while I was still living in London.'

Libby looked at him in surprise. 'Did you? Well, the name we were given was The Nightingales.'

Lenny screwed his face up. 'Don't remember no Nightingales. What was that one, now, Flo? You came with me. Addington, was it?'

'Aldington, yer daft bugger,' said Flo. 'Nothing like Nightingale.'

'Is this to do with the Heronsbourne murder?' asked Peter quietly, as Libby returned to her appointed seat.

'Yes.' Libby sent him a quick look. 'Why?'

'I might know who to ask. Are you coming back for a drink after lunch?'

'Yes, please.'

'I'll tell you then.' Peter gave her a quick smile and turned to speak to Edward.

Hetty called them all to order and presented the large joint of beef. 'Get the veg,' she instructed, and the familiar routine of Sunday lunch swung into action.

Much later, after as much of the clearing up as Hetty would allow had been done, Libby, Ben, and Edward walked down the drive with Peter and Harry to their cottage. Fran and Guy had pleaded off, saying Balzac would be eating the furniture by now.

'Tell me, why'd you want to know about care homes?' asked Peter, while Harry went to fetch drinks.

Libby gave him an abbreviated version of Gary's tale.

'So Fran and I wondered if anyone would remember that particular home,' she concluded.

'I could ask,' said Peter, looking down at his hands.

'Peter's mum Millie,' explained Harry.

'What?' Edward looked puzzled.

Peter sighed. 'My mother. Hetty's younger sister. She's in a care home. I know the matron, or whatever she's called.'

'He has to keep in touch,' said Harry.

'Do you think she might know?' asked Libby.

'She might. When did it close?' Peter accepted his glass from Harry.

'As far as we can work out, about fourteen or fifteen years ago.'

'That's about the time Millie – went away,' said Ben awkwardly.

'So it's worth asking,' said Peter. 'I'll ring her tomorrow.'

The subject was dropped and conversation became centred on Ben's trials with The Hop Pocket.

★

On Monday morning, Libby couldn't settle. She called Fran to tell her what Peter had said, then got off the line in case he tried to get through.

In fact, it wasn't until almost midday that he rang.

'I don't know if it's any help,' he said, but Nicole – that's the matron . . . supervisor, or whatever, doesn't remember a Nightingales, but she's given me a list of the ones she does remember.'

'That have closed down?'

'Of course.' Peter sounded impatient. 'There's the Aldington one Flo and Lenny remembered, and half a dozen others. Abbeydown Methodist – doesn't sound likely, does it? Barton House, Seaview, and the one I thought was most likely, Nyebourne.'

'And? That's only four.'

Peter sighed gustily. 'Oh, all right. Tower House and Milton End.'

Hmm.' Libby was busily scribbling. 'I think you're right. Nyebourne is the likeliest. But on the other hand, she could have made the whole thing up.'

'Which sounds the most probable to me,' said Peter. 'I passed on your thanks to Nicole, by the way.'

'Oh, sorry.' Libby felt the familiar pink creeping up her neck. 'I'm really grateful, Pete.'

'I know, you old trout. Just don't forget to tell me what happens next.'

Libby sat thinking for a long time after Peter had rung off. The more she thought about it, the less she believed the story of the hotel, or possibly care home. Sure, the café had received references, but were they genuine? She picked up her phone again and called Patti.

After a long and rather rambling explanation, Patti said: 'And what exactly do you want me to do?'

'I just wondered if you knew anything about care homes in Nethergate?'

'Yes, of course I do. But not that far back. I wasn't here then. And Nethergate has its own vicar.'

'Oh. Do you know him? Or her?'

'I don't honestly think I can ask the vicar that sort of question, Libby. We aren't on those sorts of terms.'

'Oh,' said Libby again. 'What do you think I should do, then?'

'I don't know. Ask at the café where she worked, perhaps?'

'The police have already done that.'

Patti sighed in exasperation. 'I can't help, then. Talk it over with Fran.'

'I have. I expect we'll go and have a root round.'

'Then you'll probably find something,' said Patti. 'Now, I've got to go. I've got a communion class this afternoon.'

Libby just stopped herself from saying 'Do they still have those?' and ended the call. Finally, she rang Fran.

'What shall we do?' she asked.

'Go and talk to the staff at the café. That's about the only thing we can do. Although the police have already—'

'Done that, I know.' Libby sighed. 'Can I come down this afternoon, then?'

'After two, then. I'm relieving in the shop until then. Not that there's much custom.'

Libby opened a tin of soup and stuck it in the microwave. Instant lunch finished, she threw on her coat and set off for Nethergate.

When she arrived, she was surprised to see Fran standing outside Coastguard Cottage.

'I thought we'd drive up to the café,' she said, climbing in beside Libby. 'It's at the top of the town.'

Libby obediently turned round in the car park behind The Sloop, and drove back up the hill to Wellington Street, which turned out to be right opposite the station, where Hal and Sal's Place was in prime position to provide succour for hungry travellers. It wasn't exactly glamorous.

Fran ordered two teas, and they sat down at one of the Formica-topped tables to wait. There was only one other customer, a man in what looked like a duffle coat and a woollen hat. After a few minutes, one of the only two staff members, a woman in a blue tunic, arrived with their teas.

'Um, excuse me,' said Libby, as the thick white mugs were put down. 'I wonder if we could ask you a few questions?'

'Questions? What about?' The woman's eyes were wide with surprise.

'Jackie Stapleton, actually,' said Fran.

'Oh, for . . .' The words were bitten off. 'The police have already been here. Why would I want to answer your questions? Silly cow got herself murdered, didn't she? We don't know nothing about that.'

'The police are trying to find out about her background, you see,' said Libby.

'And what? They asked you?' The woman laughed. 'Do me a favour.'

'Yes, actually.' Fran's tone was somewhat sharper. 'We're what they call Social Investigators.'

The woman's mouth dropped open.

'All we can find out is that she lived in a bedsit and she gave you references from a care home.'

'Yeah. That's all we know.' The woman looked slightly friendlier now.

'Did she never talk to you about her life? Her past job?'

The woman pulled out a chair and sat down. 'She talked about that bloody golf club. And some of the people where she lived. Didn't seem to like any of them. Said they was a bit up 'emselves.'

'Yes, we know that.' Libby grinned. 'She was a bit up herself, too, wasn't she?'

The woman's final resolve melted and she grinned back. 'Too bloody right! Made out like she was better then everyone else. Sounded like she come from money, like. Posh school, you know?'

'But she never said where?' said Fran.

'Nah. But it sounded like it was round here somewhere. Knew

94

the area as well as I did. But that care home – I never did work out where it was. She said it was down the bottom of the town somewhere, but it didn't make sense to me. It wasn't anywhere I'd heard of. Wouldn't put it past her to've made it up.' She shrugged. 'But there, she was here – what? Thirteen? Fourteen years? And always reliable. Funny some people, aren't they?'

Chapter Fourteen

'Didn't get us anywhere, did it?' said Libby, after they left the café, with expressions of goodwill on both sides.

'Except to confirm our impression that Jackie wasn't telling the truth.' Fran frowned out towards the sea. 'There was no care home or hotel.'

'And for the last fourteen years she's worked here and lived in Heronsbourne. At least, we think she did. She could have gone to live somewhere else and come back to Nethergate.' Libby unlocked the car. 'Now, why did she move to Heronsbourne?'

'To move to a house rather than a bedsit?'

'She could have rented a house here. She was far more of a town person.' Libby put the car in gear and set off down the hill.

'Shall we look along Cliff Terrace and see if there are any care homes?' Libby suggested as the reached the square.

'The houses aren't big enough, surely?' said Fran. 'And I though we decided she'd made it up?'

'I just thought she might have got the idea from one of them,' said Libby. 'You know, just the name.'

Fran looked doubtful. 'All right, but I don't think this is going to get us anywhere.'

Libby drove slowly along Cliff Terrace and turned round in the car park at the end, where they sat for moment looking out over the Alexandria, the Edwardian concert hall where the Oast House Company put on their Summer Shows.

'I think you're right,' she said eventually. 'This isn't getting us anywhere. Despite what Gary said, and the woman at the café, we've got no concrete evidence of Jackie's existence before she arrived in Heronsbourne, and the likeliest reason for her murder is that she upset someone really badly over the golf club business, although I can't think what.'

'I don't suppose Jackie Stapleton's her real name, either,' said Fran. 'If she was trying to conceal her background, she wouldn't be likely to keep her real name, would she?'

'What makes someone of that age try and hide her name?' Libby leant her chin on the steering wheel.

'Oh, Libby! Think of all the runaways in the big cities. All the homeless kids. She'd fit that profile perfectly. Sense of worthlessness, withdrawn . . .'

'She wasn't exactly withdrawn,' said Libby, 'but you're right. And perhaps she'd dragged herself up by her bootstraps and didn't want anyone to know.'

'So she was running away from her home life,' said Fran, 'but we've got absolutely no evidence. Poor Jackie.'

'Yes,' said Libby. 'Poor Jackie.'

'Do you want another cup of tea?' asked Fran.

'Yes, please.' Libby set off back to Coastguard Cottage.

'I wonder where she ran from?' she said, when Fran had provided them both with more tea. 'You'd think she'd go a long way from home, yet everyone seems to think she was from nearby – Kent, anyway.'

'Perhaps she ran to Kent, but came from somewhere else,' said Fran. 'Anyway, we've got no hope of finding out where.'

'I wonder if Ian would let us search her house in Pedlar's Row?' mused Libby, staring out over the darkening sea. 'And how did she afford it, anyway.'

They looked at one another in surprise.

'Now why has no one thought of that?' said Fran. 'She went from a cheap bedsit in Nethergate, working in a workmen's café, to a desirable cottage in an equally desirable village. How did she afford that?'

'You know,' said Libby, after a moment, 'she must have had other friends. I mean, did she go to all those golf club meetings on her own? And she must have gone out to other places.'

'But who would know?' asked Fran. 'Gary didn't seem to, did he?'

'Perhaps I'll ask Lewis if any of his staff knew her.' Libby fished out her phone. 'What do you think?'

'Worth a try,' said Fran, 'but personally, I think it's a dead duck.'

'I think you're right,' said Libby, and put the phone down. 'There's no way we're going to get into the golf club crowd, either.'

They sat in silence for a few minutes. Then Libby stood up, displacing Balzac, who had just settled down on her lap. 'I'm going to take all that paperwork back to Ian. I'm pretty sure he shouldn't have given it to us in the first place.'

'And it wasn't the really important stuff, anyway,' said Fran.

'Of course,' said Libby, shrugging into her coat, 'if we were in a novel, we'd immediately come across someone from her past no one had thought of yet.'

'Or a tell-tale letter from a blackmail victim,' said Fran. 'Just doesn't happen like that, though, does it?'

When Libby got home, however, she decided she would ask Lewis, even if she didn't hold out much hope.

'The other girls didn't really like her,' said Lewis, in answer to her query. 'I told you, she caused a ruction on New Year's Eve.'

'None of them ever went out with her? What about to the golf club meetings?'

'Not as far as I know. But we've got a wedding tomorrow, so I could ask. They're bound to talk about her, under the circumstances.'

'A wedding? On a Tuesday?'

Lewis laughed. 'Weddings aren't always on a Saturday these days, Lib. Do you want me to ask or not?'

'Yes, please,' said Libby meekly.

★

98

On Tuesday, Libby decided to do some much-needed housework. One of those things that tended to get glossed over in novels, she thought. She was halfway down the stairs when her phone rang.

'It's me,' said Fran, when, breathless, she answered. 'Where were you?'

'Cleaning,' said Libby proudly.

'Good Lord!' said Fran, unflatteringly. 'Well, listen. One of those unlikely things just happened. You remember I left my card with that woman in the café yesterday?'

'One of Guy's cards, yes.'

'Well, she just rang!'

'Rang the shop?'

'Yes! Guy was a bit puzzled, but rang me and gave me her name and number.'

'Blimey! There's a turn-up! Or wasn't it very useful?'

'Actually, it was. Sheila – that's her name – said she told the girl who works mornings we'd been in yesterday, as she was more friendly with Jackie than anyone else.'

'Why didn't she tell us that yesterday?'

'Didn't think of it, she said. So I thought I'd nip up there and see her now.'

'Can't you wait for me?' Libby felt cheated.

'She finishes at one. If you can get here by then you can join me there.'

Libby squinted at her watch. 'Twenty to twelve,' she said. 'I'll leave now.'

Pausing only to wash her hands and collect her coat and bag, Libby tripped over Sidney and left.

It was a struggle, she found, not to speculate on what Jackie's friend would have to tell them. Her mind wanted to construct enormous fantasies in which Jackie Stapleton's murderer was delivered up on a plate by the end of the day, which, no doubt, if they really were in a book, they would be. But in reality, she had to concentrate on her driving and petrol gauge, which was hovering dangerously close to the red section.

It was just after twenty past twelve when she arrived in the station car park in Nethergate. Fran's car was parked neatly near the entrance, and she almost ran to Hal and Sal's Place to join her.

Inside, Fran was sitting at the counter, talking to a young woman, and watched over with interest by the woman she now knew as Sheila.

'This is my friend, Libby,' said Fran, as she arrived, panting. 'Libby, this is Debbie.'

'Hello, luv,' said Sheila. 'Tea?'

Debbie smiled shyly, slid off her stool and pulled up another. The café was fuller than it had been the day before, and Libby was worried that their conversation would be overheard by the other customers.

'It's all right,' said Fran, noticing her furtive glances. 'We're taking Debbie for a drink when she finishes at one.'

'Not much I can tell you, though,' said Debbie. 'Just what you know already, I expect.'

'Go on, then,' said Sheila, 'you can come and finish your shift.' She put a mug of tea in front of Libby and grinned. Debbie slid off behind the counter.

'Does it look hopeful?' muttered Libby.

'Not sure. She looks younger than Jackie said *she* was.'

'Better than nothing, though,' said Libby.

Sheila leant her elbows on the counter. 'Sorry if I was . . . well, you know, yesterday. We got a bit fed up, what with the police, and customers asking questions. Jackie'd been here a long time, so a lot of them knew her.'

'That's all right,' said Libby. 'People often don't like us asking questions.'

'Did the customers like her?' asked Fran.

'Dunno, really. She didn't much like them what teased her.' She shrugged. 'Get a lot of that.'

'I can imagine,' said Libby. 'Not so much on Saturdays, I suppose.' She looked round the assembled customers, who mainly looked like shoppers.'

Sheila nodded. 'Going into Canterbury, this lot. 'Scuse me.' She darted out to receive some newcomers.

'We can hardly go round asking them what they think,' said Fran, nodding in the direction of the other customers.

'No, but maybe Debbie will tell us something useful,' said Libby. 'And here she comes.'

Debbie came round the corner of the counter wearing a puffa jacket and a big smile.

'Sheila let me off early,' she said. 'Where are we going?'

'We don't know this end of the town,' said Libby. 'Not as far as pubs go. Where do you suggest?'

'The Acorn,' said Debbie, leading the way out of the café. Libby and Fran turned to wave at Sheila.

The pub was just round the corner from the station and, predictably, was even fuller than the café had been.

'Jackie and me used to come in here,' said Debbie, after they had managed to buy drinks and find a table.

'Lunchtimes?' asked Fran.

'Sometimes. Mainly after work.'

'So you used to socialise a lot?' said Libby.

Debbie looked blank. 'I suppose so.'

'Did you go to Heronsbourne with her?'

'Not really. Wasn't anywhere to go, was there?'

'I suppose not,' said Libby. 'Only the pubs.'

'That's why she was so keen on the golf club, see,' said Debbie earnestly. 'You can understand it, can't you? She used to get so fed up with having to come over here every time she wanted to go out. Hardly any buses, see. Sometimes she'd stay over with me.'

'Did she? You live here, then?' said Fran.

'Oh, yes. Same place she lived before she moved. Nightingale House.'

Chapter Fifteen

Libby and Fran stared with open mouths.

'What?' said Debbie.

'Did you say Nightingale House?' said Libby.

'Yeah – why?'

'What sort of a place is it?' asked Fran.

Debbie frowned. 'Just ordinary. One of them big houses in King Edward Street. Lots of them are hotels, or divided into flats. Ours is bedsits. Quite nice really.'

Libby burst out laughing. 'No wonder we couldn't find it!'

'What's so funny?' Debbie was looking put out.

'We were looking for a care home called The Nightingales,' explained Fran, without going into details.

'Oh,' said Debbie, still looking puzzled. 'No. All the houses are called the names they used to be. You know, got names over the door.'

'Why did Jackie move out?' asked Libby.

'Oh, she'd gone before I moved in. It was her who told me to go there, though, when I first came to work here. She said it was all right, and then she took me round there. Well, round the agents first. I reckon I wouldn't have got in there without her.'

This was giving a whole new slant on Jackie's character.

'So,' said Libby, after clearing her throat and taking a breath, 'where did you go when you went out in Nethergate?'

'Ah, you know, usual stuff. Music nights at the pubs. We'd go into Canterbury sometimes. Neither of us had a car, see, so we couldn't go far. We'd get a lift sometimes.'

'Oh, who with?'

Debbie looked taken aback. 'Well, mates we used to drink with.'

'She did have friends, then?' said Fran.

''Course! Not close, but mates, you know.'

'Did you tell this to the police?' asked Fran.

'Not really. They just asked if I'd known her. Not much more.'

'You never went to the meetings about the golf club with her, then?' said Libby.

Debbie shook her head. 'Not my thing, you know? But I understood why she went. She said they were all snobs, anyway. Like the mob she worked for sometimes at that big place where they do weddings.'

'Creekmarsh,' said Fran.

Debbie nodded. 'She was going to a New Year's party there. Don't know why she was found on the golf course.'

'Well, I'm glad she had friends over here,' said Libby. 'I was beginning to think she didn't have any.'

Debbie laughed. 'She didn't, over there. Oh, she used to go for a drink sometimes with a crowd there. And of course, she was going with that bloke last year. Gary, was it?'

'Gary, yes. Did she bring him over here?' asked Fran.

'Nah! Thought himself too good for us lot.' Debbie looked thoughtful. 'She was always saying that about the Heronsbourne lot. Said she'd show 'em!'

'Did she have any other boyfriends in the time you knew her?' asked Libby.

'She went out with a couple of blokes, but never serious. Always sort of backed away after a bit.'

'No one in particular, though?'

Debbie shook her head. 'Not that I knew about, anyway.'

Libby sat back in her chair. 'Well, you have been helpful, Debbie,' she said. 'Anything else you want to ask, Fran?'

'No, thank you, Debbie.' Fran smiled at the girl. 'I hope we didn't upset you by talking about your friend?'

'No. Not that she wasn't me mate, or anything, but she was never that – I dunno. What would you say?'

'Open?' suggested Libby.

'Yeah, sort of. Always kept a bit of herself to herself, if you know what I mean.'

Libby and Fran nodded.

Debbie finished her gin and tonic. 'Well, I'm off, if you don't want nothing else.'

'Can we get hold of you if we want to?' asked Libby.

Debbie sent her mobile number to Fran's phone. 'There. Any time. Quite exciting, being talked to by the police.'

'We're not exactly the police,' said Fran.

'Next best thing,' said Debbie, with a grin. 'See yer!'

'Two separate lives, then,' said Libby, when she'd left.

'Makes a lot more sense now,' said Fran. 'But what I can't understand—'

'I know,' said Libby. 'Why the police haven't found all this out.'

'Exactly.' Fran nodded. 'They must have done.'

'Especially that business about Nightingale House,' said Libby.

'It wasn't the police that gave us the name, though. It was Gary.'

'Shall we go and have a look at it?' suggested Libby. 'It's that long road that leads down parallel to the high street, isn't it?'

'Yes, but I don't suppose there's much to look at,' said Fran, standing up. 'Your car, or mine?'

They opted for Libby's and drove out of the station car park. King Edward Street was a wide, straight street, obviously built when the town was beginning to become a tourist destination in the early 1900s. Terraces of huge, double-fronted Edwardian houses, each with a stone-work name over the front door: Gleneagles, St Michael, Windsor House, Balmoral, and yes, Nightingale House. There was little to distinguish one from another, although the number of doorbells helped. Added to the more modern additions of key boxes for the AirBnBs.

Libby pulled up opposite Nightingale House.

'Looks reasonably well maintained,' she said.

Fran nodded. 'I'd still like to know why she moved to Herons-bourne, though.'

'Seeing as she didn't seem to like it there,' agreed Libby. 'And how she afforded it. We didn't ask Debbie if she rented or owned the house in Pedlar's Row.'

'Come on,' said Fran. 'There's nothing to see here.'

It was beginning to get dark when Libby dropped Fran off in the station car park.

'A lot to think about,' she said. 'Shall I ring you tomorrow?'

'I want to know what we're going to say to Ian,' said Fran, her hand on the door handle. 'I feel he's taking us – or you, anyway – for a bit of a ride.'

'So do I,' said Libby. 'But I think he's hoping he'll get something out of it.'

On the drive home, Libby reviewed the situation. They now knew that Jackie had lived a more normal life than they had previously thought, that her social circle hadn't simply revolved around Heronsbourne and the golf club. They also had more insight into her character, although it posed even more questions. According to Debbie, she really hadn't liked the Heronsbourne residents, or in fact, anything about the place. It was before Debbie went to work at the café, but she couldn't remember if she knew when that was either. Had it been before the golf club proposals? Had she, in fact, been told?

And why, for goodness' sake, was Ian pushing her into this investigation? He must know most of what she and Fran were finding out. Her face set in a forbidding frown, she turned into Allhallow's Lane and drew up outside number seventeen.

Ben was in the sitting room, the fire was lit and Libby could hear the big brown kettle hissing softly on the Rayburn.

Ben stood up, gave her a kiss and a quizzical look. 'Shall I make tea?'

'Yes, please.' Libby shrugged out of her coat and hung it up on one of the hooks at the bottom of the staircase. 'How did your meeting go?'

'Oh, so–so. We're putting everything on hold until we've sorted out all the legal stuff.' Ben turned to fetch their mugs of tea. 'What about you? Where did you go?'

'Oh, sorry. I should have left you a note.' Libby slumped down on the sofa. 'You see, I had this phone call from Fran.'

She related everything they had found out from Debbie, watching Ben's dawning expression of disbelief.

'So what's Ian been playing at?' he burst out when she'd finished.

'Exactly what we said. The police *must* have known all of this.'

Ben shook his head, frowning. 'It's positively underhand. It's as if he's been *playing* with you!'

'Again, just what we said. Why?'

'Well, I'm going to ask him!' Ben put down his mug and pulled out his mobile.

'Do you think that's wise?'

'I'm certainly not going to ask him tomorrow night in front of everyone else.' Ben found the number. 'Voicemail,' he mouthed to Libby, moments later. 'Ian, Libby and I would like to talk to you, please, as soon as possible. And not at the pub tomorrow night.' He ended the call.

'What do you think he'll say?' asked Libby. 'Will he be angry?'

'*I'm* angry!' said Ben. 'I want to know what he's playing at.'

It wasn't until they were sitting down to dinner that Ian called back. Ben made a face.

'Yes, Ian. We do.' He listened for a minute. 'If you could call round we'd be grateful . . . No, I'm sure you can guess what we want to talk about . . . All right, sometime around seven-thirty, then.' He ended the call. 'He sounded puzzled at first. Then – blast him – amused.'

'That's how he's been every time he's talked to me, isn't it?' said Libby. 'And I thought we knew him.'

'So did I,' muttered Ben.

By the time Ian knocked on the door, they were in the front room, both slightly tense. Ben let him in.

'What's the problem?' He looked from one upset face to the other.

'Sit down, Ian.' Libby waved him towards one of the chairs at the table. 'We want to know exactly – in Ben's words – what you've been playing at.'

Ian's black eyebrows rose, his face darkening. 'Playing at?'

'Why were you sending Libby off on wild goose chases?' Ben snapped.

'Wild—' Ian looked astonished.

'You knew everything I could find out already. What was the point?' Libby's voice trembled.

Slowly, Ian's face cleared. 'Ah.'

'Yes, ah,' Ben growled.

Ian leant forward, his elbows on his knees, and looked at the floor. Eventually, he sat up.

'I'm sorry. I didn't think you'd take it like this.'

'What!' Ben burst out. 'You—'

'No, Ben,' said Libby. 'Let him explain.'

'Thank you.' He smiled tentatively at Libby. 'Yes, officers had questioned Jackie's Nethergate connections. You spoke to her work colleagues?'

Libby nodded.

'Right.' He paused. 'And they found out a certain amount. But – and you must realise, I'm not SIO on this case – I felt sure there was more to tell. So I thought the best thing to do was to ask you . . . After all, as I said before, you have a habit of being able to get at things the police can't. And in this case, it was ordinary PCs who were doing the questioning. I could hardly barge in and tell DI Winters how to

107

run his case. So I thought if I could present him with a bit more information . . .'

'All right.' Ben let out a gusty breath. 'So why couldn't you have told Libby and Fran?'

'Yes, why couldn't you? And why couldn't you muscle in on the case?' said Libby

Ian's face wore an expression Libby had never seen before. 'I didn't think they'd believe me, and there are – well, protocols.'

'Well, we thought you'd been playing games with us,' Libby went on. 'When we found out that not only had she a social life away from Heronsbourne, but you knew where she'd lived before . . .'

'Didn't I say she lived in a bedsit?'

'Oh, I can't remember. But you definitely wanted to know about Jackie's life. And you already knew it.'

'Not as much as I'm sure you and Fran found out.'

'Well, it felt pretty grubby.' Libby sat back and folded her arms.

Ian looked at her and then at Ben. 'Would it help to say I'm sorry?'

Ben made a harrumphing sound and Libby made a face.

'Look, I really am sorry. I genuinely didn't think you'd take it like this. I was going against every rule in the book, and I thought it would help.' Ian looked positively ashamed.

'All right.' Libby sighed. 'I take it you've got the car, so you can't have a drink?'

Ian's face lightened. 'I'll take a taxi.'

Ben let out a gust of laughter. 'How you do twist her round your finger!'

Ian looked shocked. 'I don't!'

'Scotch or wine?' asked Libby.

Chapter Sixteen

An hour later, the whisky was considerably lower in the bottle, and Ian had several pages of notes. One of the facts he hadn't known was Jackie's claim that she had worked at The Nightingales.

'Quite clever of her,' he said. 'There are, in fact, two upmarket retirement homes in King Edward Street, more private hotels, really, so if anyone had known the area, they could well have believed the story.'

'What amazed us,' said Libby, 'was the fact that she seemed to have two completely separate lives. The two didn't cross over at all.'

'As far as DI Winters is concerned the crime is based firmly in Heronsbourne,' said Ian, 'which is why he hasn't bothered over-much with Nethergate. And, as I said, I can't really barge in telling him how to run his case.'

'Is he concentrating on the golf club, then?' asked Ben.

'Yes. And of course, I can see why. She did cause rather a fuss there.'

'But she can only have gone to public meetings,' said Libby. 'It isn't as if she could have made an upset in the club itself, is it?'

'DI Winters thinks she could. There's been a suggestion that she had relationships with at least two of the members.'

Libby gasped and Ben looked shocked.

'That hasn't come out in anything we've heard!' said Libby.

'No. And it's one place I didn't want you getting involved,' said Ian.

'They'd stick out like sore thumbs,' said Ben with a grin.

'And there's no way of getting you in, anyway,' said Ian.

'Watch it,' said Ben. 'She's thinking.'

'Libby!' Ian said in a warning voice.

'No, listen. Where do these members live? They must go out socially, too, mustn't they?' Libby asked.

'Mostly at the club itself,' said Ian. 'That *is* their social life, which is one of the reasons there was the upset in the first place.'

'How do you mean?' Libby was frowning.

'Well . . .' Ian sat back and peered thoughtfully into his glass. Ben hastily topped it up. 'When the investigation first started, Winters, fairly obviously, went straight to the golf club. Background brought up a lot about the public disagreements, and the first people Winters interviewed were members of the committee.'

'And what did they say?'

'They were the first people to put him on to Jackie Stapleton's involvement in the club's affairs.'

'But talking to the Heronsbourne people – they all seemed to know,' said Libby.

'Yes, mainly because she talked about it, and when the protests started up, she tried to involve the locals.'

'I wish I knew how the whole thing started.' Libby scowled at her glass. Ben topped that one up too. 'No one seems to know exactly.'

'I thought the first problem was that the committee wanted to sell off the whole course?' said Ben.

'I believe so,' said Ian. 'That was for land development.'

'So it was the members protesting,' said Libby.

'And the residents. They didn't want a whole estate of new houses right on their doorsteps,' said Ian.

'And blocking their access to the sea,' said Libby. 'So that was overruled – by whom?'

'Club members. The outsiders didn't have a say.'

'So then the three new houses were put up and the clubhouse was refurbished?' said Ben.

'And that's when the fight about turning it into a venue began.' Ian nodded.

'And Jackie got entangled in it,' said Libby. 'Because of her involvement with one of the members?'

'Who used to take her there for a drink. That's apparently how it started. She couldn't understand why she couldn't go there for a drink anytime.' Ian shook his head. 'One of her main complaints was that they thought they were better than she was.'

'That sounds like what we've heard about her.' Libby nodded. 'But her friend in Nethergate knew nothing about boyfriends. She knew Jackie didn't like any of the Heronsbourne people, but not the ins and outs.'

'Worth talking to her again, do you think?' asked Ian.

'I don't think so, not at this stage.' Libby sat back and considered Ian with narrowed eyes. 'So do we go on with this?'

'Now you know I'm not making fools of you and that it's me who'll be in trouble if it all goes horribly wrong, you mean?' Ian grinned. 'I'd like you to.'

'I don't think we'd get very far without looking into the golf club aspect, though.' Libby frowned. 'The Heronsbourne people we've spoken to so far haven't helped with that, except one or two who've gone to protest meetings. Including the owners of one of the new houses.'

'Oh, yes – a friend of Osbourne-Walker's mother, you said.'

'Yes. Nice woman. Don't know anything about the other two houses, though.'

'They were all interviewed at the time. Very good vantage points.'

'Isn't there someone who could introduce us to a couple of the members?' asked Ben.

'You?' said Ian.

'Us?' said Libby.

Ben looked embarrassed. 'I thought it might help. Me being a so-called man of property, and all that . . .'

'Perfect for golf club membership,' laughed Ian. 'Have you ever played golf?'

'No, and no desire to,' said Ben, 'but I could pretend.'

'If you really mean it, I'll see what I can find out. But I really can't go rushing in, as I said. I'm going to have to tread very carefully.'

'This is all because you're not on the ground, isn't it?' said Libby.

'Could be.' Ian gazed at the fire.

'Why you didn't really want your promotion.'

He sighed. 'Yes. You know we're supposed to direct operations from behind the desk.'

'Which they tend not to do in police dramas on TV,' said Ben.

'Apparently, a sergeant is often SIO in reality,' said Libby.

'And superintendents always stay behind their desks,' said Ian.

'So you're muscling in on the sidelines,' said Ben. 'Why didn't you explain in the first place?'

'I told you someone else was in charge.'

'Hmm,' said Libby. 'So what shall we do, then?'

Ian pushed his notes aside. 'Wait until I've checked the lie of the land, if you don't mind.'

'People will want to talk about it,' said Libby. 'Especially tomorrow night at the pub.'

'Fine. People will always talk about a murder,' said Ian.

Appealed to on Wednesday morning, Fran was far less annoyed about Ian's deception.

'After all, it wasn't really, was it?' she said. 'Guy wasn't bothered. Said Ian must have had his reasons.'

'I think Ben's really bothered about The Hop Pocket, and it was a focus for his anger,' said Libby. 'Anyway, it's all smoothed out now. He's coming to the pub tonight and might be able to tell us more. If we want to go on with it.'

'Oh, I think we do, don't we?' Libby could hear the grin in Fran's voice. 'I'll come up – and no, I won't stay over. I'll see you about eight.'

Libby decided to finish what she'd started the previous day – cleaning the stairs. But she'd barely got started when, once again, the phone interrupted her.

'It's me,' said Lewis. 'I thought you'd want to know what I found out from the girls yesterday.'

'Oh! The wedding!' Libby slapped her forehead. 'Did you actually find anything out?' she asked.

'A bit. Do you want to come over?'

'I can't really, today,' said Libby. 'I've got quite a bit to do here, and I got interrupted yesterday. Had to go over to Nethergate.'

'About Jackie?'

'Yes, actually. Listen, why don't you come over to the pub this evening? Ian's coming and so is Fran. Or have you got another function?'

'No . . . tell you what, I'll get Edie to ring Hetty and I can drop her off there first. How would that be?'

'They'd both love that,' said Libby. 'We'll see you later, then?'

Libby and Ben arrived at the pub before anyone else that evening. Fran came in with Patti and Anne, having met up with them outside The Pink Geranium, Edward and Ian arrived shortly afterwards, and Peter and Lewis came in together a little later.

'So what's been going on with your murder?' asked Anne, wriggling in her wheelchair with anticipation.

'Not a lot,' said Ian, sending Libby a warning look.

'Lewis asked some of his casual staff about her, though,' said Libby.

'Did they have anything to say?' asked Ian.

'Well . . .' Lewis looked at Libby with a raised eyebrow.

She smiled. 'Yes, did they?'

Encouraged, Lewis sat forward in his chair. 'Yes, a couple of them. I got the impression that they hadn't much liked her, but they'd given her the benefit of the doubt.'

'So they'd been out with her, had they?' asked Fran.

113

'Not exactly. They'd met her in The Red Lion a few times, and the two of them that knew her best had actually worked with her at the golf club.'

'*Worked* with her?' Ian, Ben, Fran and Libby echoed.

'I hadn't heard anything about her working there,' said Ian.

'It was a few years ago, far as I could work out,' said Lewis. 'It was some President's Dinner, or something. And the main thing was—' he grinned round at the expectant faces, 'she got off with one of the nobs!'

This sparked a buzz of conversation.

'That's what I heard,' Ian said quietly to Libby.

'Yes, but not that she'd worked there,' she replied.

'No, but it begins to make sense,' said Fran. 'Now we know how she knew so much about the club.'

'And why she said they all thought they were better than her,' said Libby.

'Do we know who it was?' Ian asked Lewis.

'What, who she got off with? No. The girls haven't worked there since. They said things had changed, and anyway, they preferred working for me.' He beamed. 'I'm much nicer!'

'One of our lecturers belongs to that club,' said Edward, looking into the distance. 'He was saying it's got a bit better, but it's still a very snobby place.'

'You know someone who belongs?' Ian's voice rose in disbelief. 'Why didn't you tell me?'

'I haven't seen that much of you,' said Edward, surprised. 'Didn't think you'd be interested.'

'Well, we are,' said Libby, with a grin.

'How friendly are you?' asked Ian.

Edward frowned. 'Now, look – I'm not getting work colleagues mixed up in your cases!'

Ian sighed. 'We need to get someone in there.'

'But the police have already been in there,' said Edward. 'Don was complaining about it.'

'People don't talk to the police, though,' said Libby.

'You couldn't go in, Libby! Very much male-oriented. That's what Don was saying. They've only let women in over the last few years, and there's still a strict dress code. No trousers, for instance, and until they refurbished the clubhouse, the women weren't allowed in the bar. Had to sit in the lounge outside.' He shook his head. 'Doubt if I'd be let in, even now!'

'I'm beginning to see why Jackie felt as she did,' said Fran.

'I'm surprised more of them weren't murdered,' added Libby.

'Ian,' said Patti suddenly, 'this doesn't sound much like your official investigations.'

Silence fell as everyone looked at Ian. 'Doesn't it?' he said.

Harry provided a distraction by bursting through the door.

'What's going on?' he said, coming to a halt.

'Oh, the usual,' said Peter. 'Finished early?'

'Not much point in staying open. The kids are closing up.'

The kids, in this instance, were Harry's current staff of two work experience students from a local catering college.

'So come on. You all look very serious,' he went on, pulling up a chair while Peter went to fetch him a drink.

'Patti doesn't think this investigation is really Ian's. That's about it, isn't it?' said Fran.

'Not exactly,' said Patti, who now looked very uncomfortable. 'I just got this feeling . . .'

'Well, I hope it's not true,' said Harry, 'because *I've* got some information!'

Ian sighed. 'It isn't strictly true, Hal,' he said, 'it's just not quite the ordinary sort of investigation. More – informal.'

'Oh, good.' Harry beamed. 'Because two members of your golf club have just had dinner in the caff, and now it looks like an investigation for the whole of Libby's Loonies!'

Chapter Seventeen

Ian closed his eyes while the rest of the company erupted into excited chatter. Harry looked nervously at Ian.

'Am I wrong?' he asked.

'Not entirely,' said Fran. 'But I think Ian would prefer it to be a little more – low key.'

Ian opened his eyes and smiled at Fran. 'Precisely,' he said. 'Everybody, could you just listen for a moment?'

An anticipatory silence fell.

'Libby and Fran have been looking into the background of the victim for me. It's not something the main line of inquiry is pursuing, so we don't want it to become general knowledge.'

Put like that, it sounded eminently reasonable, thought Libby.

'It sounds to me,' said Peter, his voice slicing through the general hubbub, 'that you're not acting entirely within the rules.'

Ian gave him a rueful smile, 'You could be right.'

'So you're in danger of getting into trouble?' Peter continued.

'Not just him,' said Libby. 'Us, too.'

'So keep it quiet, eh, Hal?' said Ben.

'Oh, OK.' Harry looked sulky. 'So you don't want to know what I've found out?'

'Of course I do,' said Ian. 'Please.'

Harry sniffed and sipped his drink thoughtfully. 'In that case . . .'

'Oh, come on, Hal!' said Anne. 'Ian didn't say we didn't want to know!'

Ian laughed. 'No, I didn't. But please keep it quiet, Hal, as Ben said.'

'Oh, OK.' Harry relaxed and beamed. 'Well, these two blokes booked earlier today. Just the two of them. They were a bit smart, if you know what I mean. Not exactly suited and booted, but the old classic country gent stuff, you know? Cavalry twill trousers – or perhaps they were chinos, I don't know – tweed jackets, shirts and ties. Not my normal clientele, you might say. Anyway, I showed them to a table, quite near Anne and Patti—'

'I remember!' said Anne, and Patti nodded.

'And then they asked for a different table. The one over in the corner. Not the one near the counter, the other one. That was fine, we weren't busy. And then, when they got the menu, they asked if we had any meat meals.'

Everyone expressed astonishment.

'I pointed out that we were a vegetarian restaurant, and it did say so on the website. So they went into a bit of a huddle, then one of them said: "Very well, what do you recommend?" so I showed them the things I thought they would find – acceptable.' He sat back and grinned.

'So it was obvious they were there on the quiet?' said Edward.

'That's what it looked like. So I kept my ears open.' Harry looked smug.

'Remind me to watch what I say in future,' said Patti.

'And what did you hear?' asked Fran.

'Only snatches, but one bit, when they were getting a bit heated, was a giveaway. One said, "It's the club's reputation that worries me. You were the one who brought her there in the first place." And the other one said, "I wasn't the one who murdered her, though, was I?" After that, they just started talking about how they could keep the police out of the club and off the course. They wanted to start playing again.'

'Would you mind giving me their names?' asked Ian.

'I've only got one,' said Harry, 'the one who booked. I wrote it down for you. Here.' He handed over a piece of paper.

'Was he the one who said he didn't murder her, or the other one?'

'The other one. Mr Saville.'

'Well done, Harry,' said Ian, grinning. 'Not that I should be encouraging you, of course.'

'All's fair in love and murder,' said Harry.

'So what next?' asked Libby of Ian, as the rest of the company fell to discussing Harry's information.

'Up to you,' said Ian. 'If you want to carry on, and you feel the best way is to infiltrate Heronsbourne society . . .'

'I just want to find out what caused Jackie to take against the golf club so violently,' said Libby. 'What do you think, Fran?'

'I agree.' Fran nodded. 'Marjorie Sutcliffe bears looking into. And the proposed building on the marshes.'

'And definitely the golf club committee members. Is it worth trying to get Ben proposed?' Libby asked.

'I think it might be more trouble than it's worth,' said Ian. 'I doubt if they'd welcome you in – not immediately.'

'Oh, well.' Libby shrugged. 'I'll just have to think of something else.'

Ben and Ian exchanged glances.

'Be careful,' said Ian. 'DI Winters doesn't know you. Nor does DS Stone.'

'Hmm,' said Libby.

As they all began to drift off after Tim had called time, she drew Fran aside.

'Thursday's the weekly gathering at The Red Lion. Shall we go again?'

'When's the next quiz night?'

'I gather they're still negotiating,' said Libby. 'Not tomorrow, anyway.'

'I'll ask Guy. He'll be asking for a divorce at this rate.'

Libby looked worried. 'Really?'

'No, it's all right. After all, he got used to me being away a lot when I was involved with the theatre. I'll meet you there, shall I? Eightish?'

'Eight to eight-thirty,' said Libby, relieved. 'I'll let Jemima know we're going.'

'She doesn't live there, though.'

'But she might go over to stay with John and Sue,' said Libby. 'She's dying to be involved.'

Libby spent most of Thursday finishing her much put-off house-work and working out in her head who she wanted to talk to in Heronsbourne. There was Lewis's member of staff, of course; Edward's colleague – what was his name? Don, that was it – although they didn't even know if he lived there; possibly members of the Save the Marshes group and Harry's diner, Mr Saville.

'We could, of course,' she said to Fran, when they met up in The Red Lion car park, 'blithely march up to the door and ask to become members.'

'And how far do you think that would get us?' said Fran. 'Thrown out on our ears, that's where.'

Inside, they acknowledged the greetings of several of the drinkers they had previously met, including Jemima, John, and Sue. John immediately got up and joined them at the bar.

'What will you have, ladies?' he asked, waving at George.

They both ordered soft drinks, then went to join him at his table.

'Couldn't stay away, eh?' Dotty leant over from a table behind them.

'Makes a nice change from our Coach and Horses,' said Libby.

'And The Sloop in Nethergate,' said Fran

'So what are you after?' asked Sue. 'Found anything else out?'

'Not really,' said Fran, standing on Libby's foot. 'Although we have now met Gary.'

'Oh, good! Nice boy, isn't he?'

'Very,' said Libby. 'But what we were really curious about was the members of the golf club. So far, we haven't come across any of them. Don't any of them live here?'

119

'Oh, yes,' said John. 'You know those houses along the drive up to the club? Several of them live along there.'

'Most of the rest of them live out in the country between here and Steeple Mount,' said Sue.

'And Cherry Ashton,' added John.

'Very landed gentry,' said Libby, with a grin.

'Not much gentry about it,' Chrissie, whom they'd met at the quiz. 'Very . . .'

'Up 'emselves,' called over Dan, who had been Jackie's neighbour in Pedlar's Row.

'That was what Jackie didn't like,' said Libby, nodding. 'By the way, Dan, those cottages must be worth a bit now. I remember how much they were going for back when Fran adopted Balzac.'

'Aye.' Dan squeezed his way over to their table. 'Couldn't afford to move there now. Missus and me were lucky, if you can put it that way. Her gran died.'

'Oh, did she leave you some money – if that's not a rude question?' asked Libby, going a bit pink when Fran kicked her under the table.

'No,' said Dan with a smile. 'She died.' He made a face. 'Left us the cottage. 'Course, we had to do it up.' He buried his face in his mug. 'Always wondered how come Jackie could afford her cottage.'

'Perhaps she rented it,' said Fran hastily, before Libby could put her foot in it again.

'Dunno,' said Dan, with a shrug. 'Old boy who lived there moved out – into a home, they said, and next thing, Jackie's moved in.'

'Nice cottages, they are,' said George, leaning on the bar. 'Well, you remember, young Libby.'

'I do,' said Libby. 'We both do.'

'The other thing we were wondering about,' said Fran, 'was the Save the Marshes group.'

Libby shot her a puzzled look.

'We wondered who else belonged to it apart from Marjorie Sutcliffe.' Fran sent an inquiring look around.

120

'No one here,' said Chrissie, confidently.

'I've been to a couple of meetings,' said a voice from the back of the bar.

'Yeah, but you didn't go back,' said Dan.

There was an answering grunt.

'We asked about this before,' Libby hissed at Fran, who gave a minimal nod.

'I don't suppose any of the golf club members were there?' she continued, addressing the unseen voice.

A burst of mocking laughter greeted this.

'Actually,' said the voice, 'there was.'

There was immediate silence.

'Really?' encouraged Fran. The company parted like the Red Sea, revealing a bulky, bearded, middle-aged man on a stool at the end of the bar counter.

'Yeah.' He nodded. 'One o' the reasons I didn't go back.'

'Al! You didn't say nothing about this!' accused someone else.

Chrissie turned to Fran. 'That's Al. He used to be a greenskeeper at the club.'

Al shrugged. 'They was only there to make trouble. Just looked like a set-up to me.'

'A set-up?' Libby frowned.

'Like that Jackie used to stir up trouble. Looked like they was gettin' their own back.'

'But Jackie wasn't a member of the Save the Marshes group,' said Fran.

'No, but a lot o' the other members was.' Al turned back to his pint.

'Hang on,' said Libby, getting to her feet. 'I don't understand. What members of what?'

Al sighed. 'Folk what was protestin' with 'er at the golf club was members of the Marshes group. So I reckoned it was sort o' tit fer tat. They was out to cause trouble.'

'I'm very puzzled,' said Libby, sitting down again with a sigh.

'Anyway, thought you'd be down for the play.' Al fixed her with a gimlet eye. 'You're the one what does the pantos, ain't yer?'

'Yes?' Libby raised quizzical eyebrows.

'Thought yer would.' Al shrugged and turned back to his pint again.

Libby looked first at Chrissie, then at Sue. 'Does he mean your panto? The one Jackie used to be in?'

Sue sighed irritably. 'No, he means the golf club panto. I didn't think they were carrying on with them.'

'They do a panto?' Fran sounded incredulous. 'With all men?'

'Oh, they've got women members, but they're very much second-class,' said John.

'They do them for two nights in the clubhouse – one for members and one for the public.' Chrissie mimed the flicking of an imperious nose.

'Why on earth haven't I heard about this?' said Libby.

'I didn't know about it,' said Jemima. 'I'd have told you.'

'I didn't think about it,' said Sue. 'We've cancelled ours, and I thought after all the trouble they wouldn't be doing theirs. They don't treat it very seriously.'

'I shoulda told you.' George was polishing a glass. 'Their captain's in charge of it. That Bomber Harris. Mate of your friend Lewis.'

Chapter Eighteen

The company settled down to chat, and Libby and Fran shook their heads at each other.

'What I find incredible is that no one told us,' said Libby. 'I mean, I'm not exactly famous, but people round here do know what I do. Like that Al.'

'I don't suppose anyone thought it would have anything to do with Jackie Stapleton,' said Jemima. 'After all, most people thought you were here asking questions for the police, not as a panto supremo.'

Libby felt the familiar colour creeping up her neck. 'No, sorry. That was a bit pompous of me, wasn't it?'

'To be fair, we've only just decided we want to get inside the golf club,' said Fran.

'Is that what you want to do?' Chrissie, who seemed to have joined their party, looked surprised.

'Well, yes,' said Libby. 'Jackie was killed on the course, wasn't she? So it makes sense that it might have been a member. The police thought at first she'd been at a party in the clubhouse. They've been in the club talking to everybody. And we know she'd been in there with a member,' said Fran. 'Before all the protests.'

'Really?' John, Sue, and Chrissie looked astonished.

'She never said.' Chrissie looked affronted. 'Just went on about what a load of – er – snobs they were. Only she didn't say snobs.'

'And she never brought any of her friends from Nethergate over here?' asked Fran.

'Didn't know she had any.' Chrissie sniffed. 'S'pose she must've done, though. Must've gone out with someone.'

'Oh, I don't know.' Libby sat back in her chair. 'This whole thing is mad. It's so mixed up. I don't know what we're doing here, to be honest.'

'Aren't you going to find out what happened, then?' asked Chrissie. 'Find out who did it?'

"Course she is,' said George comfortably from behind the bar. Libby glowered at him.

'It would certainly be a way in to the club,' said Sue, thoughtfully. 'But you'd have to be introduced.'

'That's the thing,' said Libby. 'No one seems to know any of the members, which is mad. They live here – so does everyone else.'

'They keep themselves to themselves,' said John.

'So we've gathered,' said Fran. 'But what about children? They must have children. Don't they go to school here?'

'We don't have a school anymore,' said George. 'Most villages don't. Kids go to Nethergate.'

'That lot mostly go private,' said Chrissie.

'Not all of them,' put in Dan, leaning over from his table. 'My kids go to Nethergate and a lot of the posh kids go there, too. Mind, big school's different.'

'So they just don't mix,' sighed Libby. 'Sounds like some of the seaside towns and the DFLs.'

Everyone nodded gloomily.

'What's the DFLs?' someone asked.

'Down From London-ers,' said John.

'Coined in Cornwall,' said Fran. 'Supposedly because people from London came and bought up local houses.'

'And local people couldn't afford to live there any more,' said Sue.

'And they don't mix with the locals,' said Libby. 'Although it's nowhere near as bad as it used to be. I know quite a few nice DFLs.'

'And we can't expect everything to stay the same,' said Fran.

The current locals gave her a dubious look.

124

'Anyway,' said George, 'the members are locals. Some of the committee members have been here for ever. That Harris. His dad was captain for years.'

'Bomber's a nickname, right?' asked Libby.

'Yeah.' George grinned. 'What's his name now? Go on, Al – you know.'

'Martin,' said Al, without looking up.

'Anyone want another drink?' asked Libby suddenly

She took orders from John, Sue, and Jemima. Fran came with her to the bar.

'So, Al.' She positioned herself next to him. 'You used to be a greenskeeper at the club?'

Al grunted.

'Did you retire?'

'Surplus to requirements.'

'Really?' Libby and Fran looked at each other.

Al sighed. 'When they was sellin' up. Got rid of a load of staff.'

'But they didn't, after all. Why didn't you get your job back?'

''Ad words, di'nt we?' Al's face was now suffused with colour.

George placed the glasses, on a tray, in front of them. 'Al's got a bit of a temper when he's riled,' he said. 'Not that he wasn't in the right of it. Treated them all shameful. I'd have told them what I thought of them if ever they'd come in here – not that they would.'

Libby paid for the drinks, adding a refill for Al to the total.

'I'd get on to Lewis,' said George. 'I'm not saying he's bosom mates with Bomber, but he knows him.'

'I will, thanks, George. And thanks, Al.'

He lifted his glass to her.

'By the way,' she said, as she turned away. 'Did you know a member called Saville?'

He looked back at her in surprise.

'Saville? 'Course. He's the bloody vice-captain.'

'OK,' muttered Libby, as they went back to their table. 'Now we know.'

'So would they be the people who wanted to close the club?' said Fran.

'Not if Martin Harris was that involved with the club's history.'

'But they had already got into discussions with the builders,' said Fran. 'Someone must have done that. And surely it couldn't have been done without the people at the top – and that's what the captain and vice-captain are.'

'Perhaps Jackie talked Saville into it?' said Libby, handing out drinks.

Chrissie wanted to know what they found out.

'And we wondered who it was who wanted to close the club,' Libby concluded.

'It wasn't the whole club,' said Sue. 'Only the course. For the building land.'

'So they would have kept the clubhouse?' Fran frowned. 'Isn't that a bit weird?'

'But,' said Libby excitedly, 'it explains Jackie's attitude! Don't you see? She thought it was just going to be a lovely drinking club, with no stuck-up golfers, and then all of a sudden, her hopes were dashed! And I wonder when her relationship with Saville collapsed?'

'Is it important?' asked Sue. 'Wouldn't the police have questioned them all?'

Fran gave Libby another warning look. 'Yes, of course they would,' she said. 'Perhaps we're looking for something that doesn't exist.'

Libby, looking astonished, opened her mouth. Fran's glare became even more marked.

'What would your panto have been this year?' she asked Sue quickly.

'*Sleeping Beauty*,' said Sue. 'But it's becoming more difficult every year. We haven't got enough people, really, so someone has to write us a special version, and, to be honest, we haven't got anyone who can do that very well.'

126

Luckily, this developed into a general conversation, with a few rather pointed remarks directed at Libby, who managed to ignore them all. After another half an hour, Fran began sliding into her coat.

'Time I went,' she said. 'What about you, Lib?'

'Yes, I ought to go, too,' said Libby, desperate to know what Fran was up to.

Goodbyes were said all round, and Fran and Libby made their escape. Libby was conscious of Al watching them all the way to the door.

'OK,' she said. 'What was that all about? What did you mean, looking for something that doesn't exist?'

Fran walked to the edge of the car park. 'It occurred to me that the more interest we expressed in the golf club, the more gossip would start which would reach the members.'

'Isn't that what we want?' Libby followed her friend, pulling her coat collar up round her ears.

'It would warn them,' said Fran. 'They want to protect the club and get back to playing golf. That's what Harry overheard. And when you think about it, Jackie's involvement with the club started several years ago, and to all intents and purposes, she was nothing more than an annoying busybody these days.' She turned to look at Libby. 'When was she actually active in her protests against the club?'

'I – I don't know.' Libby looked startled.

'No – exactly. As far as we know, all she was doing these days was complaining about it.' Fran turned back to stare across the road towards Pedlar's Row. 'I'm far more interested in how she came to be living down there.'

'So you think it all goes back to Nethergate?'

'Or before. Who was she really? Where did she come from?'

'But we've got nothing to indicate that it came from that far back. The motive, I mean.'

'Someone was protecting themselves,' said Fran firmly.

Libby let the silence stretch out. 'Fran,' she said eventually, 'Is this . . .'

Fran turned to look at her and grinned. 'No, it isn't one of my "moments",' she said.

Fran had in the past experienced several odd 'moments' of psychic perception, which she didn't much like. They seemed to have stopped in recent years, but Libby couldn't help asking.

'We've said, haven't we, how muddled this whole case is,' Fran went on. 'Think about it. We, and the police have been scrubbing around among her friends – if you can call them that – here, those in Nethergate, the golf club, even the Save the Marshes group. She touches them all, but there's no real depth to any of the connections.'

'So what do we do?'

'I don't know. I feel even more that we shouldn't carry on, unless we can find out who she really was.'

'Oh, hell!' said Libby.

'If you want to carry on, you could always ask Lewis about his friend Harris.' Fran grinned again. 'And I could always try and join the Marshes group. After all, I am more or less a local.'

With that Libby had to be content. She drove home slowly turning over everything Fran had said. Never before in their various investigations had she felt quite so much at a loss. She appreciated Fran's warning that the members of the golf club would get to hear about their questions and close ranks, as if they hadn't already done so, and she reluctantly agreed that although Jackie had been disliked, there seemed to have been nothing in her life either in Heronsbourne or Nethergate that provided a motive for murder.

Friday took Libby into Canterbury for a weekly shop. She was just loading her bags into the boot of the car when her phone rang.

'Lewis! What do you want?'

'That's nice, I must say!' Lewis sounded amused.

'Sorry. I'm in the supermarket car park.'

128

'Oh – well, I won't keep you a moment. I just wanted to apologise.'

'Eh?' Libby stood up suddenly.

'I didn't say I knew who Saville was on Wednesday.'

Light dawned.

'Oh! So you didn't! Why?'

'I don't know. Didn't think it mattered?'

'Oh, Lewis! And you didn't mention at any time that you were friends with Bomber Harris.'

'Eh? Who told you that?'

'Someone in The Red Lion. Is it true?'

Lewis sighed gustily into his phone. 'I'm going to get involved in this whether I like it or not, aren't I?'

Libby laughed shortly. 'You should never have asked my advice, should you?'

'No. Listen – do you want to come over tomorrow for lunch?'

'Why can't you come to Steeple Martin?'

'I thought you might want to meet Martin Harris.'

Later that afternoon, her phone rang again.

'Libby,' said Fran, 'I've just found something out.'

'Oh?' Libby sat back on her heels and poked the fire she'd been nurturing.

'You know I said I'd try and join the Marshes group? Well, I looked into it this morning and got Marjorie Sutcliffe's number.'

'Blimey!' said Libby.

'Yes, well, she invited me over to see what they were doing. Or trying to protect. We met at the top of Pedlar's Row, and she took me down on to the Marsh.'

'That's where I bumped into her.'

'I didn't mention you, or Jackie. But she told me how those builders were after the Marsh for housing, and then she went on to talk about the church and the yew tree.'

'St Cuthbert's, yes.'

'Yes. And then she said that it was a shame the vicar had left the group.'

'The vicar?'

'Yes. Apparently he was a retired vicar who showed an interest. Bought one of those new houses. But after Jackie came along to a meeting, he was never seen again.'

Chapter Nineteen

'Blimey!' said Libby. 'And do we think this is relevant?'

'Well – it could be, couldn't it?'

'Yes, but it doesn't do to jump to conclusions. After all, we're bound to think about dodgy vicars after the last business.'

'True. That's what I did think about, to tell the truth.'

'I suppose Guy wouldn't let you off for another Saturday, would he?'

'I don't want to push my luck. Why?'

Libby told her about Lewis's "confession" and invitation to lunch.

'I'd better not,' said Fran. 'But you could always call in here afterwards, couldn't you? Probably more instructive than my information, anyway.'

'Maybe,' said Libby. 'Actually, I've just remembered. Dotty Barlowe mentioned the person who bought the end house next to theirs. Now, did she say he was a vicar?'

'I don't know,' said Fran. 'I wasn't there.'

'I think,' said Ben later, 'you were right. Don't jump to conclusions. Just because there's a retired vicar living on the golf course, it doesn't mean that he used to abuse young girls, or that Jackie was one of them.'

'No, I know.' Libby dished up salmon fillets and new potatoes. 'And what about Lewis's friend from the golf club? I just don't understand why he didn't mention him in the first place.'

'Not everyone tries to connect everything to a murder,' said Ben, helping himself to peas. 'Just don't dig too deep. You don't know what you might hit.'

When Libby arrived at Creekmarsh the following lunchtime, she was aware of Edie's sharp gaze fixed on her.

'Hello, Lib,' said Lewis, enveloping he in a hug. 'This is my mate Martin.'

A stocky, sandy-haired man stood up and held out his hand. 'Hello, Libby.'

'Hello.' Libby shook the proffered hand and bent down to kiss Edie.

'Watch 'im,' Edie whispered.

'Edie's done lunch,' said Lewis. 'How about a drink first?'

'I'm driving, thanks, Lewis,' said Libby.

'And I'm off to have me own lunch,' said Edie, standing up. Lewis looked startled. 'Bye, all. Come and say goodbye, Lib, eh?'

'I thought she was staying,' said Lewis.

'You ought to know her better,' said Libby.

'Yes.' He frowned at her.

'So I gather you rather wanted to meet me,' said Martin Harris, leaning back in his chair.

Libby was puzzled. His face was nondescript, his studiedly casual clothes obviously expensive, but his accent only marginally more refined than Lewis's own.

'Martin comes from our part of London,' explained Lewis. 'I didn't meet him until I moved down here.'

'We bumped into each other after that business of the skeleton,' said Martin. 'You were involved with that, weren't you?' His small eyes locked on to Libby's. She nodded. 'And you're involved with our murder, too, Lewis tells me.'

Libby refused to look at Lewis, and simply shrugged. 'Simply looking into background.'

Lewis got up and fetched a bottle of red wine. 'Sure?' he said to Libby.

'I'm fine,' said Libby. 'Tell me about your panto, Martin. I was surprised to hear about that.'

'Panto?' said Lewis.

'Ah, only a silly little thing – just an amusement for the members.' Martin laughed self-consciously.

'Oh? I heard you did a performance for the locals, too?' Libby beamed at him brightly.

'Er – yes. Not this year, though. We thought it would be a bit—'

'Insensitive?' suggested Libby, and was pleased to see the colour deepen in Martin's face.

'Well, yes.'

'Was Jackie ever involved in it? In previous years, of course.' Libby accepted the glass of mineral water Lewis offered.

Martin was looking more uncomfortable than ever. He cleared his throat. 'Yes. Some years back.'

'Ah.' Libby nodded. 'Was that when she was in a relationship with someone at the club?'

Martin's breath came out in a rush. 'She knows everything,' he said plaintively to Lewis. 'You didn't tell me—'

'I didn't know.' Lewis placed a large dish of shepherd's pie on the table. 'All I know is she advised me to tell the police Jackie had been here New Year's Eve, then she's asking questions all over the place. When we – she – found out you and someone called Saville had been to dinner at The Pink Geranium . . .'

'How?' Martin was wide-eyed.

'The owner's one of my best friends. And so's the Chief Inspector in charge of the investigation.'

'Oh, shit . . .'

After that, things went more smoothly. It transpired that Jackie Stapleton had been hired by Martin a couple of times as casual waiting staff, along with others, for special events, such as the President's Dinner. It hadn't been Doug Saville but the treasurer at the time who had taken a fancy to her, and subsequently brought her into the lounge for drinks on occasion. At about that time, said Martin, tucking into a second helping of shepherd's pie, the subject of non-members being allowed in had come up at the committee. Some

133

thought it ought to be allowed due to the fact that the club was running at a loss, and extra income was needed. And, of course, that led to the argument about selling up altogether.

'And Jackie heard about it?' asked Libby.

Martin nodded gloomily. 'Vince – our treasurer – told her all about it. It wasn't until the new clubhouse was proposed that she started interfering.'

'As a venue, you mean?'

Martin nodded. 'It was all about profit. We'd voted down selling the course, even though we'd had a very good offer.'

'From Rochester and Someone?'

'Brown, yes. But we gave them the corner of the land that wasn't really part of the course, to build three houses. Then the arguments started about the clubhouse.'

'And all this time, Jackie was seeing this Vince?'

'Yes. And then we started the panto, and of course, she *had* to be in it, didn't she?' Martin pushed his plate back grumpily.

'What was the idea of that?' asked Lewis. 'Seems a bloody funny idea for a snooty golf club.'

Martin scowled at him. 'Someone thought it would be good public relations. If we did it for the locals.'

'But they've got their own!' said Libby.

'I know. Bad idea. But the members enjoyed it. Bit of fun, you know?'

'Hmm.' Libby sat back and looked at the ceiling. 'Lewis said you came from the same area as him and Edie. But I heard that your father was captain before you – for years.'

Martin groaned and Lewis laughed. 'The family came from London,' he said. 'Martin tries to live it down.'

'Ah.' Libby eyed him speculatively. 'So tell me. Was Jackie a thorn in your flesh all the time?'

Martin nodded. 'We tried to ban her, but Vince wasn't having it. In the end, of course, when the real trouble started—'

'About the venue idea?'

'Yes. Well we threw her out – barred her – and Vince resigned.'

'Now I understand why she hated you all so much,' said Libby.

Martin looked uncomfortable.

'But no one hated her enough to bump her off, eh, Martin?' said Lewis.

'No.' Martin sighed. 'She wasn't one of us . . .'

'And that's what she couldn't stand,' said Libby. 'Well, thank you, Martin, you've been very helpful.'

'I have?' Martin looked surprised.

'Yes.' Libby nodded. 'Now all we have to find out is why she was like that with everybody.'

Lewis topped up Martin's glass. 'She was a bit of a cow,' he said.

'Yes.' Martin was thoughtful. 'I thought it was just us.'

'Oh, no,' said Libby. Then, 'did none of the people in the new houses join the club?'

Martin hesitated. Then he said, 'no. Oh, we offered them membership, but none of them took it up. I was surprised actually.'

'I know Dotty and Eddy Barlowe,' said Libby. 'They don't seem the golf club type. But I don't know the others.'

'Godfrey Peterson and Mr and Mrs Hughes. Can't remember their first names.' Martin cleared his throat.

'Did they seem golf club types?' asked Libby.

Martin's colour deepened again. 'Not sure what that is.'

Libby and Lewis grinned.

'So Jackie hadn't been to the club for some time, then?' Libby pushed her own plate away.

'No, although she was always around if there were any protests going on. And, of course, she got involved with that group that tried to save the church.'

'That was nothing to do with you, though, was it?'

'The church and that tree used to be on our land. They managed to get the council to redraw the boundary, and now they're on the marshes.'

'The Heronsbourne Flats,' said Libby.

'Is that what they're called?' asked Martin. 'We didn't care, anyway. They were only in the way.'

'But they'd have been dug up if you sold the land for redevelopment.'

'Well – yes.' Martin looked down at his hands.

'Coffee?' said Lewis, after a moment.

'I won't, thanks, Lewis,' said Libby. 'I've got another appointment.'

'In Nethergate?' Lewis raised an eyebrow.

'Yes, in Nethergate.' Libby grinned at him. 'I'll just go and say goodbye to Edie.' She stood and held out a hand to Martin Harris. 'Thank you for meeting me, Martin. And I meant it. You were a great help.'

Libby made her way to Edie's private sitting room.

'What did 'e say?' she asked.

'Oh, he was fine,' said Libby. 'Very helpful.'

'Hmm,' said Edie. Libby didn't ask.

In Harbour Street, she looked into Guy's gallery. He waved.

'Gone home,' he called.

She walked slowly along the sea wall and paused to look out over the unfriendly sea.

'How did it go?' said a voice behind her.

Libby turned and saw Fran smiling at her from the door of Coastguard Cottage.

'Oh, fine. Give me a cup of tea and I'll tell you.'

She followed Fran inside and into the kitchen.

'What did Lewis have to say, then?' Fran asked, switching on the kettle.

Libby reported.

'And what did you find out from the Marshes group?' she asked.

'Well.' Fran turned round and leant against the sink. 'Marjorie's a bit – strange, isn't she?'

'I thought so,' said Libby. 'But what did she say?'

'Basically, she told me abut the group. It wasn't set up to protect

136

the golf club, it's been going for some time, apparently, to protect the marsh as a habitat for wildlife and a Site of Special Scientific Interest. And, of course, the church and the yew tree.'

'Was there a threat to those before?'

'Several times, from different quarters. And when the golf club was due to be sold off, they were worried because it stands right on the edge of the marsh next to the course itself. But now, if the marsh itself is developed it will be all be dug up and pulled down, so she's trying to get a preservation order or something slapped on it.'

'And how did Jackie come into it?'

'Once she'd got on to the subject, I couldn't shut her up. Jackie joined after all the arguments about the club had more or less stopped. All she did was wind people up, Marjorie said. She just seemed to want to start an uprising.' Fran poured boiling water into mugs. 'The thing that annoyed Marjorie most was that after the first time Jackie turned up – shooting her mouth off, Marjorie said – this vicar who'd joined them looked most offended and was never seen again. She thought having a vicar on the membership would be good for their image. And he was very clever, she said.'

'I can imagine Jackie offending a member of the clergy,' said Libby, amused. 'But didn't Marjorie get in touch with him afterwards?'

'Yes, but she said he wouldn't see her or speak on the phone.'

'Perhaps he thought it would become too rowdy for the likes of him.'

'Maybe. I just wondered.'

'I can see you did.' Libby took her tea into the sitting room and went to sit on the window seat. 'But as I said, it doesn't do to jump to conclusions. What did she know about this vicar?'

Fran sat down in her chair by the fire. 'Only,' she said, 'that he'd been living abroad.'

Chapter Twenty

Libby stared at her. 'Ah.'

'It just struck a chord,' said Fran. 'But, as you said, doesn't do to jump to conclusions.'

'No.' Libby took a thoughtful sip of tea. 'And every vicar who's been living abroad isn't necessarily a paedophile.'

'No.' Fran gazed at the fire. 'Would it be worth finding out about him, though?'

'This isn't like you,' said Libby. 'It's usually me wanting to find out about people.'

'It's rubbing off on me,' said Fran with a grin. 'Anyway, how could we? He doesn't sound very sociable.'

'I wonder if he goes to church in Nethergate? Patti says she doesn't really know the vicar there, and won't go digging for us. And we can hardly tip up for morning service or whatever.'

'Pity we don't know any church-goers in Heronsbourne,' said Fran. 'I didn't even know there was a church there.'

'Neither did I until Patti told me. I wonder if Dotty Barlowe knows? She's his next-door neighbour. And what about the neighbours the other side. Martin Harris mentioned them. What did he say their names were?' Libby frowned. 'Hughes, that's it.'

'What about them?' asked Fran.

'Maybe they go to church?'

'I don't see how that would help. We don't know them, either.'

'Maybe,' Libby said, 'I could call in on Dotty on the pretext of leaving the car to explore the beach, and get chatting about the neighbours? She seems to like a good gossip.'

Fran looked at her solemnly for a moment. 'That's not a bad idea. Could I come?'

'When would Guy let you off?'

'Monday morning?' suggested Fran.

'You're on!' said Libby.

Dotty would be only too pleased to see them on Monday morning.

'Call in when you arrive and we'll have coffee. How about that?' she said.

'Lovely,' said Libby. 'About eleven?'

She picked Fran up in Nethergate at ten forty-five.

'What are we going to ask her?' Fran asked.

'Play it by ear,' said Libby. 'She was at The Red Lion last week, so she knows the sort of questions we're asking.'

Dotty, as before, welcomed them at the door of Spindrift with a beaming smile.

'Oh, it's so nice to have visitors,' she said. 'We don't know enough people here yet. Edie would come round, but it's a bit far for her to walk, and she doesn't like to keep asking her son for lifts.'

'What about the other ladies you meet at The Fox?' Libby asked, as they followed her up the stairs.

'Yes, sometimes. Not often, though.' Dotty ushered them into her spectacular sitting room, which Fran duly admired.

'What about your neighbours, though?' she asked. 'All being newcomers together?'

Dotty pulled a face.

'Not really our sort. Sally and Paul Hughes are all right, but she's a bit of an invalid.' Dotty sniffed. 'Though I reckon it's all in her mind.'

'What about the other side?' asked Libby, coming away from the window, where Fran was still admiring the view.

'Oh, him.' Dotty snorted as she went into the kitchen. 'I told you, didn't I? He's a retired vicar. Godfrey Peterson. Barely speaks to anyone, as far as I can see.'

'I heard about him,' said Fran. 'I met someone from the Save the Marshes group, and she said he used to belong to it. 'I wonder if that's why he moved here,' said Fran. 'The peace and quiet, and hardly any neighbours?'

Dotty shrugged. 'Maybe. I've only spoken to him once or twice. We went round to introduce ourselves after we moved in, but he didn't even invite us in.'

'How do you know he's a retired vicar?' asked Libby. 'Does he wear a dog collar?'

'No.' Dotty laughed. 'One of the girls at The Fox who belongs to that Save the Marshes told us. That Marjorie was ever so chuffed to have him in the group. Thought it added a bit of class.'

'What about the Hugheses? They're retired too, are they?' said Libby, deeming it sensible to change the subject.

Dotty nodded. 'Him and my Eddy chat a bit sometimes. Eddy was an engineer – motor trade, you know – and Paul was in the same sort of line. Actually, I ought to give Eddy a shout as we're having coffee. He's got a little sort of workroom up there in the third bedroom. He does little projects. Makes stuff for the grandsons.'

She went back to the staircase, which Libby now saw continued up to the top floor, and yelled: 'Eddy!'

Eddy appeared in a check shirt and oil-stained jeans, a smile on his ruddy face.

'Libby and Fran came to park their car,' Dotty explained. 'They're going to walk down to the beach. So I asked them in for coffee.'

'Coffee! Lovely,' said Eddy, rubbing his hands.

'Well, you'd better wash them,' said Dotty, noticing the oil anointing his chubby fingers.

They all laughed.

'Dotty was saying you and your next-door neighbour had both been engineers,' said Libby. 'At least that's one thing you've got in common.'

'Not quite the same line, though,' said Eddy, speaking from the kitchen sink. 'He was railways.'

'Must be difficult not speaking to the other one, though,' said Fran.

'Not really.' Dotty shrugged. 'Sally and Paul are nearly always there, so there's always someone to take in a parcel. Mind, we've had to take in a few for old Godfrey.'

'Fan of online shopping, is he?' said Libby with a grin.

'Aren't we all, these days?' said Dotty. 'No, these are more personal like. Handwritten parcels, if you know what I mean.'

'Foreign, too,' added Eddy.

Libby managed to stop herself glancing at Fran, who said nonchalantly, 'Oh, yes, Marjorie Sutcliffe said something about him living abroad.'

'That explains it, them,' said Dotty. 'Wonder what a vicar would be doing abroad?'

'They don't have missionaries any more, do they? The Church of England?' said Libby.

'Perhaps he was Catholic?' suggested Eddy. 'Although they don't retire, do they? They keep on being priests.'

'Oh, well, it doesn't matter,' said Dotty. 'He doesn't interfere with us, so we leave him alone.'

'Does a bit of bird-watching,' said Eddy, blowing on his coffee before sipping it. 'Seen him on his balcony with his binoculars.'

'Great place for it, I suppose,' said Fran, before Libby could put her foot in it.

'Don't know what he thinks he can see at night,' said Dotty.

'Owls?' suggested Fran.

'Does he do that often?' asked Libby, who could barely restrain herself.

Dotty shrugged. 'Only seen him a couple'a times, but then, we don't sit out there often at night.'

'Sometimes in the summer,' said Eddy. 'We have a G&T out there after dinner, don't we, ducks?'

'He's not out there then,' said Dotty. She laughed. 'He might have to speak to us!'

'I don't suppose the golfers are out there, then, are they?' said Fran.

'They are in June,' said Dotty, 'still light then, see?'

'And we get a bit of noise from the club sometimes,' said Eddy. 'That's why we was against 'em turning the place in to a nightclub sort of thing.'

'I can imagine,' said Libby. 'After all, you came for the peace and quiet, didn't you?'

'Was your part of London very noisy? It was a bit where I was.' added Fran.

And so, deftly, the subject was moved away from Mr Godfrey Peterson, and after a decent interval, Libby and Fran were able to take their leave.

'So, was that helpful?' asked Libby, as they walked down the footpath towards the beach.

'A bit, I suppose,' said Fran. Neither of them could resist casting a swift glance at the reverend gentleman's balcony.

'Not likely to have nipped out on New Year's Eve to bash Jackie over the head,' said Libby.

'And no connections locally,' agreed Fran.

'And the Hugheses don't seem to mix much, either,' said Libby. 'So the new houses don't seem to provide any suspects.'

'Wonder what Mr Peterson's really looking at through his binoculars?' mused Fran.

'And is he really a vicar?' Libby turned to look at her friend.

Fran laughed. 'Look, it's not him we're investigating! Don't get sidetracked.'

'Intriguing though, don't you think?' Libby thrust her hands into her pockets and frowned at the muddy path in front of her.

'Mildly,' said Fran. 'Come on, what are we supposed to be looking for down here?'

'Scene of the crime?' suggested Libby.

'That was on the golf course,' said Fran.

'Yes, but there are supposed to be cut throughs from the beach. Shall we look for them?'

The beach, when they reached it, was a mix of greyish-looking sand and pebbles. The tide was out, and on the sullen-looking sea they could see a few seabirds.

'Here, look.' Libby clambered up a shingled bank. 'Between these two dunes.'

The shallow dunes, covered in sparse vegetation, concealed a deep, sandy dip, bordered on the sea-side with more vegetation.

'This is it – the bunker,' she said. 'And look. There's a little bit of police tape.'

Sure enough, a flicker of blue and white showed at the far side. They stared at it in silence for a while.

'Easy enough to come down the path to get here,' said Fran.

'And easy to get here from the beach.' Libby pulled at her lower lip. 'What puzzles me is how someone managed to get her into the bunker without being seen. It's right by the beach, and there were loads of people here at the party by all accounts.'

'Mmm.' Fran nodded. 'But they did. Must have been someone at the party, after all. A stranger would have been noticed.'

'Shall we walk along the beach a little way?' suggested Libby. 'We might see another point of access.'

The beach was much the same all the way along. The low dunes protected the golf course from being visible, except for the few breaks between them where there was access. A creek at the end divided this beach from the mud flats of the marshes.

'How did the party-goers get here?' said Fran. 'Across the marsh?'

'I suppose so. Or down the footpath past Dotty's house.'

'Would a stranger know this route?' Fran looked puzzled.

'No – it would have to be a local.' Libby glanced at the sky. 'It's going to rain again. Let's go back.'

They turned and made their way back along the beach.

'It has to be unplanned,' said Libby. 'If it wasn't, why pick here? There must have been easier places . . .'

'Heaven knows,' said Fran. 'Looks as though her past has nothing to do with it, doesn't it?'

'It does, rather. I suppose someone could have caught up with her after she'd left . . .'

'And then what? Brought her body back here? How? Unless the police found tyre tracks on the golf course.'

'Wheelbarrow down the footpath?' Libby said hesitantly.

'Come on, Lib! Don't be fanciful.'

They paused to peer into the bunker again, then resumed their trek up the footpath. As they reached the new houses, the first drops of rain began to fall.

'Well, we've done a lot, even if we haven't achieved much,' said Libby, setting the car bumping along the track towards the main road. 'What shall we do next?'

'No idea,' said Fran, moodily. 'I just wish we could talk to someone else who'd known her.'

'We've talked to young Debbie at the café,' said Libby. 'And some of the people she drank with in the pub. And we don't think it was someone she knew pre-Heronsbourne. So, who?'

Chapter Twenty-one

Libby reported to Ian when she got home.

'I don't see where else we can go,' she said. 'It looks to us as though Jackie's killer must be among the people at the New Year's party on the beach. We couldn't see how a stranger could have got down there.'

'No, Winters thought the same,' said Ian.

'Does he know what we've been doing?'

'It's been mentioned.' Ian sounded amused.

'Oh. And does he know about Jackie and this Vince person at the golf club?'

'Yes.'

'Hmm,' said Libby. 'You see? We're not going to find out anything you – or DI Winters – don't know already.'

There was a short silence.

'All right, leave it at that,' said Ian. 'But if you do hear anything else, let me know. After all, you're both known to be interested in the case now, so people may well get in touch. Will you be going over there this week?'

'No reason to,' said Libby. 'We've got a quiz evening tonight – at home. Some of The Red Lion people will be there, I expect.'

'I expect the subject will come up, then.' Ian paused. 'And you never know, I might drop in on my way home. Edward will be there, won't he?'

'If you do that no one will speak to me,' said Libby. 'You could stick to Edward and Philip, I suppose, and not talk to Fran and me.'

'Right, I'll see you later,' said Ian, and rang off.

When Libby and Ben arrived at the pub, the teams from The Red Lion and The Poacher had already arrived, as had Fran, Jemima, Edward, and Philip from their own team. They were greeted cheerily by a number of voices. Sid from The Poacher strolled over, glass in hand, while Ben went to fetch drinks.

'Hear you're involved in another murder?' he said.

Libby sighed. 'Sort of. It's all right – nothing over your way. Nothing over our way, either.'

'That girl who was found on the golf course, wasn't it? She worked in that café in Nethergate.'

'That's the one. Did you know her?'

'Not personally, but one of our regulars thought they did.'

'Really?' Libby's eyebrows shot up. '*Thought* they did?'

Sid nodded. 'Thought he recognised her from years ago. Couldn't have been her, though. Different name.'

'Would he talk to me?' asked Libby, after a moment, wondering how much she should say.

'Expect so,' said Sid with a grin. 'He knows who you are. Belonged to that ukulele group.'

'Oh, heavens!' groaned Libby, remembering another prior investigation. Fran, alerted, came over. Libby explained.

'Can you set it up, Sid?' Fran asked.

'No need. Always comes in for his lunchtime pint.'

'Shall we go over tomorrow?' Fran turned to Libby.

'I suppose so.' Libby smiled at Sid. 'Here we go again.'

Chrissie and a few members of George's team came to ask if there was any news, to which they gave negative answers, then Tim called for everyone to take their seats as he was about to start.

They were well into the second round when Libby noticed Ian at the bar. She turned as far away from him as possible, and nodded at

Fran, who ignored both Libby and Ian in her normal serene manner.

This time the team from The Fox won, to Philip's chagrin.

'It was the sport round again!' he complained. 'Don't we know anyone who's a mad keen sports fan?'

Everyone shook their heads.

'Only Tim,' said Ben. 'And we can't have him.'

'We can ask him, though,' said Philip, making his way to the bar, where Edward was talking to Ian. Ian made space for him and strolled over to the team's table.

'Second, again?' he said.

'Lack of a sports expert,' said Ben.

'Ah. Can't help you there.' He smiled across the table. 'Fran, Libby.'

'Ian.' Libby cleared her throat. 'Can I have a word?'

'What did I tell you?' he said when she had explained about Sid's regular. 'Said it would come up.' He patted her shoulder. 'Let me know.'

'That sounded a bit patronising,' said Jemima, her eyes following Ian back to the bar.

'It did, didn't it?' Libby scowled at Ian's back.

'Does it feel as though he's still pulling our strings?' said Fran.

'Yes.' Libby heaved a sigh. 'But I don't think he sees it like that.'

'No.' Ben came up behind them. 'To him, you're his secret weapon. I think he wants to get to the bottom of the whole thing before this DI does.'

'That's a bit petty of him,' said Fran.

'The trouble is,' said Ben with a grin, 'your interest has been piqued. You aren't going to give up now.'

Tuesday dawned surprisingly sunny. It was, however, several degrees colder, Libby realised, as she went out to the car.

It was a nice change, she reflected, to be driving in a different direction from her usual route into Nethergate. As she drove down the little hill towards Shott, she admired the frost-covered green in front of The Poacher.

Fran was already seated at the bar. Sid came up with a friendly smile.

'Coffee?' he offered. 'Then I'll introduce you.' He nodded towards an elderly man in a heavy tweed coat and cap seated at a table in the window.

'What do we ask him?' murmured Libby.

'Play it by ear again,' answered Fran.

Sid appeared at Libby's side and presented her with a mug of coffee, then led them towards the man in the window.

'Here we are, Fred. Remember our Libby?' Sid pulled out chairs for Fran and Libby. 'And Fran, of course.'

'Oh, aye!' Fred stood up and swept off his cap. 'Nice to see you again, ladies. 'Nother pint, Sid, ta.'

They all took their seats while Sid went off to fulfil Fred's order.

'Now, then. Sid said you wanted to ask me about that girl who was murdered.' Fred's eyes, surprisingly bright, twinkled at them from a weathered face.

'Thank you for talking to us, Fred.' Libby looked Fran, who nodded. 'Sid said you thought you recognised her.'

'Well, see, I goes into the caff she works in when I go to do me shopping. And she looks just like a girl I used to know. Older, o' course. Wasn't though. Different name.'

'Where was it you knew this girl?' asked Fran.

'Oh, over Felling way.' Fred sat back and unbuttoned his coat, unaware of the quickening interest in his listeners. Sid silently put down a pint glass in front of him, and as silently, drifted away.

'Did you work over there?' asked Libby.

'Carpenter, see? Master carpenter.' He preened a little. 'Did some work for a bloke over there.'

There was a loaded silence while Fred took a sip of his new pint.

'I don't suppose it was Ted Sachs, was it?' asked Libby, trying to sound nonchalant.

148

'Now how would you know that?' Fred grinned delightedly. 'Didn't actually work *for* 'im, but we both worked for the same bloke for a while.'

'So how did you come across the girl you thought was Jackie?' asked Fran.

'She were with a crowd of youngsters. Drank in the local – although I reckon most of 'em were too young.' He sniffed. 'Bit of trouble there was over there, then.' He thought for a moment, then brightened. 'Then I started working for a bloke in Canterbury. Much better money.'

'Do you remember the name of the girl in Felling?' asked Libby.

'Well, it weren't Jackie!' he chuckled. 'Now then, what was it?' He frowned. 'I know! Rose! That's it. Or – no, I tell a lie! Rosa. Never knew her last name.'

'Right.' Libby sighed. 'What made you think it was Jackie Stapleton?'

'Looked like her – I said. Wrong colour hair though. And come to think of it, she was fatter.' Fred noticed Fran's expression. 'Mean to say, not fat. But – er – plump.'

He took another hefty swallow of beer. 'Mind, if it had been her, she would have recognised me. Always used to have a bit of a chat, like, when I saw her in the pub over there.' He shook his head. 'No, it wasn't her.'

'Never mind,' said Fran. 'We're just trying to find out about Jackie's background. No one seems to know.'

'Sorry I couldn't help,' said Fred. 'Poor girl. Never did like them golfers.'

After ten minutes of desultory chat, Libby and Fran got up to go.

'Nice to meet you, Fred,' said Libby.

'Hope you find who done it,' said Fred. 'See you again.'

'Now what?' said Fran as they stood in the car park. 'That didn't help, either.'

'Unless Jackie was his Rosa in disguise,' said Libby doubtfully. 'Changed her name, dyed her hair, lost weight . . .'

'Just didn't sound right, though, did it?'

149

'Would have been the right background, if she'd been in with that lot in Felling.'

'It was Ted Sachs's name that did it, wasn't it?' said Fran.

Ted Sachs had been a builder very much involved in a previous adventure. Libby had no desire to come across him again any time soon.

'Let's face it, it would have been a bit too much of a coincidence if it had been,' she said.

'Just as it would have been if she had been a victim of a rogue priest.' Fran grinned at her. 'That's what you were thinking about the Reverend Peterson, weren't you?'

Pink crept into Libby's cheeks. 'It did cross my mind.'

'I knew it! But it would be a bit daft to reappear in the same area where you'd caused so much trouble.'

'I know.' Libby sighed. 'Back to square one, then.' She looked at her watch. 'Shall we pop in to see Cass at the nursery?'

Cassandra, Libby's cousin, lived with Mike Farthing of Farthing's Plants, the nursery she helped him to run not far from The Poacher.

'I don't think so, if you don't mind,' said Fran. 'I ought to get back to give Guy a break. He's just got a commission, so I need to take over in the shop. We miss Sophie, now she's started her PhD.'

Sophie, Guy's daughter, and occasional significant other of Libby's son Adam, lived in the flat over the shop when she was between university stints.

'OK. I think I want to go back normality myself. I'm a bit fed up with chasing wild geese.' Libby unlocked her car. 'Are you coming up for a drink tomorrow?'

'I don't think I'll do that, either.' Fran smiled ruefully. 'I seem to have spent a lot of time up there recently. You'll have to come down to us for a change. Saturday?'

'Sounds like a plan,' said Libby. 'See you then.'

'So what's been happening with your murder?' asked Anne, when Libby and Ben joined her and Patti the following evening in the pub.

'Nothing much,' said Libby. 'No one knows anything about this girl – woman, I should say. She tipped up in Nethergate sometime back, moved to Heronsbourne, and that's virtually all anyone knows.'

'No friends?' Anne was aghast.

'A few, but they were acquaintances more than friends. She didn't seem to be close to anyone.'

Ben put Libby's half of lager in front of her. 'And despite this one's digging into everything in sight, nothing's turned up.'

'Are you going to resign again?' asked Patti.

'Just let it die a death,' said Libby, 'if you'll pardon the pun.'

She recounted the events of the last few days. Patti echoed Fran's thoughts.

'It honestly would be too much of a good thing if it all linked back to something else you've looked into,' she said. 'Just too Miss Marple-ish for words.'

'I know. But in a way, the whole reason Ian wanted us to have a look was because of our local connections. I mean, Jackie could well have been one of the girls caught up in the nastiness in St Aldeberge. She was the right age.'

Patti frowned. 'That's all done and dusted. Don't go digging that up again.'

'I wasn't going to. But that's what Ian wanted us to find out.'

'What, about St Aldeberge?' Patti looked horrified.

'No! Just giving an example,' said Libby. 'Let's talk about something else.'

Chapter Twenty-two

'You know,' said Libby on the phone to Fran on Thursday morning, 'I much prefer it when people ask us in to look at things. When there's a more personal connection. This is just so confusing – and we're not the police, so people can refuse to talk to us.'

'Lewis did ask your advice in the first place,' said Fran.

'Not the same,' said Libby. 'Anyway, got to think of a new project. Thought about a painting of the marshes. What do you think?'

'For the shop?'

'Well, if Guy wants it. It's more or less local, isn't it?'

'I suppose so. I'll ask him.'

After ending the call, Libby mooched into the conservatory and stared moodily at the already stretched paper waiting for her on the easel. Ben appeared in the doorway.

'Trying to summon up enthusiasm?' he asked.

'Yes. I want to do the marshes.'

'You'll have to go down there then.'

'Only to take some pictures. And,' said Libby, brightening, 'there are bound to be some on Google!'

'Giving you an excuse to go and sit in the sitting room and light the fire,' grinned Ben.

'I was thinking,' said Libby, settling down with her laptop in front of the fire. 'Do you think Gerry and Colin would like a painting for their flat? Gerry said he liked the ones in Steeple Farm.'

'He was just being polite,' said Ben. 'Shall I put some soup on for lunch?'

Gerry and Colin were recent friends who lived, temporarily, in one of the flats Colin had created in a building he had renovated in the centre of the village.

'When are they back from Spain?' asked Libby.

'When they've sorted out whatever business they had over there,' said Ben. 'They both lived over there for some time.'

'But Colin had done all that, hadn't he? He's been here longer than Gerry. And they wanted to start house-hunting so they could be in by spring.'

'They'll be back soon enough,' said Ben. 'Now, about that soup?'

Lewis called that evening.

'Solved a mystery for you!' he said smugly.

'Oh?' Libby struggled to sit upright on the sofa. 'Which particular mystery?'

'Your reverend gentleman.'

'He's not mine! He just lives next door to Dotty.'

'Yeah, well, he's not an English vicar. He comes from America!'

'Really? How on earth did you find that out?' Libby was fully alert now.

'We've got a party of Yanks here for a weekend – some conference or other. Anyway, they went out for a look round the village – you know how they always love our villages – and saw him coming up the path from the new houses.'

'I didn't think he ever went out,' said Libby.

'Well, he did today. And this bloke recognised him!'

'And? Don't be provoking, Lewis.'

'Apparently, he ran this place called the House of the Sacred Flame. How about that!'

'Well!' said Libby. 'Fancy that.'

'Thought you'd like to know,' said Lewis. 'Oh, and my girls don't know much about that Jackie, by the way. Although one of them did say she — Jackie — had said she used to do waitressing in her teens.'

'She didn't say where?'

'No, that was it. Now I'd better go. They'll be wanting their nightcaps. Oh, and I nearly forgot. Is your mate still looking for a house?'

'As far as I know. Why, have you found one?'

'Yeah, Might have.'

'I'll tell him when I hear from him,' said Libby.

'What was all that about?' asked Ben, putting the television on mute. Libby told him.

'Oh, one of those mad American TV churches?' said Ben.

'That's a bit harsh,' said Libby. 'A lot of them are very well respected.'

'So why's he over here?' asked Ben.

'How do I know?' Libby settled back into the sofa. 'Anyway, obviously not a renegade Anglican priest.'

'Wonder if he's trying to set up a branch in Kent?' mused Ben.

'Someone would know about it,' said Libby. 'No, I reckon perhaps he came from round here years ago, and he's come back to retire.'

'And Jackie used to be a waitress?'

'The way Lewis put it, it sounded more like part-time to earn pocket money. Turn the sound back up, Ben.'

On Friday night, Ben and Libby went to see Dame Amanda Knight's pantomime at the Oast Theatre. The previous year, she had presented it at the Alexandria in Nethergate, with the help of Libby and Fran. This year, she was reprising it in Steeple Martin, with a cast partially made up of Libby's usual company. Ben had overseen the sound and lighting and set construction, but had not been needed for the whole of January. The run was due to end tomorrow, so this was more or less their last chance to see it.

Dame Amanda, or Abby, as she liked to be called, met them in the foyer.

'Feels a bit silly, welcoming you to your own theatre,' she said, kissing them both.

'Feels a bit odd coming to watch,' said Libby. 'I've missed it.'

'I did ask you to be in it,' said Abby.

'I wouldn't have been able to stop myself poking my nose in,' said Libby, laughing.

'Tell me about this new murder you've got yourselves mixed up in,' said Abby, leading them to the bar, where one of the Oast House Company's members was officiating.

'Oh, we're not really mixed up in it,' said Ben. 'Libby and Fran were just asked to find out some background material.'

'No excitement, then,' said Abby.

'No, thank goodness,' said Libby. 'We've found out a lot more about Heronsbourne, though!'

'Where's that?' Abby frowned and Ben explained.

'Quite near Nethergate then.' Abby gave them a glass of wine each and ordered interval drinks. 'I expect you'll see some friends here tonight, won't you?'

'Bound to,' said Libby, as someone came up behind her.

'Hello Libby,' said Sarah Elliot.

Chapter Twenty-three

'Good Lord!' Libby's mouth fell open in surprise to see the three women standing behind her. 'Ben, Abby, this is Sarah Elliot, her mum Angela, and her aunt Amy. Ladies, this is my partner Ben, and Dame Amanda Knight. It's her panto.'

Everyone shook hands all round, then Abby excused herself.

'Must go and ginger up the troops,' she said. 'See you later.'

'What brings you here?' asked Libby, when she had gone, and Amy was ordering interval drinks.

'We knew about your theatre and your famous pantomimes, so we decided to come and see. Then we discovered you weren't doing this year's,' said Sarah.

'But we decided to come anyway,' said Angela.

'How's young Thomas?' asked Libby, thankful that she could remember Sarah's baby's name.

'He's fine. He's with his dad, we thought he was a bit too young for panto yet!' said Amy.

Just then the first bell rang to indicate the imminent start of the show. As they began to make their way into the auditorium, Sarah caught Libby's arm.

'Can I have a word with you later?' she asked in an undertone.

'Interval?'

'Great.' Sarah moved to catch up with her mother and aunt.

'What was that?' muttered Ben.

'Wants a word,' whispered Libby. 'Mysterious.'

She had met the three ladies during the most recent investigation in which she and Fran had been involved, and, in fact, when she had met Jemima. But she now resolved to put the mysterious word out of her mind and enjoy the pantomime, even though she had seen it the previous year. But that was the thing about pantomime, you could see the same story every year, and it would always be different.

And this one was different. The script had been modified, and she thought guiltily, the new cast, comprising Tom, the Dame, and Bob and Baz the double act, were far better than their predecessors had been.

They came out into the foyer bar having thoroughly enjoyed themselves, and looking forward to the second half. Ben went to collect their pre-ordered drinks, and once again, Sarah was clutching her arm.

'I'm sorry to buttonhole you again,' said Sarah. 'Oh, look, here's Ben with your drinks.'

Libby signalled madly with her eyebrows, Ben handed over her glass of wine and melted back into the crowd.

'OK, Sarah. What is it?' Libby did her best not to sound impatient.

Sarah looked at her feet. 'I'm sorry. I've just been worrying about this ever since last year.'

'What's up?' Libby made her tone gentler. 'Come on, tell me.'

Sarah looked up, rather pink about the face. 'You remember I didn't tell you everything at first?'

'Yes. But it didn't matter in the end. We got the killer.'

'Yes.' Sarah frowned. 'And that *was* a shock.'

'I'm sure.' Libby put her head on one side and waited. 'Well?'

'There were a couple of friends of mine I didn't mention back then.' Sarah cleared her throat. 'Carole Spinner and Jill Stevens. I just wondered if you'd come across them during the – er – case.'

'No, I've never heard of either of them.' Libby's interest was now piqued. 'Do you think they were part of the whole nasty business?'

'I think they were, yes. Oh, they didn't run away from home, or

157

anything, but they started missing school and they stopped mixing with the rest of us.' Sarah looked down again. 'And Jill had been almost my best friend.'

'Did she try to get you to join in?'

'Oh, yes. But I didn't – as you know. I tried to talk Jill out of it, but she just laughed.'

'So she wasn't unhappy about it?'

'Not at first. But then after a bit she was – well – withdrawn. When we saw her, of course, which wasn't often. And then she left school. So did Carole.'

'Well, there weren't any unidentified bodies at the end of the case,' said Libby, 'so they must have just gone off the radar.'

'Is there any way I could find out?' asked Sarah diffidently. 'I wouldn't know how to go about it.'

'Neither would I,' said Libby. 'I'll make a couple of unofficial inquiries to see if their names came up, but that's about all I can do.'

Sarah nodded. 'Well, thank you for listening. I wish I'd mentioned them in the first place.'

'Always the same,' said Libby. 'People don't tell the police – or even me – everything because they're scared of getting themselves or someone else into trouble.' She finished her wine. 'Let's join the others. They'll think we're plotting something.'

'Tell you later,' she murmured to Ben, as they prepared to go back for the second half, which proved to be even more hilarious and anarchic than the first.

They met Dame Amanda in the foyer, and said goodbye to Amy, Angela, and Sarah before meeting the rest of the cast.

'I'm glad I talked to you,' said Sarah, as she was leaving. 'It was hearing about that girl on the golf course that brought it to mind, and as you're involved with that . . .'

The synapses were firing as Libby turned back to Ben and Abby and prepared to be congratulatory to the cast.

'What's up?' asked Ben, as they went to the bar to buy drinks. 'You're distracted.'

158

'Tell you later,' she repeated. 'But I'm kicking myself.'

It was another half an hour before they were able to detach themselves from the theatre crowd. Libby linked her arm through Ben's as they walked down the Manor's drive, which also served the theatre.

'So, tell me,' said Ben.

'I'm afraid I wasn't terribly pleased when she finally managed to spit it out,' said Libby. 'She is a bit of a flake, I'm afraid.'

'Yes, and?'

'She wanted to tell me about something she hadn't told me during the last business.' She looked at him. 'About two other girls who'd also been involved. And who she hadn't heard of since they left school. And, it seems, neither has anyone else. And I suddenly thought . . .'

Ben stopped walking. 'What if one of them is Jackie Stapleton?'

Chapter Twenty-four

'I'm not going mad, then?' Libby looked anxiously into Ben's face.

He reached out and hugged her.

'No, of course you're not. And to be honest, I don't know why no one's thought of it before.'

'Actually,' said Libby, looking a little shamefaced, 'I did. I even thought the American vicar person could be Turner – you know, the vicar from St Aldeberge.'

'As I believe you said,' Ben resumed the walk down the drive, 'that really would be a coincidence too far, wouldn't it? And why would he risk coming back here anyway?'

'Exactly,' said Libby. 'But then, why did she? If Jackie *is* one of those girls, she didn't go far. She was in Nethergate ten or fifteen years ago, and it would only have been twenty years ago that she was in St Aldeberge.'

'Perhaps she wasn't brave enough to go somewhere completely new? Or perhaps someone set her up there – in Nightingale House?'

'And you realise who that could have been?' said Ben, stopping again.

'Oh, bloody hell!' Libby's hand flew to cover her mouth. 'Nick Nash.'

Nick Nash had been the victim in the most recent investigation. He had been an acquaintance of Colin's from Spain, which was initially how they had become involved.

'Well, he did keep coming back to the area, apparently. He could easily have set her up in that place,' Ben went on.

'And,' said Libby, getting quite excited, 'he could have then set her up in Pedlar's Row! Perhaps she was blackmailing him!'

'It also explains why she was so secretive about her past,' said Ben.

By this time they were walking along the high street, and just as they were approaching the pub, the door opened and Colin and Gerry came out.

'Libby! Ben!' Colin almost rushed forward to hug them both. Gerry followed, amused at his partner's effusive greetings.

'Tim's just closed, so why don't you come up to the flat for a drink?' he said. 'Or are you in a hurry to get home?'

Ben and Libby exchanged glances.

'Oh, go on, then,' said Libby with a grin. 'We were only talking murder.'

'What?' Colin stepped back.

'Come on, Col. Granny Mardle told you they were mixed up in another murder,' said Gerry, ushering them all across the road. Granny Mardle was Libby and Ben's next-door neighbour, who had helped bring Colin up.

'Oh, yes. You can tell us all about it,' said Colin, and led the way through the entrance and up the stairs to the flat.

'Now,' he said, when they were all served with drinks in his comfortable sitting room. 'What's it all about?'

Between them, Libby and Ben gave a much-abbreviated version of the events of the last few weeks, without mentioning Sarah's revelations and their concerns about Nick Nash.

'So you've given up now?' said Gerry, when they'd finished.

'I think so,' said Libby. 'Now tell us what you've been doing.'

'Just clearing up in Spain,' said Colin. 'All Gerry's stuff is now being shipped over and going into storage.'

'Oh, that reminds me,' said Libby, putting down her glass. 'You know our friend Lewis at Creekmarsh? Well, he said he'd heard of a house for sale.'

Colin and Gerry both leant forward eagerly.

'Really?' said Gerry. 'Where? What's it like?'

'He didn't say. But you could give him a ring in the morning and ask him.'

Gerry sent Colin an excited grin. 'Where's Creekmarsh?'

Colin, who had never been there, deferred to Libby, but Ben took it on himself to explain.

'So do you think it's near there?' asked Colin.

'Maybe,' said Libby. 'But you've been keeping an eye on all the estate agent's websites, haven't you? I would have thought you'd have seen everything that was available.'

'Perhaps it's not on the market yet,' said Ben. 'You know how Lewis gets hold of things.'

'Yes,' said Libby thoughtfully. The other three looked at her, puzzled. 'Look,' she went on, 'I'll give him a ring in the morning, shall I? Then I can let you know.'

'Lovely!' said Gerry. 'Another drink?'

'No thanks, we'll get on our way,' said Ben, standing up. 'Great to have you both back.'

'OK,' he said, when they were once more on their way home, 'what suddenly struck you?'

'About the house?' Libby thought for a moment. 'Well, it's nothing really, but after we'd been talking about the possibility of Jackie being involved with Nash, I just thought perhaps it had belonged to one of the other people who'd been involved in that business. Someone who'd had to leave quickly.'

Ben chuckled. 'Now that *would* be a coincidence,' he said.

Libby rang Lewis on Saturday morning.

'Can I ring you back, Lib? I'm seeing my Yanks off.' He sounded harassed.

'OK – but where's this house you mentioned?'

'House? Oh, for your mate! Yeah, well, you know it! Dotty Barlowe's neighbour's place.'

'The vicar?' Libby yelped.

'No, wally! The other side. Can't remember their name. Got to go.' The line went dead.

Libby sat looking at her phone for a long time.

'What's the matter?' Ben emerged into the sitting room.

Libby looked up. 'I don't believe this,' she said. 'Another bloody coincidence. I'm sick of coincidences.'

'What is it?' Ben perched on the table in the window.

'You know that house?'

'Which house? I know hundreds.'

'The one Lewis told me about for Gerry.'

'OK – yes. The one that belonged to a villain who scarpered?' Ben grinned.

'Shut up. Well, it doesn't. It belongs to Dotty and Eddy Barlowe's neighbours.'

'Remind me – Dotty and Eddy Barlowe?'

'People who live next door to the American Rev.'

'Oh, yes – Edie's friend. So what? The American Rev is moving?'

'No – the other side. Somebody Hughes, I think. But why didn't Dotty tell me?'

'Why should she?' said Ben reasonably. 'You haven't expressed any interest in moving.'

'No, I suppose not.' Libby pursed her lips thoughtfully. 'Perhaps she doesn't know.'

'Well, Lewis knows, why shouldn't she? Look, give her a ring and ask. Quite legitimate – you've got friends who are looking for a house in the area. By the way, do you think it would be suitable for them?'

'Actually, yes, I do. And it's got a terrific view. I wonder if Dotty would object to a couple of men as neighbours. And another thing. I wonder why they want to move? They've only been there five minutes.'

Ben gave an exasperated sigh. 'For goodness' sake, ring and ask!'

Libby found Dotty's number and rang. After a minute, she was just about to ring off, when a rather breathless Dotty answered.

'Oh, I'm sorry! Did I disturb you in the middle of something?'

'No, that's all right!' puffed Dotty. 'I was upstairs doing the bedroom. Never take my phone with me!'

'No, me neither,' said Libby. 'Well, if you've got a minute, just a quick question.'

'Go on, then.'

Your neighbours – the Hugheses, wasn't it?'

'Sally and Paul, yes.'

'I may have got this wrong, but Edie's son Lewis heard their house was going on the market. I was surprised as they haven't been there that long.'

Dotty laughed. 'No, he's right. Why, you interested?'

'No, but some friends of ours might be. It doesn't seem to be with any estate agents, yet. Is it official?'

'Oh, yes. I told you Sally's a bit of an invalid, didn't I?'

'Yes, you did mention it.'

'Well – this isn't the best place for an invalid, is it?'

'No, I suppose not.'

'So she's missing the bright lights. Shops and people anyway. She's from London, too, back in the day. Paul's quite happy, but while she isn't – you can imagine!'

Libby laughed. 'I can indeed. So how can I show Gerry and Colin details?'

'I'll email our original details.' Dotty said proudly. 'I can do all that stuff these days.'

'Brilliant!' said Libby. 'Thank you so much, Dotty. Got a pencil? I'll give you my email address.'

'Text it, Libby. Easier.'

She sent the required text, and turned to Ben.

'Did you hear any of that?'

'I heard what you said, yes.' He looked up from his tablet, on which he was reading the morning's papers.

164

Libby told him what Dotty had said.

'Not actually a coincidence, then,' said Ben. 'All quite logical. All these people live in the same small, quite isolated area. Bound to know one another.'

'But fancy one of them having a house for sale just as our friends are looking for a house – oh. Put like that it doesn't sound so unlikely.'

'Exactly.' Ben stood up. 'Ready for another cup of coffee? And we're going down to Nethergate tonight, aren't we?'

'Coffee, please, and yes, we are. So what else are we going to do today?'

'I thought you had a painting to finish?' said Ben wickedly.

'I never even started it,' said Libby.

While Ben made the coffee, she checked her emails and found Dotty's details. Then phoned Colin.

'Listen,' she said, as if he wasn't. 'I've got the original details of that house I told you about.'

'What do you mean – original?'

'It's one of the new houses next door to the golf course at Heronsbourne.'

'Golf course?' Colin sounded dubious.

'Oh, there's a sort of hedge of shrubs dividing them. I've been there – it's lovely. I've got the details of the middle one of the three, but the one next door is the same. Have I got your email address?'

'Probably – I've got yours. I'll email you and you can reply with the details.'

It was half an hour later, when Libby was staring gloomily at her easel in the conservatory – again – that her phone rang.

'Libby, it's Gerry.' He sounded excited. 'I've just spoken to your friend Dotty.'

'How did you manage that?'

'You forwarded her email, so we emailed her and asked for her number. Anyway, she's going to ask her neighbours if we can view their house! Honestly, Libby, it looks fabulous. Just what I was look-ing for.'

'What about Colin, though?' asked Libby. 'He didn't sound too keen.'

'Oh, he changed his mind when he saw the pictures. I'll keep you posted.'

Libby wandered back to the sitting room.

'They're going to see the house,' she told Ben.

'I assume you mean Colin and Gerry and the house next door to your Dotty?'

Libby poked him in the arm. 'You know I do. What shall we do next?'

'You were in the conservatory.'

Libby poked him again.

They drove down to Nethergate later that afternoon. Libby joined Fran in Coastguard Cottage and Ben went to drag Guy from the shop and into The Sloop for a pint.

'I have news,' said Libby, settling in the window seat with Balzac on her lap.

'And you didn't phone to tell me?' Fran looked amused.

'I thought it could wait.' Libby attempted to look superior.

'Will we need tea to help it along?'

'Yes, please.' Libby smiled.

Fran retreated to the kitchen and put the kettle on.

'Go on, then,' she said, coming to lean in the doorway.

Libby told her of the events since the previous evening's meeting with Sarah Elliot.

'Wow,' said Fran, handing Libby a mug and sitting down in her armchair. 'So – conclusions?'

'The obvious one is perhaps Jackie is one of the girls Sarah told me about.'

'What were their names again?'

'Carole Spinner and Jill Stevens.'

'And they would be – what? Same age as Sarah?'

'I suppose so. Ish, anyway.'

166

'And they just left school? No evidence of mysterious disappearance?'

'She didn't say so.'

'Well.' Fran frowned into her tea. 'The obvious assumption is Jill Stevens, isn't it?

'Why?'

'Same initials. J. S.'

Chapter Twenty-five

'Oh!' Libby looked startled. 'Of course! That's what people do, isn't it. Use the same initials.'

'Apparently. Used to be because of them being stamped on suit-cases and wallets and so forth. Not that people do that these days.'

'No, but it makes sense.' Libby stared at her friend in admiration.

'And what about the house for sale?'

'Nothing in that. Not to do with the murder, anyway. Oh – and I didn't tell you what Lewis said, did I?'

She repeated Lewis's findings on Godfrey Peterson and Jackie's former waitressing days.

'That adds weight to Jackie having been one of the unfortunate St Aldeberge girls. The girls there waited on those men that attended the vicar's meetings. But it rules Mr Peterson out of the equation. House of the Sacred Flame. Rather pretentious.'

'I don't know – it has a ring to it!' said Libby mischievously.

Fran and Libby's previous investigation had involved the abuse of children and teenagers, and seemed to be cropping up in this one only too often, as Fran remarked.

'Not to be wondered at, really,' she said. 'The same area, and the victim's a young woman. Bound to be parallels, if not an overlap.'

'I suppose so. I was complaining to Ben about coincidences, but it isn't surprising, is it?'

'The only surprising thing is how many murders there are in this fairly small area of Kent, and how often you stumble into them,' said Fran. 'More tea?'

'Are we going to do anything about any of this?' asked Libby when her mug had been refilled.

'Nothing to do, is there?' Fran poked the fire.

'Find out about Jackie's relationship with this Vince-person Martin Harris mentioned?' said Libby.

'Nothing to find out. Sounded as though Harris told you everything there was to tell.'

'Mmm. But none of it had come out before. Perhaps there's even more to tell.'

'Look, it was at least three or four years ago, and Harris said that Vince, whoever he was, had resigned.'

'I wonder if there was any more behind it than just the trouble over Jackie?'

'Oh, Libby! Stop trying to make mysteries. Jackie was a troublemaker. She affected a lot of people one way or another and we've uncovered a lot of them. Ian knows it all, so the police can look into it if they want to.'

Libby fixed her friend with a look. 'He doesn't know about Carole Spinner and Jill Stevens.'

'The police will probably think they're irrelevant.'

'I think I'll mention it anyway next time I see him,' said Libby. 'You know – in passing.'

Fran looked dubious. 'On your head be it,' she said. 'And now I'd better start dinner.'

'Shall I help?' asked Libby.

Fran sighed. 'No. You'll upset the cat.'

Ben and Guy returned from the pub and Fran served up lasagne and salad, followed by apple and blackberry pie. While they were sitting over coffee, Guy demanded an update on Libby's activities.

'Nothing special,' said Ben. 'She's supposed to have given up, but she's still ferreting.'

169

Guy raised a questioning eyebrow. 'Of course. How?'

Libby opened her mouth.

'I'll tell you later,' Fran butted in hastily. 'It's all right. I'm not going diving into the devil's maw.'

'Very poetic!' said Libby.

'Oh, she is,' said Guy, reaching over to squeeze his wife's hand. 'You've no idea.'

'Come on, Guy,' said Ben, standing up. 'Let's clear the dishes. Leave the women to gossip.'

'Hey!' said Libby. 'We never gossip!'

'It was a not so subtle way of getting Guy on his own so he can give him an edited version of what's been going on,' said Fran, when the men had gone into the kitchen.

'I thought he would have done that while they were in the pub,' said Libby. 'Honestly, they're so – so – chauvinistic!'

'Just old-fashioned. Good job they get on so well,' said Fran.

Libby sighed. 'It is, isn't it. And at least they don't try to stop us doing things. Well, not much, anyway.'

'We're not going to do anything at the moment, though, are we?' said Fran.

Libby flashed her a look. 'N-no. I suppose not.'

Ben and Libby drove back to Steeple Martin on Sunday morning. On the way, Libby told Ben what Fran had thought about Jackie's previous life.

'Absolutely logical,' he said. 'Will you tell Ian?'

'Fran doesn't think the police will think it's relevant. The two girls, I mean. That case is closed.'

'But as she said, it's perfectly understandable that there should be links between the two cases. If I was a policeman, I'd certainly think so.'

'I said I'd mention it if I see him.' Libby turned to look out of the window at the grey sky. 'Miserable out there.'

They left Ben's 4x4 in Allhallow's Lane, popped in to number seventeen to feed Sidney, and decided to walk across the fields to The Manor.

'I like our fields,' said Libby, tucking her arm into Ben's. 'Cosier than those marshes. I was wondering if the golf course would be a bit too bleak for the boys. No trees. Just golf course, marsh, and mud flats.'

'I thought you liked it?' said Ben.

'I do. But I don't think it's everybody's cup of tea.'

Not entirely to her surprise, Libby was greeted enthusiastically by Gerry as soon as she and Ben opened the door to Hetty's kitchen.

'Hang on!' she said, laughing. 'Let me get my breath.'

She went to kiss Hetty, and said hello to Flo, Lenny, Edward, Peter and Harry, and Colin.

'Full house today,' she commented

'At least I can tell you all together,' said Gerry. 'Col made me wait until Libby was here.'

'So what is it?' asked Harry. 'Have you found a house?'

Gerry's face fell and Colin laughed. 'Now you've stolen his thunder! How did you know?'

'I didn't – took a wild guess.'

Ben and Edward between them were distributing wine. 'Come on, Gerry,' said Ben. 'Tell all.'

'Did you all know Libby's friend Lewis told her about a house that was for sale in Heronsbourne?' Gerry began.

'Was you looking fer one?' asked Flo.

'Yes, we were. So Libby found out about it, and put us in touch.' He paused to take a sip of wine.

'The upshot is – we went to see it this morning,' said Colin.

There were exclamations of surprise from everyone.

'And we're buying it!' concluded Gerry, his face alight.

'I must say you make up your mind quickly,' said Libby, among the assertions of pleasure and congratulation. 'You were the same when you first saw Steeple Farm. What did you think?'

'The view is spectacular,' said Colin. 'I can see us spending all our time by the French windows or on the balcony.'

171

'And our bedroom looks out the same way,' said Gerry. 'It's absolutely perfect. You're so clever to have found it, Libby.'

'It fell into my lap, really,' said Libby. 'And I was worried you might find the marshes too bleak.'

'It's beautiful,' said Colin. 'And there's a pub at the end of the drive – perfect! And your friend Dotty says you can walk right across the marsh to the mudflats.'

'You can. Just don't try crossing the golf course!'

'What did you think of Dotty?' asked Ben. 'I've not met her yet.'

'Lovely woman,' said Gerry. 'Wasn't so sure about the vendors though. Or the woman, at least.'

'Sally, is it?' said Libby.

'Hypochondriac,' sniffed Colin. 'Doesn't like the country. Don't know why they moved there.'

'Struck me that the husband might have persuaded her,' said Gerry. 'He seemed all right.'

'Quite pally with Dotty's Eddy, I gather,' nodded Libby.

'Don't like the sound of the other neighbour, though,' said Colin.

'He doesn't go out much,' said Libby. 'Dotty says they never see him.'

'Good.' Gerry nodded with satisfaction. 'All round, pretty perfect.'

The rest of the company were demanding to know more about the house, which Colin now revealed had the unprepossessing name of Links View. 'I think we'll be changing that.'

'Don't you have to inform the post office or something?' asked Edward.

'Not in this case,' said Colin. 'The builders registered the three houses as numbers one (that's us), two, and three, The Drive.'

'Is this anything to do with the murder?' asked Edward, while Colin and Gerry described the delights of number one, The Drive to the company.

'Nothing at all,' said Libby. 'Except that I met Dotty, who lives in number two, while I was asking Lewis and Edie what they knew about the golf club.'

'What about the vicar? You mentioned him once before.' Peter helped himself to more wine.

'He turns out to be the head of some church in America called the House of The Sacred Flame,' said Ben, 'so he's out of things, too.'

'What are you left with?' asked Harry.

'Nothing.' Libby shrugged, not wishing to go into details about Sarah Elliot's schoolfriends. 'The police will have to get along without us.'

Peter, Harry, Edward, and Ben exchanged disbelieving glances, and Libby moved round the table to take part in the discussions on the new home.

'Any idea when you'll move in?' she asked.

'The Hugheses and us need to get on to our solicitors straight away,' said Gerry.

'That'll be my solicitor in the morning,' said Colin. 'Mrs Hughes seemed very keen to get things going right away.'

'But they'll have to find somewhere else,' said Flo. 'Can't do that in five minutes.'

'No problem, apparently,' said Colin. 'They own a flat in London which they've rented out on a short-term lease, so they can turf the poor tenants out whenever they want.'

'She was obviously half-expecting this,' said Libby.

'Looks like it,' said Gerry. 'Beats me why she wanted to move in the first place.'

'What I said.' Libby nodded.

'Mind you,' said Gerry, 'she did say something about "making up to your mate" to her husband. Sounded as though they got the place through a friend.'

'I didn't hear her say that,' said Colin.

'You were out on the balcony,' said Gerry. 'But then, I suppose we've got it through a friend, too.'

'Come and get the veg, gal.' Hetty approached the table bearing a joint of pork with a covering of crisp crackling. Libby got up to do as she'd been told.

Colin and Gerry declined the invitation to Peter and Harry's later this afternoon, claiming they had a lot of preparation to do.

'They're so excited, bless 'em,' said Harry, as they distributed themselves around the sitting room of the cottage. 'Won't see 'em around so much soon, will we.'

'I was just thinking said Libby, and forestalled the usual groans with a raised hand. 'No, listen. Did you hear what Gerry said? About making up to a friend?'

She repeated Gerry's comment. 'I was wondering if those houses were offered to friends, sort of under the counter. Maybe that was why when Dotty came to buy one she could only get the middle one.'

'So you think the reverend gent got it under the counter, too?' said Harry.

'I don't know. It was just a thought.'

'Considering the shenanigans that went on with the golf club – selling off the course, then just that little bit, and all the arguments about the clubhouse itself, it wouldn't surprise me,' said Ben, accepting whisky from Peter and handing one to Libby.

'You know I said I had a colleague who was a member of that club?' said Edward.

'Yes?' Everyone turned to look at him.

'I could ask him what he knows about it. Casually, you know!' He flashed them his broad white grin. 'Say I've got friends who—'

'Are thinking of buying! Of course!' said Libby excitedly.

'Oh, Edward!' Peter shook his head at him. 'Now you've set her off again.'

'The solicitors will see if there's anything dodgy in the previous sale,' said Ben.

'I do hope there isn't,' said Libby. 'I really want them to get that house.'

'So that you can go poking around?' said Harry.

'No! Because they really want it. I don't do everything just to help my – er – investigations.'

'I think you mean nosiness, you old trout,' said Harry. 'Now, shut up about it and let's talk about something else.'

Chapter Twenty-six

It snowed on Sunday night.

'I wonder what The Drive is like under snow,' said Libby, gazing out at Allhallow's Lane with her hands clasped round a mug.

'Is it a tarmac surface?' asked Ben, who was listening to the radio with half an ear.

'Yes, I think so.' Libby frowned. 'Easy to drive down, anyway. I suppose the golf club would have made sure of that.'

'Mmm.' Ben wasn't really listening.

'I shall ask Colin to check that,' said Libby. 'And do you suppose it's a leasehold? It could be, under the circumstances.' She looked across at Ben, who was deep in the overnight cricket scores from the other side of the world, and sighed.

She called Fran.

'And I was wondering,' she finished up, 'whether Pedlar's Row got itself snowed in. Which would mean John and Sue would be cut off.'

'And this matters why?' asked Fran.

'I was just wondering,' said Libby. 'And how would Jackie have got out? Come to think of it, how did she get to work? She didn't have a car.'

Fran sighed. 'There's a direct bus route to Nethergate. You know that.'

'Oh, yes.' Libby brooded for a moment. 'And I'd still like to know how she got hold of that cottage. Was she renting – or did she buy it?'

'Why don't you ring Debbie at the café and ask her? She might know.'

'Because you've got her number not me.'

'I'll text it,' said Fran. 'Let me know how you get on.'

Debbie's phone went straight to voicemail, so Libby left a message asking her to call back.

'Of course it did,' said Ben, accepting a second mug of tea. 'She'll be at work, won't she?'

'Oh, yes.' Libby wandered disconsolately into the conservatory, and very swiftly out again. 'Cold in there,' she said.

Ben shook his head at her. 'I'm going over to the Pocket,' he said. 'Just to check everything's all right. You never know with snow. Do you want to come?'

'No, thanks. I think I'll phone Colin.'

'I wouldn't,' said Ben. 'He'll be busy with solicitors. He said, don't you remember?' He frowned. 'Have you seen my boots?'

'Conservatory,' said Libby. 'I think I'll phone John and Sue, then. Just see how they're coping with the snow.'

Ben sighed.

'Yes,' said Sue, when Libby called. 'We have to shovel the snow along the path to Pedlar's Row, and the residents there have to clear that. Lucky we don't get much snow, isn't it?' She sounded perfectly cheerful about it.

'We were wondering about The Drive,' said Libby. 'Some friends of ours are going to buy one of the houses there.'

'Really?' Sue sounded surprised. 'But they've only been there a couple of years. Who's going?'

'Sally and Paul Hughes.'

'Oh – never really got to know them. Isn't she an invalid?'

'Apparently.' Libby charitably didn't repeat the general consensus that Sally Hughes was a hypochondriac. 'Not the best place for an invalid.'

'No. So that's why they're going?'

'I think so. That's why I wondered . . .'

'I expect they're snowed in,' said Sue. 'That's an unadopted road, too.'

'Oh, well, Gerry and Colin are young and fit, so it won't bother them. I'd better phone Dotty and see if she's OK.'

Sue laughed. 'Oh, she'll be fine! Doesn't seem to let anything bother her.'

'No, I got that impression,' said Libby. 'I wonder how the vicar will cope?'

'No idea,' said Sue. 'I doubt he'll get his posh car out.'

'Has he got a car? I somehow thought he hadn't.'

'Oh yes – a sleek black job with tinted windows. Not that we see it much.'

I wonder why he was walking along The Drive, then, when Lewis's American saw him? thought Libby. Aloud, she said, 'As long as you're OK and you don't need anything?'

'No thank you, Libby, you're very kind. Actually we've had a few people on asking if we're OK, including Jemima.'

Not kind, thought Libby, as she ended the call. Just nosy.

It was nearly half past eleven when Debbie rang back.

'Coffee break,' she said cheerily, 'so I can't be long.'

'That's fine,' said Libby. 'I just wanted know if you knew anything about Jackie's cottage in Pedlar's Row.'

'I know it's nice,' said Debbie. 'Not much else.'

'Did she rent it? I can't imagine she owned it – they're expensive properties.'

'Couldn't quite work it out. I asked her once and she looked sort of – I dunno – pleased with herself. She said she didn't have to worry about that. Which was a funny sort of answer, don't you think?'

'Certainly was.' Libby's mind was going nineteen to the dozen.

'Anyway, it was something to do with her mate at the golf club. I know that much.'

'Her – *mate*?' Libby gasped.

'Yeah. I thought you knew about him.'

'If you mean Vince?' Libby hazarded.

'Don't know his name. I don't know anything about him, she hardly mentioned him. But I'm pretty sure the cottage was something to do with him. Bit iffy, I thought.' Debbie was silent for a moment. 'In a way, I'm not all that surprised she got herself topped. She wasn't like the rest of us.'

Libby thanked her and ended the call, immediately calling Fran again.

'Guess what!' she said breathlessly, as soon as Fran answered.

'I can't, but I'm sure you're going to tell me,' said Fran in a weary voice.

Libby told her.

'Now listen to me.' Fran sounded serious. 'You are not to go diving into this on your own – and no, I'm not going with you – you'll get yourself into trouble. You've always disapproved of the heroine who goes into the cellar in the middle of the night, haven't you? Well, this is the same. Jackie was murdered, for goodness' sake. This isn't a game.'

'Oh.' Libby stared into the distance for a moment. 'What do we do, then?'

'Tell Ian,' said Fran promptly. 'If he thinks it's worth passing on to DI Whatshisname, he will.'

'Do I do it now, or wait until I see him socially?'

'Wait. It isn't urgent, is it?'

The snow didn't look as horrific as it had earlier, so Libby decided to make an expedition to the high street. Perhaps she could persuade Ben to buy her a sandwich in the pub as Harry didn't open The Pink Geranium on Mondays.

She picked her way slowly along Allhallow's Lane to the high street, where the snow had retreated to sullen looking grey stripes in the gutters.

'Libby!' A voice hailed her from the other side of the street. Turning, she saw Colin waving at her.

'Come and have coffee!' he called.

Nothing loath, she crossed the road and slipped on the piled up snow.

'Ben's in the Pocket,' she said, catching her breath. 'He went to check for leaks.'

'I'll go and get him,' said Colin. 'You go up.'

By the time she got to the flat, Gerry had the door open, and the smell of fresh coffee wafted out.

'We've sorted everything out,' he said, 'but we'll wait for Colin and Ben.'

'Oh?' said Libby, shrugging out of her coat. 'We were wondering if it was a leasehold, actually.' She raised an eyebrow.

Gerry grinned and tapped the side of his nose.

Colin and Ben arrived immediately Gerry had given Libby her cup of coffee.

'And now tell us what happened with the solicitors?' said Libby.

'It'll take a few days,' said Colin, 'but all the basics are in place.'

'The interesting thing is what you said earlier, about a leasehold,' said Gerry.

'And is it? A leasehold?'

'It was,' said Colin. 'But the freehold is being offered to the owners.'

Libby and Ben looked at each other, frowning.

'Surely that's quite normal?' said Ben.

'For free?' asked Gerry.

'Free?' echoed Libby.

'For nothing?' Ben looked aghast. 'How much was the original annual fee?'

'Very little,' said Colin.

'And did the golf club – presumably the leaseholders – undertake any maintenance for that?'

'Maintaining The Drive. That's about it,' said Gerry.

'And now the owners have to do that?' asked Libby.

'Presumably. We couldn't find anything, but our solicitor is look-ing into it. He was puzzled, too.'

'Did you see who the original signatory for the golf club was?' asked Ben.

'No – should we have looked?' asked Gerry.

'You'll have to excuse Ben,' said Libby with a grin. 'He's a land-lord, after all.'

'Oh, yes, a bloated plutocrat!' laughed Colin. 'What's the prob-lem, Ben? We just thought it was a bit odd. I don't think it affects the title to the property.'

'I just think it's worth making an in-depth inquiry, that's all.' Ben was, in fact, looking concerned. 'And asking the golf club for a for-mal disclaimer to the land.'

'You think there's something funny going on?' asked Gerry.

'I think maybe there *was*,' said Ben. 'When you consider all the problems they were having over the sale of the club. I think perhaps they wanted to keep some kind of control over the land when they first had the houses built.'

'And now things have settled down they don't need to?' said Libby.

'Possibly,' said Ben. 'Definitely needs looking into.'

'But not enough to scupper the sale?' said Gerry, looking worried.

'Oh, no,' said Ben. 'As long as your solicitor's on the ball.'

'He is. He sorted this lot out for me.' He waved a hand, indicating the whole of what had been the Garden Hotel and was now Hardcastle House, 'named after my parents, not me,' as he assured everybody.

'Oh, good,' said Libby. 'You sounded so pleased about it. I'd hate to see it fall through.'

'So would we!' said Gerry. 'And I get the impression that Mrs Hughes can't wait to get out!'

Colin laughed. 'Apparently, she'd been on to their solicitor at the crack of dawn today. Can't understand why it should all take so long.'

'I don't suppose she noticed when they were buying Links View,' said Ben, 'if they were still living in their London flat.'

'And they probably bought off-plan,' said Libby. 'I expect the Rev did, too, as Dotty and Eddy got the only one that was left.'

'Oh, yes!' said Gerry. 'You could ask your friend about the lease-hold business, couldn't you?'

Libby exchanged a doubtful look with Ben. 'I don't think we're that close.'

'Well, if you could just mention it,' said Gerry, disappointed.

They spent another half an hour chatting, mostly about Gerry and Colin's plans for Links View, until Ben said he needed his lunch. He and Libby declined to stay and share their hosts' meal, and departed.

'Do you really think there's something dodgy going on there?' asked Libby, as they made their way back home.

'Not really dodgy,' said Ben. 'Just a bit peculiar, and worth checking out. I don't suppose that Harris chap would tell us anything?'

Libby laughed. 'Ben! Now you're doing it!'

'Doing what?'

'Poking your nose in!'

'No, I'm not!' Ben looked affronted. 'Just looking out for a friend.'

'I wish we could find out about the Vince person, though,' said Libby. 'He seems to have been very close to Jackie.'

'You were told he resigned from the golf club, though, weren't you?'

'Yes, but someone must know where he is.' Libby thought for a moment. 'Who could I ask?'

Ben turned to look at her. '*Now* who's poking their nose in?'

Libby spent the rest of the afternoon trawling the internet for current information about the golf club and Vincent Halliday, its former treasurer. Neither yielded anything useful.

At sometime before six o'clock, just as Ben had started to prepare dinner, Libby's phone rang.

'Hello, Patti. What can I do for you?' asked Libby.

'This is a bit odd,' said Patti hesitantly. 'Do you remember Connie Barstowe and Elaine Roberts?'

'Of course I do! Your village biddies who were so certain there was a madman murdering people in the village.'

'Well, they've been round again. Saying there's someone who didn't come up in the previous investigation.'

'What?'

'And they wondered – or Connie did – if it's him who murdered Jackie Stapleton. Although they didn't know her name.'

'Why on earth would they think that? Who was it?'

'They wondered if Jackie was another one of the "missing girls", as Connie put it. And they thought the murderer might be one of the Reverend Turner's business friends.'

'But *why*?'

'Because he played golf.'

Chapter Twenty-seven

'Bit tenuous, isn't it?' said Libby slowly.

'Ye-es. That's why I said it's a bit odd. They want to talk to you again.'

'Oh, good grief! You don't think they just want to be part of the action?'

'If it was just Connie, I'd probably say yes,' said Patti, 'but Elaine isn't like that.'

'No.' Libby sat remembering the shy little lady who was so much in awe of her friend. 'What do you think?'

'It wouldn't hurt, would it? Put their minds at rest.'

'All right. When?'

'Tomorrow morning? If you aren't busy?'

'At some point I've got to go and check over the theatre now that Abby's lot have gone. Ben's already been, but he's mainly done the tech side. I've got to go and check dressing rooms and stuff. I daresay I can do that tomorrow afternoon.' Libby called through to Ben. 'All right if I check the theatre tomorrow afternoon?'

'Whenever,' called Ben.

'Tomorrow morning, then,' she said Patti. 'Ten-thirty? Don't bother to ring back if the time's OK, only if it isn't.'

'What's that all about?' asked Ben, when she wandered into the kitchen.

'Connie and Elaine from St Aldeberge want to talk to me again.'

'Oh, no! More mad murderers?'

Libby smiled sadly. 'Actually, it makes a horrible sort of sense, although I was a bit dismissive to Patti.'

'What then?' Ben dug an exploratory knife into the potatoes.

'They were wondering if another of their missing girls could be the victim, and one of Nasty Nick's businessman friends who played golf could be the murderer.'

Ben's eyebrows rose. 'That's a bit of a coincidence too far, surely?'

'Just like us wondering if Dotty's vicar neighbour could be the Rotten Rev from St Aldeberge. If you look at all the facts, as I said, it makes a horrible sort of sense. Except that Dotty's neighbour comes from the States.'

'Are you going?'

'Yes. And then I'll dump the whole lot in Ian's lap. All of this has been dumped on me – I didn't go looking for any of it.'

'You did ask young Debbie to let you know if she knew about the cottage in Pedlar's Row,' Ben reminded her.

'Yes, well . . .'

'But I agree. Just tell Ian about everything you've learnt – including the business of the leasehold, if you like – and leave it at that.' Ben gave her a quick hug. 'And now – dinner.'

On Tuesday morning, having heard nothing to the contrary, Libby drove to St Aldeberge.

'Groundhog Day,' said Libby, when Patti opened the vicarage door. 'Are they here yet?'

'No, you're early. Coffee?'

'Yes, please. Look, I'm going to dump this all on Ian, you know that, don't you?'

Patti gave her a half-smile. 'I expected you to. And he'll probably dismiss it all as nonsense.'

Patti was just pouring coffee when there was a knock on the door.

'Go into the sitting room,' she said to Libby, and went to answer it.

A minute later, she ushered in her visitors. Connie Barstowe, an upright woman with close-cropped grey hair, and Elaine

Roberts, short and stout, with improbably brown hair, who smiled nervously.

'Hello, ladies!' said Libby brightly, shaking hands with them both. 'Nice to see you again.'

'I don't know about that,' said Connie, seating herself on the sofa. Elaine perched beside her.

'Not that it isn't lovely to see you, Mrs – Libby,' Elaine said with a reproachful look at her friend. Connie glared back.

'Just we reckon there's more nastiness gone on,' Connie said. 'We don't think you found out about all those girls. Found out about a few of them, and just left the rest.'

Libby and Patti stared open-mouthed at the older woman.

'Connie!' Elaine spoke more sharply than Libby had ever heard her. 'That's very rude, and it wasn't down to Mrs Libby, it was the police.' She sat back and folded her hands. Connie turned a dull red and tossed her head.

'Elaine's quite right, Connie. And it's very bad manners to speak like that to someone you've asked to help you.' Patti, too, sounded angry.

Connie mumbled something and looked pointedly away. Libby suppressed an urge to laugh.

'Elaine,' she said, 'you tell me about it.'

'Well,' she began, with a wary look at Connie, 'there was a lot of talk in the village after – after—'

'Yes, there would be,' said Libby. 'Go on.'

'And it seemed everybody had something to say about it all.' Elaine was gaining confidence. 'People were remembering other girls they hadn't heard of since, er, since then.'

'But this girl was murdered only a few weeks ago, not back then,' said Patti.

'Yes, but she could of run away, like those others,' Connie came back sharply.

'And what about this man who played golf?' Libby asked Elaine, ignoring Connie.

'Oh, that weren't nothing. People were talking about the men who went to the Reverend Turner's meetings. Because we heard all about what went on, didn't we?' She turned to her friend.

Connie nodded. 'And we started thinking about all the other so-called "businessmen". And we all knew some of them.'

'And the man who played golf?' reiterated Libby.

'Actually, there were a couple of them,' said Elaine. 'People only knew because they used to turn up in those golf trousers, you know?'

'Plus fours?' Libby was startled. 'They were still wearing those?'

'Very old-fashioned club, obviously,' said Patti. 'Surprised they wanted to turn it into a venue.'

'Ah, but that was voted down,' said Libby. 'So, ladies, you've no hard evidence about the murdered woman being from here, nor the murderer being a member of Turner's infamous club?'

Elaine looked sheepish and Connie indignant.

'What about that coloured girl?' she snapped.

All three other women made sounds expressive of distaste.

'You mean a black girl?' said Patti gently.

'That's what I said, didn't I?' Connie said. 'She went, didn't she?'

'She was murdered, Connie,' said Elaine. 'They found her murderer.'

Libby looked across at Patti, who shook her head.

'He could have been part of it all, couldn't he?' Connie argued.

'No, he was just a boy,' said Elaine. 'Not part of anything.'

'What was her name, Elaine?' asked Patti. 'Do you remember?'

'Not exactly . . . Givings, or something. Her mother moved away. Sheep farmers, they was.'

'Well, we'll check it all out,' said Libby, 'and Patti will let you know if anything else happens.'

Patti saw the ladies out, Elaine apologetic and Connie defiant.

'God, she's a pain,' said Libby, as Patti came back into the room. 'Sorry, Patti.'

'No, I agree. Typical of certain members of her generation, complete refusal to keep up with the times. And yet you look at your

Hetty and Flo. Completely different.' Patti picked up mugs. 'More coffee?'

'Yes, please. I'll come into the kitchen,' said Libby.

'And what about the black girl?' asked Patti. 'Anything in that?'

'Didn't sound like it.' Libby sat down at the kitchen table. 'Unusual – black sheep farmers.'

'Shall I try and look it up?' said Patti. 'What did she say – Givings?'

'Or something like it,' said Libby. 'I will, too. But I don't think it's got anything to do with Jackie Stapleton's murder. Come to that, neither did their other so-called information.'

'Bricks with straw,' said Patti, putting a mug down in front of Libby.

'Usually me doing that,' said Libby.

Back at home, she called Ben at the Estate Office up at The Manor.

'Have you ever heard of a family of black sheep farmers?'

'Black sheep? Do you mean dodgy farmers?'

'No! Black farmers.'

Ben sounded puzzled. 'No – why?'

'Oh, nothing much. It came up in conversation with those women at Patti's. One of them is a real old witch.'

'You didn't get anything, then?'

'No, all supposition, and, as Patti said, bricks with straw.'

'You'd know all about that,' said Ben, and Libby could hear the grin.

'All right, all right.' Libby sighed. 'Are you coming home for lunch?'

'No, Hetty's making sandwiches. See you later.'

'OK,' said Libby.

'Oh – your black sheep – why not ask Bob? He buys a lot of his meat direct, doesn't he? Like those turkeys you got involved with.'

Now that, thought Libby, is not a bad idea. As Abby's pantomime had finished, Bob had relinquished his role, and should be back at

188

work in his butcher's shop. She decided to pay him a visit after lunch.

It was still grey, but not especially cold. The last of the snow had disappeared, and several people were out and about. Libby waved at a few, and exchanged greetings with a couple more in the butcher's shop.

'What can I do for you, young Libby?' asked Bob cheerfully.

'Have you recovered from the panto?' asked Libby.

'Just about. Hope you're coming back next year, though. We missed you.' He reached under the counter. 'Got some of those nice homemade sausages today.' He displayed them hopefully.

'Yes, I'll have a couple of those,' said Libby. 'But I wanted to ask you something.'

'I might have known.' Bob grinned as he wrapped up the huge sausages in greaseproof paper.

'It's a bit delicate,' said Libby.

Bob raised an eyebrow, and jerked his head towards the door, where another customer was entering.

'Hello, May,' he said, 'Don't mind Libby. She just came for a chat. What can I get you?'

'You going to do the panto next year, Libby?' asked May. 'Missed you, we did.'

'That's what I was telling her.' Bob winked at Libby. 'Now, May?'

When May had been served and left the shop, Bob handed over Libby's sausages. 'What is it?' he said as he took her money.

'Have you ever heard of a black sheep farmer in the area?'

Bob raised both eyebrows in surprise. 'Do you mean the Geddings?' he said.

Libby gasped. 'So you do?'

'Of course. Best salt marsh lamb in the business,' he said. 'Why?'

'They were mentioned over in St Aldeberge this morning.'

Bob narrowed his eyes. 'I hope it wasn't anything to do with this murder?'

'Er—'

189

'Only they lost a daughter a few years back. Don't want to bring it all up again.'

'No, of course not,' said Libby, going rather pink. 'Sorry.'

'Nice family,' said Bob. 'Live over near where your girl was found.'

'What, Heronsbourne?' Libby's head was reeling.

'Yeah, near that golf course. On the marshes.'

Libby remembered the sheep grazing among the tussocks on the marsh when she had bumped into Marjorie Sutcliffe.

'They actually live on the marsh?'

'Near there, anyway. What's the interest?'

'Some old biddy mentioned a black girl being murdered. Nothing to do with us – her murderer was caught. And ages ago, anyway.'

'That was the Geddings girl. Nasty business. Racially motivated, by all accounts,' said Bob.

'Poor things,' said Libby, shuddering. 'They're all right now, are they?'

'Doing well,' said Bob. 'Not that I know them well, of course. 'Want to try some of the lamb?'

Libby took a couple of lamb chops, thanked Bob, and left the shop. As she wandered back home, she ruminated on Bob's information. Apart from the coincidence of the Geddings living at Heronsbourne, there was nothing whatsoever to connect it with the current investigation. When she got back home she'd call Patti and tell her.

But when she got home, her phone rang as she was putting her purchases in the fridge.

'Libby, it's Sue Cantripp.'

'Hello, Sue. Nice to hear from you.' Libby moved the big kettle on to the Rayburn.

'Jemima's coming over tomorrow and we wondered if you'd like to join us for tea. Lemon drizzle cake?'

Sensing a desire for information, Libby couldn't contain a chuckle. 'Lovely – my favourite. What time?'

'Three? Three-thirty?' Sue sounded relieved, and Libby wondered why.

'That suits me,' she said. 'I'm going out in the evening.'

'Great. Oh, and your friend Fran, too, if she'd like to.'

Definitely information gathering, thought Libby, as she ended the call and made her tea.

Chapter Twenty-eight

As Fran had declined Sue Cantripp's invitation, Libby arrived at Hobson's – which was looking less attractive under a lowering grey sky – alone. This time, she gave the grazing sheep a more searching perusal, but they looked just like any other sheep. 'Probably Romney Marsh sheep,' she told herself wisely, knowing absolutely nothing about sheep.

As before, she was ushered into the sitting room, where John was ensconced in his fireside chair. He rose as she entered and grinned.

'Don't blame me,' he said. 'It's these two being nosy.'

'John!' expostulated Sue.

Jemima laughed. 'Quite true,' she said. 'We haven't heard anything about the murder for days. So we thought we'd get the skinny from you.'

'Nothing much to tell, I'm afraid,' said Libby, seating herself on the large sofa, while Sue went to fetch the same tray as before, this time with tea things and a delicious-looking lemon drizzle cake.

'Have the police made no progress?' she asked, putting it down on the coffee table.

'I don't know, frankly.' Libby leant back and sighed. 'This is nice.'

'And you and Fran haven't either?' asked Jemima.

'No, nothing.' She took the cup Sue handed her. 'Thank you. I'm still wondering about Jackie's cottage in Pedlar's Row, though. Was it hers, or did she rent it? And how did she afford it? They're quite pricey, those cottages.'

'I never thought of that!' said Sue, looking surprised.

'Some fancy man, I shouldn't wonder,' said John.

'John!' said Sue again.

'No, he might be right,' said Libby. 'Someone else suggested the same thing. Someone to do with the golf club, perhaps?'

'But I thought she hated the golf club?' said Jemima.

'Not always, we've discovered,' said Libby. 'She apparently had quite a thing going with one of the members a few years back. And then found that unless she was with him, she couldn't go in. And we assume that's what set her off.'

'I suppose it makes sense,' said Sue, sounding doubtful. 'How long ago was it?'

'We don't know, exactly.' Libby accepted a slice of cake. 'And we can't go barging into the club to ask.'

'What about your friend Lewis?' asked John. 'Did he ask Bomber Harris?'

'He introduced me,' said Libby. 'Nothing much.' She decided not to reveal anything of Martin Harris's revelations, nor any of the speculations about Vincent Halliday. 'By the way,' she went on. 'Those sheep out there – do they belong to the Geddings?'

John and Sue looked surprised. 'Yes!'

'Why?' asked Sue.

'Our local butcher was singing their praises and sold me a couple of lamb chops,' said Libby. 'I was surprised when he told me they were Heronsbourne Flats sheep.'

'Oh, yes,' said John. 'Won prizes, they have. Very well regarded.'

'And she's a lovely woman, Alice,' said Jemima.

'You know her?' Libby turned to her.

'Another one whose garden I've ruined,' grinned Jemima. 'I usually pop in when I come and see John and Sue. She's not much of a one for socialising.' She cocked her head on one side. 'Would you like to meet her?'

'Oh, no,' said Libby hastily. 'She would think I was being intrusive – especially if she knew who I was.'

193

'You have a point,' said Jemima, smiling knowingly. Libby turned quickly back to John and Sue.

'Any more activity from the Save the Marshes group?' she asked. 'Fran was quite keen to join.'

'Now that's one who took against Alice Gedding,' said John, scowling.

'Who? Not Marjorie Sutcliffe?'

'The very same. She was angry enough when her pet vicar left the group – you'd think she'd be more charitable,' he grumbled.

'What had Mrs Gedding done to offend her?' asked Libby, already being sure of the answer.

'She's black, isn't she.' John sounded quite confrontational.

'Oh.' Libby looked Sue for an explanation.

'Alice wanted to join the group – understandable, really. She grazes her sheep here. Got quite a reputation.' Sue sat back and folded her arms. 'The way that woman's going, she'll have nobody left in the group.'

'That's not good,' said Libby. 'How's it going? Do you know?'

'No.' Sue shrugged. 'We can't get through to the solicitor. Marjorie tries to say it's her business, not ours.'

'But surely—' began Libby.

'Oh, I know.' John nodded. 'So we've got in touch with another solicitor – Alice Gedding's with us – and we've approached some other people with a legitimate claim. And the people who originally got it made an SSSI.' He raised an eyebrow at Libby.

'Yes, I know – a Site of Special Scientific Interest,' said Libby. 'What you need is to find a species that needs to be saved.'

'Exactly.' Sue looked smug. 'And we think we have.'

'Oh?' said Jemima and Libby together.

'Some moth or other,' said John. 'Looks promising.'

Libby stayed another hour, then apologised and said she had to go. 'And thank you for the tea and cake – I haven't been invited out to tea since I was a little girl!'

Sue laughed. 'But what a nice tradition!'

194

Jemima went with her to her car.

'You don't think the marsh protest has anything to do with Jackie's death?' she asked.

'I can't see it, can you? She just made a bit of a fuss as she seemed to do everywhere she went.' Libby unlocked the car. 'And despite my asking about Mrs Gedding, she hasn't got anything to do with it, either. It was one of those old women in St Aldeberge sniping about her daughter.'

'That's the trouble, I suppose,' said Jemima. 'Every time you mention anything, people jump to conclusions.'

'And ask questions,' said Libby, with a grin.

'Alice is an awfully nice woman,' Jemima added reflectively. 'You'll have to meet her one day.'

'Yes, I'd like to. And if you see her, tell her Bob the butcher is selling me her salt marsh lamb!'

Libby cooked her salt marsh lamb chops for dinner that night, and she and Ben agreed they were excellent. They wandered down to the pub later, and found Patti, Anne, Colin, Gerry, and Edward already gathered round their usual table.

After settling with drinks, Libby told Patti about Alice Gedding.

'Everyone says she's a very nice woman. She's involved with a fight against the development of the marshes with Jemima's friends, John and Sue.'

'What – the Save the Marshes group?' asked Anne.

'No – apparently Marjorie Sutcliffe, the organiser – I told you about her, didn't I? – chucked her out.'

'Why?'

'Because she's black,' said Libby, sending Edward an apologetic smile.

'You wouldn't believe it, would you?' said Edward, in an exasperated voice. 'I still come across it, even in my exalted position!' He smiled back ruefully. 'Poor woman. I'd like to meet her. You'll have to arrange it, Libby.'

195

'She's probably married, Edward,' said Libby mischievously.

'I didn't mean that!' Edward drew himself up, looking affronted.

Libby laughed. 'I know. I was teasing.'

'So, any more news about the murder?' asked Gerry.

'No,' said Libby. 'I think Fran and I are out of it now.'

'Mind you, there are still some of my parishioners trying to get some mileage out of it,' said Patti with a sigh.

'Oh?' Colin looked interested, so Patti regaled them with a description of Connie Barstowe's endeavours to link the murder to those uncovered in the previous investigation.

'It's what Jemima said to me this afternoon, some people automatically think that I know more about these situations than they do. Even when I don't.' Libby sniffed and took a healthy swallow of her drink.

About an hour later, Ian arrived, accompanied by Peter.

'I popped into The Pink Geranium to see if any of you were in there,' said Ian, as Peter went with Ben to the bar to fetch drinks. 'Harry won't be long. He isn't busy.'

Ben put Ian's coffee in front of him and delivered fresh supplies to the others.

'Anything to tell us?' asked Anne eagerly.

Ian laughed. 'Nothing I can tell you!'

'No progress, then?' asked Peter.

'No.' Ian looked round the group. 'What about you. Any news?'

Colin and Gerry told him about their inquiries with their solicitor and Patti told him about Connie Barstowe's thoughts.

'Not so much thoughts as certainties,' said Patti. 'Libby and I took it all with a pinch of salt.'

Ian looked at Libby. 'Did you?'

'Yes. And this black girl she was talking about, turns out she has a very respectable mum who farms sheep on Heronsbourne Flats.'

'Ah.' Ian nodded. 'Alice Gedding.'

Everyone stared at him in surprise.

'You know her?' said Libby.

'Indeed.' Ian sighed. 'During the last investigation, the murder of her daughter was obviously looked into, in case it had any relevance.'

'And her murderer was caught, apparently?' said Patti.

'He was.' Ian shut his mouth firmly.

'So there's nothing in this mysterious golf-playing person Connie was hinting about?'

Ian shrugged. 'Some of the members of the Reverend Turner's infamous meetings were businessmen, and likely to play golf. We didn't track them all down.'

The conversation became general, but Libby noticed Ian leaning across to Colin and Gerry and obviously asking them something. He caught her eye and grinned. 'All right,' he said. 'I'm interested in the terms of the leasehold on these properties. Do you think your friend who lives there would talk to me?'

Privately, Libby thought Dotty would be delighted. Aloud she said, 'I'm sure she would. Shall I ask her?'

'If you would,' said Ian. 'And I might have a chat with Alice Gedding, too.'

'But you said—' began Libby.

'Just for background,' he said carelessly.

'Informally,' said Libby, glancing at Edward, who shook his head at her.

Harry caused a diversion by bursting through the door and demanding refreshment.

'Listen,' he said. 'I've just had those two golfing blokes on again.'

'What for?' asked Libby.

'To book a table, of course!' Harry raised his eyebrows. 'What else?'

'They know about us knowing you,' said Libby. 'And Ian. So why risk coming here again?'

'Oi! Perhaps they like the food!' said Harry, offended.

'Or perhaps they want to do a bit of digging of their own,' said Ian. 'When are they coming?'

'Tomorrow. Eight o'clock. Want me to book you in?' he added hopefully.

'No – just keep your eyes and ears open, and if they start asking questions, give me a ring.'

'You definitely think the murder's something to do with the golf club?' Libby asked Ian quietly, when the conversation became general once more.

He looked down into his coffee cup. 'Or someone involved with the club,' he said. 'What else have you found out?' He looked up at her. 'And don't tell me you haven't.'

Libby flushed, and told him about Debbie's revelations about Vincent Halliday. 'At least,' she finished. 'I assume he was the Vince referred to.'

'Hmmm.' Ian sat back in his chair. 'Trouble is, we can't find him.'

'Oh, heavens! Not someone else who's run away to Spain!'

Ian gave her a crooked smile. 'You never know!'

Colin leant over. 'Not Spain again?'

Ian swivelled in his chair. 'Ever heard of a Vincent Halliday in your Mediterranean days?'

Colin and Gerry both shook their heads.

'Oh, well,' said Ian. 'It was worth a try.'

Suddenly Libby clapped her hand to head. 'Oh, God! I've just remembered!' She sent Patti an apologetic glance. 'Sorry, Patti.'

'What have you remembered?' asked Ian sharply.

'Those girls – the girls Sarah mentioned.'

'Sarah?'

'Elliot – you remember? She had belonged to the church. Well, she remembered two friends of hers from about the same time. Carole something and Jill Stevens. And they used to attend the meetings. And they disappeared.'

Chapter Twenty-nine

Ian looked dubious. 'And she remembered this why? She didn't happen to know you had been asking questions about the murder of Jackie Stapleton?'

'Well – yes. But she wasn't making it up, I'm sure of it,' said Libby, aware that everyone was looking at her.

'And it didn't occur to you that she was doing exactly what Patti's old lady was doing?'

'Trying to get in on the act,' said Harry, grinning at her.

'No, it didn't,' said Libby. 'And Ben and I thought of something afterwards, didn't we, Ben?'

'Erm – yes,' said Ben unwillingly.

Ian sighed. 'All right. Tell me what she said.'

Libby pulled her chair round to face Ian.

'Sarah said they didn't run away from home, or anything, but they started missing school and they stopped mixing with the rest of the girls. And Jill had been almost her best friend. So I asked if this Jill had tried to get her to join in, and she said yes, but she hadn't. Sarah, that is. And she tried to talk Jill out of it, but she laughed.'

'Anything else?'

'I asked if she wasn't unhappy about that, but she said not at first. But then after a bit she was withdrawn. And then she left school. So did the other one, Carole.'

'I think I followed that,' said Ian with a smile, 'but if Carole was Carole Spinner – that was the name, wasn't it? – she was located. She really was just a simple runaway. Didn't get on with her stepfather. So, Ben. What did you think?'

Ben pulled a face. 'Actually, I said suppose one of them was Jackie Stapleton. And then Fran came up with the fact that this Jill Stevens had the same initials.'

Ian stared at Ben with an arrested expression.

'Right,' he said eventually. 'Anybody like another drink?'

Ben, surprised, stood up. 'I'll get them.'

'Thanks,' said Ian. 'And I'd better make some notes.'

Libby and Ben exchanged puzzled glances.

'What was all that about?' asked Harry, who had been excluded from the conversation.

'Oh, more possible leads, I suppose,' said Libby. 'But there've been so many, all leading nowhere . . .'

'Like what?' Edward joined in.

'Oh, there was the old boy at The Poacher, who thought he'd recognised Jackie as a girl he knew in Felling. Turned out she looked completely different and her name was Rosa.' Libby sighed. 'Then there was Vince from the golf club, and Martin Harris who was the first person to introduce her there. And Hannah Barton, whose boyfriend, Gary, Jackie pinched. And whoever got her the expensive cottage in Pedlar's Row. And all the people at the New Year's Eve party on the beach, of course.'

Ian, who had been listening with amusement, said, 'And don't forget the old ladies from St Aldeberge.'

'And the suspicious American vicar,' said Ben, back at the table.

'Thanks.' Ian accepted a new cup of coffee. 'And don't worry about it, Libby. I'll have another look at all of this, and if I can join up any of the dots, I'll let you know.'

Libby nodded and turned her chair back to the assembled company. Patti raised an eyebrow.

'I'm surprised there hasn't been any news in the media,' she said. 'Surely the official investigation should have progressed further than this by now? It's been weeks.'

'Oh, it has,' said Ian. 'Just not necessarily in the right direction.'

'You're not trying to undermine your own DI?' said Edward. 'Shame on you.'

'No, just trying to lend a helping hand while remaining unobtrusive,' said Ian. 'Not necessarily successfully.'

As everybody was leaving, Ian stopped Libby.

'I'm going to try and visit Alice Gedding,' he said. 'Would you like to come with me? I'm going to take Edward, too.'

'Officially? You can't do that, can you?'

'Oh, no, not officially. Would you like to come?'

'Yes, but I don't see how you're going to manage it,' said Libby.

'Leave it to me,' said Ian.

'What do you make of all that?' Libby asked Ben as they walked home.

'I haven't got the faintest idea,' he said. 'His attitude throughout this has been most odd.'

'It has,' Libby agreed thoughtfully. 'More like a private detective. You don't think he's going to retire and become a PI instead?'

'Shouldn't think so for a minute. I think it's more likely to be to prove that he's better on the ground than stuck behind a desk.'

'Poor DI Winters,' said Libby. 'Bit sneaky, isn't it? I never thought Ian was sneaky.'

'I'm sure he's passing on anything relevant,' said Ben. 'I'm more interested in this visit to Alice Gedding. What *is* going on there?'

'You don't think he's matchmaking, do you?' Libby's eyes lit up.

'Oh, Libby!' Ben snorted with disdain and opened the door.

The next day she found out.

Ian picked up Libby, who climbed into the back of the car behind Edward.

'No, I don't know what he's got up his sleeve, either,' he said, in answer to her question. 'He's behaving very oddly.'

'That's what we were saying last night,' said Libby.

201

'I heard that,' said Ian, sliding in behind the steering wheel.

He drove them towards Heronsbourne, but turned off to the left before they reached The Red Lion. Libby realised they were going along the edge of the marsh towards the sea, when Ian veered off to the left again and drew up in front of a red brick, foursquare house. Off to the right, Libby could see what looked like farm buildings.

As Ian held the car door open for Libby, she saw a smiling woman in blue dungarees come out of the house.

'Ian!' she said, smiling. 'Lovely to see you.'

Edward and Libby stood aside, bewildered, as Ian and the woman, who was obviously Alice Gedding, hugged each other. Then he drew Libby forward.

'And this is my friend Libby Sarjeant,' he said.

'Alice,' said the woman, holding out a hand. 'I've heard all about you. I thought you might be coming to see me.'

'And this is my neighbour Edward.'

Edward shook the hand held out to him. 'Good to meet you,' he said.

Alice led the way into her house.

'Kettle's boiled,' she said. 'Tea or coffee?'

Edward and Ian opted for coffee, and when Libby hesitated, Alice grinned and said, 'And tea for Libby?'

Before long they were seated in a comfortable, slightly shabby sitting room.

'I'd better explain,' said Ian. 'Libby and Edward are wondering why I've dragged them out here, and you're wondering why I haven't come on my own.'

A sudden suspicion flashed into Libby's mind. A relationship?

Alice turned to Libby and Edward. 'Ian and I have known one another for a long time,' she said. 'He helped me when—' she hesitated.

'When Alice's daughter died,' Ian went on. 'You two have heard about that.'

'Only briefly,' said Libby.

202

'Well, we kept in touch.' Alice smiled at Ian. 'And when this awful business about Jackie Stapleton came up, he got in touch again.'

Libby turned slightly accusing eyes on Ian, but refrained from comment.

'I'll explain later,' he said, 'but meanwhile, I thought I'd introduce you two to Alice as she's heard rather a lot about you in the past couple of weeks.'

Alice leant forward and put her hand on Libby's. 'You mustn't mind,' she said. 'He was worried that you might get distracted. I know a lot of the people you've been talking to, you see. And you might have been swayed by my reactions.'

'I'm beginning to see,' murmured Libby, patting Alice's hand. 'But Edward hasn't been investigating?'

'Well, no.' Ian looked slightly guilty. 'But I've talked about him to Alice rather a lot.'

'I'd almost begun to think he had a crush on him!' laughed Alice. Edward looked horrified.

'So what are we here for, exactly?' asked Libby. 'Not that it isn't lovely to meet you, Alice,' she added. 'Jemima Routledge and John and Sue Cantripp have been singing your praises.'

'Just a pleasant break in the investigation?' suggested Ian.

'I don't believe that for a moment,' said Libby.

'How about I take Edward out to look at the farm,' said Ian, 'and leave you and Alice to have a chat?' He looked interrogatively at Alice, who nodded.

'That'll be fine,' she said. 'All right, Libby?'

Libby, at a loss, nodded.

Ian and Edward, who hadn't said a word since they came indoors, left the room.

Alice folded her hands in her lap and looked down at them. Libby contemplated her rather beautiful, fine-drawn face, and still wondered. At last she looked up.

'Can I ask how you first heard about me?' Alice asked.

Libby squirmed. 'Um—' she said.

Alice smiled. 'From what Ian said, I gather it was something to do with someone in St Aldeberge?'

'Yes.' Libby took a deep breath and explained about Connie Barstowe. 'You see, when we were investigating the murder out there last year, she had quite a lot to say about the victim.'

'I know.' Alice nodded. 'And she decided this murder was connected to the whole business.'

'Yes.'

'Which is exactly what she did with my daughter.' She stared into the distance for a few minutes. 'Poppy was sixteen when she died. And there was a lot of gossip because a year or so before there had been a lot of talk about the strange club at the church, and then the disappearance of the vicar.'

'So it was after that?'

'Oh, yes. And at first, the local police didn't take it seriously. And then . . .' She stopped.

'Don't go on if it's difficult,' said Libby.

'No, it's all right.' Alice turned to face Libby. 'I found her body. Not buried or anything – just left in our farmyard.'

Libby gasped. Alice smiled sadly.

'I know. Anyway, I called 999, and Ian and another policeman arrived – along with all the other people – and very quickly they arrested a boy who had been bothering Poppy for ages. I'm afraid it was because . . . because she was black.'

'I see.' Libby wanted to say 'it must have been awful for you', but decided it was too trite for words

'And Ian was a tower of strength. My husband had left when Poppy was eight, and I'd been running the farm almost single-handedly, so I hadn't really had enough time to be a proper mother, and I'd let her run a bit wild.' Alice suddenly covered her face with her hands. 'I felt so guilty.'

Hesitantly, Libby leant over and put her hand on Alice's arm. 'I'm so sorry.'

After a moment, Alice looked up and smiled tremulously.

'Thank you.' She took a breath. 'Anyway, he put me in touch with all sorts of people who could help, and the long and short of it was I sold up and bought this place. And now I've increased my flock.'

'And won prizes, I hear,' said Libby. 'My butcher recommends your meat. We had a couple of your chops this week.'

'Good.' She sat up straight and lifted her head. 'And when Ian heard you might be looking into the Save the Marshes group, he told me. Did you know about that?'

'I know all about Marjorie Sutcliffe,' said Libby grimly.

'I thought you would. She threw me out – and Jackie – because she had a real live vicar in the group. Who, incidentally, left at the same time as we did. We rather assumed it was because I was black and Jackie was, in Marjorie's words, "a common little trouble-maker." And she's obviously spread that around.' Alice frowned.

'How do you know?'

'I've had a couple of rather nasty anonymous letters.'

Libby gasped again.

'Don't worry,' Alice went on, 'Ian knows about them. But he's kept Poppy's death at the back of his mind, just in case someone decided to make capital out of it.' She looked at Libby. 'And now she's been brought to your attention so it looks as though someone has.'

Chapter Thirty

Libby sat still, frowning. 'I'm not sure I understand. Why should anyone be seeking to make capital out of it?'

'I'm not sure, either,' said Alice. 'As far as I'm concerned, it simply means that the whole business has been brought up again. What Ian thinks is that Jackie's death is being linked to all those deaths twenty years ago, and now, so is Poppy's.'

'But Poppy's, at least, isn't linked at all. So why?'

Alice shrugged. 'Malicious gossip?'

'But to what end? It doesn't make sense!' Libby's voice was rising.

'I know. And I told Ian that – but he's got some bee in his bonnet.'

'And he's been encouraging me – me and my friend Fran – to look into it all more and more. And we can't see quite what we're supposed to do.'

'Yes, he told me. And he said you were a bit resistant to his suggestions too!' Alice laughed. 'I'm not sure he liked that.'

'He's so used to me charging off on my own, you see.' Libby looked sheepish.

'And we can never normally do anything to stop her.' Unnoticed by Alice or Libby, Ian and Edward had re-entered the room.

'Ian!' Libby reproached.

'Sorry.' Ian looked anything but apologetic. 'Have you bonded over your disapproval of me?'

Alice laughed. 'Libby can't see why you're interested in Poppy's death all over again either.'

'She'll find a way to link it all together, you'll see,' said Edward. 'Sorry for butting in.'

Alice looked across at him. 'Has Ian told you about my disreputable past?'

Edward smiled. 'Hardly disreputable.'

'We saw you've got a couple of early lambs?' said Ian.

'Early, yes,' said Alice. 'That's why we're keeping them in. The others aren't due until March or April, and they'll mostly lamb outside.' She sighed. 'As long as we've still got a marsh to lamb them on.'

'John and Sue Cantripp said you've joined them in consulting another solicitor,' said Libby.

'Yes, and it looks quite hopeful,' said Alice. 'Our solicitor thinks the builders applied for permission almost on the rebound after losing out on the golf course. And what with the SSSI designation, and this discovery of the moth—'

'Moth?' echoed Ian and Edward.

'Protected species,' explained Alice, 'and then St Cuthbert's and the yew—'

'The what?' said Edward.

'I'll tell you later,' said Ian. 'Or Libby will. I bet she knows.'

'Well, it was lovely to see you all,' said Alice. 'I don't get many visitors.'

Edward looked as though he was going to say something, but Ian forestalled him.

'We'd better leave Alice to get on,' he said, and bending down, kissed her cheek. 'I'll be in touch.'

Alice stood up, too, and impulsively kissed Libby's cheek. 'I do hope you'll come again,' she said.

Edward held out his hand, and Libby was sure she saw something pass between them, but then Ian was hustling them out to the car.

'Well,' said Libby, as they were driving away, 'not that it wasn't lovely to meet Alice, and she's a really nice person, but you could have told me all of that yourself.'

Edward turned round from the front seat and grinned at her. 'I think he wanted to introduce me.'

'You *were* matchmaking!' said Libby.

Ian met her eyes in the driving mirror. 'I just thought two very nice single friends of mine might like to meet one another.'

'And me?'

Ian's voice gentled. 'You're very good at making friends, Libby. And Alice needs a friend.'

'But why? John and Sue and Jemima all like her – they told me.'

'She thinks there's feeling against her in the community because of Marjorie Sutcliffe.'

'That's rubbish,' Libby expostulated. 'That woman's losing support hand over fist, so I'm told. Although it's a pity, because the fight against the planning permission needs all the help it can get.'

'What's this about St Cuthbert's and – a yew, was it?' asked Edward.

Libby told him what she knew. He lapsed once again into silence.

'So, Ian. When are you going to tell me what's in your mind?' said Libby after several minutes had passed.

'Cards on the table time?' She could hear the smile in his voice.

'Yes, please. We've already had a couple of run-ins over this business. Isn't it time you levelled with us?'

'Meaning you and Fran?'

'Exactly.'

'I'm going to drop Edward at home first, then we could drive down to Nethergate,' he suggested.

'You practically drive past Nethergate on the way home,' said Edward. 'Why don't you pick Fran up on the way, then the three of you can put your heads together in your place.' He turned to Libby. 'I might even provide you with lunch!'

Libby beamed.

'Ian?'

'That's very nice of you, Edward,' he said. 'Can you give Fran a ring, Libby?'

Fran, although taken aback by the invitation, agreed with alacrity.

'What's it all about though?' she asked.

'Cards on the table time, Ian said. But I'm more confused than ever.'

Fran was waiting outside Coastguard Cottage when they arrived, and climbed into the back of the car with Libby.

'Where are we going?' she asked.

'Grove House,' said Edward. 'Ian can host a round table conference, and I'll bring you lunch.'

Fran raised her eyebrows at Libby, who gave her a smug smile.

Grove House was a small, perfect Georgian manor house divided into two apartments and situated near the village of Shott, only two or three miles from Steeple Martin. Edward had bought the ground floor flat just after the renovations, and Ian had purchased the top floor some time later. Ian drove up to the big front doors and parked with a flourish.

Edward disappeared into his flat, and Ian led the way up the stairs into his own domain. In the big sitting room, with its view over surrounding countryside from the balcony and French windows, they sat down at the round table in the window.

'Right,' said Ian, getting notebook, pencil, and tablet out of a briefcase. 'Where would you like me to start?'

Fran and Libby exchanged glances.

'At the beginning?' suggested Libby.

'What do you think of as the beginning?' asked Ian. 'When you came into the story?'

'No,' said Fran. 'The discovery of the body.'

'Ah.' Ian looked down at his tablet. For a moment he was quiet. 'With the ubiquitous dog walker, then?'

'Yes,' the women said together.

'Very well.' Ian swiped the screen on his tablet. 'On New Year's

Day, a resident of Pedlar's Row, Heronsbourne, walked his dog, as usual, down to the beach. He always went along the beach and, as the dog was often let off the lead, it frequently strayed on to the golf course.'

'Pedlar's Row!' said Libby.

Ian smiled. 'Nothing suspicious about that. But he recognised the victim. He called the police, and two officers went along to the scene. Within an hour, the whole circus had arrived, including DS Stone, who promptly referred it to DI Winters. And, of course, it ended up on my desk.'

'What about this resident?' asked Fran.

'He and his wife have recently retired and bought one of the cottages. He only knew the victim as a neighbour, and had seen her in The Red Lion, where they assumed she wasn't particularly popular.'

'Did he know what number she lived at?' asked Libby.

'He did. Obviously, the team went there, and found very little to help them. George at the pub was interviewed and confirmed her identity as Jackie Stapleton. It was quickly established that there had been a party on the beach the night before, and that was where DI Winters started his investigation.'

'Right.' Libby was frowning. 'So when Lewis reported that she had been a guest at his place that night, Winters must have already known quite a lot?'

'Very little. You yourself have found out how what? – secretive? – she was. Very little except a general dislike had been uncovered and, of course, all the publicly available material, such as her interference in the whole golf club debacle. So by the time you appeared, a lot of background information had been uncovered, but nothing in the way of a viable suspect or motive.'

'Which was where Libby came in?' Fran grinned at her friend.

'You *both* came in. I had kept out of the day-to-day running of the case as much as possible, but I was getting frustrated. After all, I knew a lot of the people in Heronsbourne, and Lewis, of course, and I felt there was a lot more to be learnt if the surface was scraped. But

I couldn't do it. Frankly,' he said, leaning back in his chair and sighing, 'I was relieved when you appeared. So I suggested you – er – became involved.'

'Without telling DI Winters?' said Libby.

'DI Winters doesn't know either of you, and would, anyway, have been decidedly unwilling to allow you to have anything to with the case.'

'I said you were trying to undermine him, poor bugger,' said Libby.

'Not at all!' Ian laughed. 'Anything you ferreted out that I felt was helpful, I managed to pass on – without arousing suspicion. Winters is known for being a stickler for procedure, although DS Stone is more – shall we say – lateral thinking?'

'So you've been passing it all on to DS Stone?' Fran was looking faintly disapproving.

'Some of it. Very delicately, of course.' Ian's tone was somewhat mocking.

Libby scowled at him. 'So you *have* been using us, just as Ben and I thought.'

Ian's expression became frosty. 'No more than I have used information supplied by any other informant. Yours is usually discovered through unorthodox means. This time, I asked for it.'

Fran and Libby were silent.

Ian sighed. 'Look, I've asked you to do no more than you would have done on your own, have I? And I'd be in trouble if I was found out.'

'That I'd like to see,' muttered Libby.

Ian burst out laughing. 'So would a lot of people! And again, I apologise if I've offended you, either of you.'

Following a perfunctory knock, Edward put his head round the door. 'May I serve your lunch, your honour?'

Ian grinned at him and moved his tablet and notebook to one side. 'Please do. You have brought a plate for yourself, haven't you?'

Edward came in and set a tray on the table. 'I didn't want to intrude.'

'Fetch one of mine, then,' said Ian. 'You deserve to hear this.'

When they were settled and Edward had offered sandwiches and salad, 'Not very wintry, sorry,' and Ian had fetched some bottles of beer, a jug of water, and glasses, they returned to what Ian referred to as 'the inquest'.

'Tell us what the official investigation has unearthed so far,' said Fran. 'If you're allowed to.'

'Sadly, they had already talked to your friend Debbie at the café—'

'She told us,' said Libby.

'But they hadn't unearthed the information about someone from the golf club. Although she could have had some kind of relationship with several at the golf club. They are now looking into the possibility of irregularities in the sale and transfer of land for the three new houses.'

'Oh, I do hope Dotty isn't going to get into trouble.' Libby stared mournfully at her sandwich.

'As far as I can see,' said Ian, pouring beer, 'it only affects the two end properties.'

'So there is something dodgy there?' said Libby.

'It looks like it,' said Ian, 'but again, as far as I can see, it doesn't come into Jackie's murder.'

They all ate silently for a moment.

'And what about the girl Sarah Elliot remembered? The one I told you about last night?'

'Ah.' Ian swallowed a mouthful of beer. 'I passed that on, and, in fact, it's with our Rachel for investigation.'

'Rachel Trent?'

'Indeed. On her way to becoming Detective Inspector Trent. As she was very much involved in the last investigation, that seemed sensible.'

'But she's not connected to this investigation?' asked Fran.

'I didn't say that,' said Ian.

Chapter Thirty-one

'So that's a new lead?' said Fran.

'It could be, but DS Stone didn't think DI Winters would bother with it. Which is why I've given it to Rachel. If she finds anything, it can be officially passed on.'

'Where does Alice come into all this?' asked Edward, after a moment.

Ian pushed his plate away. 'When it came out that Jackie had been thrown out of the Save the Marshes group by the Sutcliffe woman, as well as Alice, I wondered. I know the reasons were different – Jackie was a troublemaker and Alice is black – but it struck me that there could be a connection. I had no idea what, but Alice's daughter was murdered.' Ian stared broodingly into his glass. 'I know her murderer was caught, but, as you heard, Libby, it had first been suggested that there might be a link with the girls who had disappeared. Nobody looked into that. I tried to, but was soon warned off.'

Fran, who had heard nothing of the morning's visit, was quickly put in the picture by Libby and Edward.

'I may be chasing rainbows,' said Ian, 'but I couldn't help feeling that there was a vague connection.'

'I can't see how we could find that out,' said Fran.

'No, neither do I.' Ian gave them a crooked smile. 'Rachel will do her best.'

'So what about all the other people who've contributed to the inquiry so far?' asked Libby. 'Are any of them any use?'

'Everyone who has helped build a picture of Jackie as a person was useful, of course. DS Stone told me that you'd got more out of them than the whole official inquiry.'

Libby beamed. 'That's nice! But have they looked into who owned her cottage? I keep asking people, and no one seems to know if she was renting or she owned it.'

'According to the documents lodged at the Land Registry it's owned by a JS Wilson, so no clue there. And there were no obvious rental payments showing in Jackie's bank account. DS Stone hasn't yet traced JS Wilson.'

'Didn't Debbie think it was something to do with Jackie's putative golf club lover?' said Fran.

'If it was him, he has even more questions to answer,' said Ian. 'But as I told you, he seems to have vanished.'

'Spain again, I thought,' Libby told Fran.

'Colin wouldn't know, I suppose?' Fran turned to Ian, who shook his head.

'If he's still alive, it would be under a different name. We've spoken to his ex-wife, who hasn't any idea.'

'I didn't know he'd been married,' said Libby. 'If we're talking about Vince.'

'Why should you?' said Ian. 'You don't have to know *everything*!'

Edward stood up and loaded the empty sandwich platter on to his tray. 'Anyone want coffee?'

Ian and Fran accepted, but Libby stuck with beer.

'And where should we be looking now?' she said. 'For the murderer, I mean? Now we've cleared away the dead wood?'

'OK,' said Ian. 'You tell me. Where would you start?'

Fran and Libby went quiet. Finally, as Edward returned with coffee, Libby looked up, twisting the beer glass in her fingers.

'I think,' she said, 'I'd want to know if she could possibly be one of the girls Sarah Elliot told us about. And if not one of them, precisely, if she had come from St Aldeberge.'

Ian nodded. 'I agree. Fran?'

'If that was followed up, I'd want to know if anyone living here had also come from St Aldeberge.'

'Bearing in mind,' said Ian, stirring coffee, 'that members of the Reverend Turner's club didn't only come from St Aldeberge. At least a couple of them didn't, including the sergeant from Felling – Peacock. Remember?'

'Who is now living in Spain,' sighed Libby.

Sergeant Peacock had been implicated in the case of historic abuse they had run into during the last investigation, which Connie Barstowe and Sarah Elliot seemed to be trying to link to the murder of Jackie Stapleton.

'We did try and link the cases up ourselves at first,' Libby went on, 'but there didn't seem anything to link Jackie to St Aldeberge.'

'There didn't seem anything to link her to anywhere,' said Fran. 'And it isn't as if traditional things like DNA or fingerprints are any use. Not without something to compare them with.'

'Exactly,' said Ian. 'Which is one of the reasons your ferreting can be so useful.'

'Except that we haven't found anything this time,' said Libby.

'What about the illegal land transfers, or whatever they were?' said Edward.

'That wasn't us,' said Fran. 'That was Colin and Gerry.'

'To be fair,' said Ian, 'it was Libby who put them on to the house.'

'There was the information you got from Martin Harris,' said Fran.

'Which merely led to Vincent Halliday, who has subsequently disappeared.'

'Would you,' Fran said to Ian, 'be able to question someone involved in the last case?'

'Do you mean someone we convicted? No, not now. It hasn't come to trial yet.'

Libby sat up. 'That's it! That's the motive!'

Fran clicked her fingers. 'Of course! If there's someone in Heronsbourne who was linked to the business in St Aldeberge, they would be scared of being recognised and taken to court. For assisting a murderer, or something similar.'

'Well done.' Ian looked from one to the other. 'How do we go about finding out?'

'God knows,' said Libby.

'That's what you're good at,' said Ian. 'Finding out the things we can't.'

'Our ferreting, you mean,' said Fran.

'As I said, it can be very useful.'

'But we've ferreted all over the place, and come up with nothing. As *I* said,' said Libby. 'What do you suggest?'

'How much is going to be passed on to DI Winters?' asked Fran.

'Rachel will pass on whatever she finds out,' said Ian. 'And I shall review the evidence and send a suitably edited report.'

'Editing us out?' inquired Libby.

'Maybe a little.'

'Doesn't seem fair,' said Edward. 'They've done such a lot of work.'

'The problem is that Winters would have a rooted objection to following up on anything not brought out by normal procedures,' said Ian, 'which, as I've tried to explain, is why I may have been, as Libby and Ben put it, a trifle underhand, and apparently "using" you. Yes, I was – but in the nicest possible way.'

Libby spluttered

'We'll take that as read, then,' said Fran with a wry smile. 'But I don't see where we can ferret now. We've tried Save the Marshes, and the customers at The Red Lion, we've exploited Lewis's connection with Martin Harris, we've talked to Debbie at the café in Nethergate, Jemima's friends John and Sue, from whom we got Hannah and Gary – where now?'

'JS Wilson,' said Libby promptly.

'Who?' Fran looked puzzled.

'Ian told us – Land Registry says that's who owns Jackie's cottage.'

'Oh – yes. But how?'

'The official inquiry has tried,' said Ian, 'but nothing so far.'

'And who lived there before?' asked Edward.

'As far as we can find out, until seven years ago, an old boy who'd been there for as long as anyone remembered.'

'And the search of the premises?' Edward continued.

Ian looked at him with amusement. 'Are you getting involved, now?'

Edward grinned. 'Why not? I've been helpful in the past!'

'They *have* searched her cottage, haven't they?' pursued Libby.

'Of course they have. And found nothing. No old letters or photographs, no books. Couple of shopping lists.'

'Mobile? Laptop?' suggested Fran.

'Neither, although there were chargers for both.'

They all looked at each other.

'Pinched,' said Libby.

'Stolen,' said Edward and Fran.

'Quite,' said Ian.

'That hasn't been released to the press,' said Fran.

'No. And we tried to trace the mobile, but it was obviously a throw-away job.'

'You were right, secretive is the word,' said Libby. 'So – do we think, sorry, do *you* think, Jackie was blackmailing her murderer? Possibly with the cottage – if you know what I mean?'

'I think it's very likely.' Ian turned to Edward. 'What do you think?'

'I think it's an obvious place to start,' said Edward, 'but I haven't got the faintest idea how you go about it.'

'Neither have I,' said Libby gloomily.

'There's one obvious thing,' said Fran.

'What's that?' asked Edward.

'Ask Sarah if she thinks Jackie is Jill Stevens. Show her a photograph.'

'Of course!' said Libby. 'Why didn't I think of that?'

'It will have to be a post-mortem photograph,' said Ian.

'What – her being cut up?' said Libby, horrified.

'No, of course not. I meant a photo of her – dead.'

'Oh.' Libby giggled. 'Sorry.'

'Has there been a press release showing a picture?' asked Fran.

'No,' said Ian thoughtfully. 'Perhaps it's time that was done.'

'A "have you seen this girl?" sort of thing?' said Libby.

'More a "do you know this woman?" sort of thing,' said Ian.

'Good idea,' said Edward. 'More coffee?'

Later, Ian drove Libby and Fran back to Steeple Martin. Libby had offered to drive Fran home after they'd had time to mull on – and talk over – today's events.

'I still haven't worked out why Ian's connecting Alice Gedding's daughter to the whole thing, though,' said Libby.

They were sitting in front of the fire in the sitting room, having eschewed the idea of tea due to being full of beer and coffee. Ben was at The Manor, so they were undisturbed.

'Neither do I,' said Fran, 'although on the face of it, I can see why the Aldeberge ladies linked her to the previous case, although only in the light of what came out then. At the actual time of the events twenty years ago, there was nothing to connect them.'

'All very complicated,' said Libby. 'And I can sort of see why Ian's been setting us to chase hares.'

'So what are we going to do?' asked Fran.

'Show the picture of Jackie's dead face to Sarah Elliot,' said Libby. 'And perhaps try and find out who JS Wilson is?'

'I don't see how we can do that. The police must have tried to find out through official channels.'

'And she didn't appear to be paying rent, so they can't check up on bank records.' Libby sighed. 'We could ask the neighbours. There's that chap who used to live there, who remembered Balzac. What about him?'

'That would mean another trip to The Red Lion,' said Fran slyly.

'It's Thursday today,' said Libby. 'They get together on Thursday, don't they? We could go tonight?'

'Could we persuade Guy and Ben to come too? I'd feel less conspicuous then.'

Libby thought for a moment. 'If I can talk Ben into it, we could all drive down to yours, pick up Guy and go and have something to eat – perhaps in The Sloop?'

'Sounds like a plan,' said Fran. 'You call Ben first.'

Ben, sighing with resignation, agreed with the stipulation that Libby drove.

'Then I can have a drink,' he said.

Guy, being informed that Ben had agreed to go, also said yes. Libby put the kettle on, and they settled down to wait for Ben's arrival. They discussed the possibility of eating at The Fox, but decided that it might complicate matters, and The Sloop, having nothing whatsoever to do with the inquiry into Jackie Stapleton's death, was more appropriate.

It was, therefore, just after half past eight when they arrived at The Red Lion. George greeted them all delightedly, and immediately fell into discussion about the quiz with Ben and Guy. John and Sue Cantripp welcomed Fran and Libby, and invited them to their table, where they also found Dotty and Eddy. Standing in a group next to them, were Hannah and Gary with Chrissie from the quiz team and several others, including the big and burly Dan.

'Oh, good!' said Libby beaming. 'Dan, we wanted to ask you a question.'

The whole group went quiet, and Dan looked decidedly nervous.

'Do you remember who lived in Jackie's cottage before she did?'

Dan looked relieved. 'Oh, yes!' he said. 'Lovely old boy. He'd been there forever, always looked after himself. Kept the place spotless. Old-fashioned, mind, but cosy. Was a real shock when he went.'

'He died?' asked Fran.

Dan looked shocked. 'Oh, no! Went into a home. Not a nursing home, more a—' He turned to his friends. 'What did they call it?'

219

'Retirement home,' came the chorus.

'You don't remember where, I suppose?' asked Libby.

'Nethergate,' he said promptly. 'Got the name somewhere.'

'What's his name – I suppose he's still alive?' put in Fran.

'Oh, yes. Bit frail now. But still alive, old Joe.'

'Joe?' repeated Libby.

'Joseph Wilson,' said Dan.

Chapter Thirty-two

Fran was better at concealing reaction than Libby.

'Do you think he'd speak to us?' she asked calmly. 'Or the police?'

'He might,' said Dan. 'Talked to them last time.'

'Last time?' asked Libby, recovering from shock.

'When you took that cat away,' said Dan with a grin.

'His memory's OK, then?' said Libby.

'Oh, yes! Especially for things that happened years ago. If you go and see him, say I sent you.'

'Nyebourne,' came a quiet voice from somewhere around Dan's waist.

Dan roared with laughter. 'Thanks, love!' he said, indicating a small woman sitting at the next door table. 'The wife. Emily.'

'Thank you, Emily,' said Fran. 'That's the name of the retirement home, is it?'

Emily beamed. 'That's right. King Edward Street in Nethergate. Don't know if you know it?'

'Oh, yes,' said Libby and Fran together.

'I live in Nethergate,' added Fran.

'Really?' Emily turned bright, boot-button eyes on Fran. 'I used to live there, too. Before I met this great lump.' She dug Dan in the thigh. 'I knew Nyebourne from when I lived there, and it was me that suggested it to Joe when he decided he couldn't live on his own anymore.'

'Oh, it was his own idea, then?' asked Libby.

'Oh, yes.' Emily was obviously settling down for a good long chat. 'I used to pop in on him almost every day when Dan and I still lived in town. And then he started having difficulty opening jars and bottles because, his arthritis was getting so bad. And other little things – he couldn't reach the top shelves of cupboards, and he was too doddery for ladders. That sort of thing. So we talked it over, and then I took him to see Nyebourne. And that was it!'

'And did he rent his house to Jackie?' asked Fran.

'No, he didn't know her. I understood she got it through an agent.' Emily looked at them both with inquiring eyes. 'Didn't she?'

'There's no record of anyone renting it to her,' said Libby. The owner's still registered as JS Wilson, but no one seemed to know who that was. Until Dan just told us.' She turned to Dan. 'Do you mind if we tell the police what you told us—' she turned back to Emily. 'Both of you?'

''Course not,' said Emily. 'Glad to help. Wish we'd known it was important before.'

'Yeah,' said Dan, nodding vigorously. 'Would'a told you.'

'Any help?' asked Sue, as Ben and Guy left George and came over to the table.

'Yes,' said Libby. 'You didn't know old Joe, I suppose?'

Hannah piped up from the other group. 'I did.'

All eyes turned towards her, and she came over to the table.

'And I don't suppose you know how Jackie became his tenant?' said Fran.

'I thought it was through an agent.'

'I think we'd better go and see old Joe,' said Libby.

Dotty leant forward. 'And have you found out anything about our house?' she said. 'Your friend Colin told us there was something a bit funny about the leasehold. We got a bit worried.'

'Only your next-door neighbours',' said Ben. 'Are you freehold?'

'We are now,' said Eddy. 'The golf club offered us the freehold after we'd been here a few months. We assumed they'd done the same to the neighbours.'

222

'But we've never been on the sort of terms with either of them so's we could ask,' said Dotty.

'Who signed everything on behalf of the golf club?' asked Fran suddenly. 'Do you remember?'

Dotty and Eddy looked at each other, frowning.

'Holliday, wasn't it?' said Dotty.

'Halliday?' suggested Libby.

'Could be,' said Eddy. 'I've got the paperwork at home. I'll look it up if you like.'

'Don't worry,' said Fran. 'I'm sure you're right.'

'You're still looking into Jackie's murder, then?' asked Sue.

'Well, yes,' said Libby.

'Of course they are,' said Guy. 'You can't stop them.'

Fran glared at him.

John laughed. 'The ladies, eh?'

Sue, Fran, and Libby all turned on him in surprise.

'I beg your pardon?' said Sue in freezing tones.

John subsided in confusion. Oddly, this provided a welcome release of tension, and conversation became more general.

'We've got to go and visit old Joe,' said Libby to Fran.

Fran nodded. 'And try and find Halliday.'

'But if he's in Spain . . .'

'Somehow, I don't think he is,' said Fran.

'Is that a "moment"?' asked Libby.

'No, not at all. I just don't think he's far away.'

Libby regarded her seriously. 'Sounds like a "moment" to me,' she said.

After another three quarters of an hour, Ben bent down and whispered in Libby's ear.

'Have you found out what you wanted?'

Libby turned to Fran. 'Have we found out?'

'Yes. Do they want to go?'

'Yes,' said Libby. 'Shall we?'

They took a cheerful leave of their Heronsbourne friends and left.

223

'Do you want to come in for a nightcap?' asked Guy when they arrived at Coastguard Cottage.

Libby parked in the car park behind The Sloop and joined the other three in Fran's sitting room, where Balzac had already appropriated Ben's lap.

'What do we think, then?' asked Libby, having been provided with tea while the others had alcohol.

'Visit Joe. Find out who's been paying Jackie's rent,' said Fran.

'But surely the police will have done that?' said Guy, frowning.

'You would have thought so,' said Ben.

'Perhaps DI Winters has and just not told Ian,' said Libby.

'It would be in the files,' said Fran. 'I can't understand how it's been missed.'

'And find out about the new houses,' said Guy. 'Sounds as though there's definitely been something odd going on there.'

'I wonder where the Save the Marshes group comes in,' said Fran. 'If it does.'

'And the save the church and yew tree,' said Libby. 'Although I suppose that's incidental.'

'Don't go making more mysteries,' said Ben. 'You've got enough to deal with.'

'Shall we try to see Joe tomorrow?' asked Fran. 'Or did you want me in the shop, Guy?'

Guy shrugged. 'Fine with me. We aren't busy, and I've got that commission to get on with.'

'Ooh, commission?' said Libby, distracted.

'Yes.' Guy frowned at her. 'And so have you. From me.'

'Oh.' Libby shrank back on the window seat, and the other three laughed.

'No, you go ahead,' said Guy. 'I'm interested to see why so much hasn't been followed up, if you see what I mean.'

The following morning, Libby drove to Nethergate and picked Fran up.

'You don't suppose,' she said as she drove to King Edward Street, 'that DI Winters is deliberately concealing stuff?'

Fran looked at her in surprise. 'Where did that come from?'

'Well, all these things that haven't been done,' said Libby, slowing down to look for a parking space. 'Following up Joe, and the person who introduced Jackie to the golf club . . . and looking into people who might have a link. I mean, we haven't found it that difficult, have we?'

'N-no.' Fran stared up at the stately houses lining King Edward Street. 'There, look. Nyebourne.'

'I've got to park first,' said Libby irritably.

By the time the car was parked, some distance from Nyebourne, Fran had obviously thought over what Libby had said.

'I hate to think it, but I suppose you could be right,' she said. 'It would explain a lot about Ian's attitude.'

'Is he just suspicious, or has he got proof?' mused Libby.

'He seems to have kept in touch with DS Stone,' said Fran. 'Perhaps she alerted him?'

'That wouldn't go down well,' said Libby.

'Maybe he suspected something and asked her?'

'Let's just find out what we can and leave it to him to sort it out,' said Libby. 'I just hope Winters doesn't come after us.'

Nyebourne proved to be on the end of a terrace, and obviously had a fairly large extension behind. The entrance hall was spacious and smelt of lavender polish. A smartly-uniformed, middle-aged woman appeared from a doorway behind a curved reception desk and smiled at them.

'Can I help you?'

'We were hoping to see one of your residents,' said Libby.

'Joseph Wilson,' added Fran.

The woman's carefully groomed eyebrows rose. 'My, Joe's popular! You're the third set of visitors he's had in a week!'

'Really?' Fran smiled and Libby envied her *savoir faire*. She was completely thrown.

The woman laughed. 'Oh, perfectly unexceptional. Visitors from his old home.'

'From Heronsbourne?' said Libby, finding her voice. 'Oh, I expect we know them, then.'

'I should think you could go straight up,' the woman said. 'He usually keeps to his room in the mornings.'

'Thank you,' said Fran, looking round vaguely.

'Do you mind if I don't take you up?' asked the woman. 'We're a bit short-staffed. You can go in the lift, or up the stairs. Left-hand corridor, and it's number nine.'

'Not very security conscious,' muttered Fran, as they mounted the wide staircase. 'Reminds me of The Laurels.'

Fran's aunt, from whom she had inherited Coastguard Cottage, had been resident in a similar home.

'More of a nursing home, that was, though,' said Libby.

'True.' Fran shook off unpleasant memories as they stopped outside number nine, complete with nameplate, *Mr Joseph Wilson.*

Libby took a deep breath. 'Here goes.' She knocked.

'Come in,' said a cheerful voice.

They looked at each other and Fran opened the door.

The room was large and light. Two long windows were set in the wall opposite the door, while a television set stood catty-cornered to the right of them, and a sofa and a comfortable-looking armchair were positioned in front of it. To their left, set well back, were a double bed, a chest of drawers, and a wardrobe. The paintwork was fresh, and the curtains and loose covers a muted floral pattern. Getting up from the armchair was an elderly man.

'Hello!' he said, holding out a gnarled hand. 'I don't know you, do I?'

Joe Wilson was small, slightly bent, and almost bald, apart from a ruff of white hair standing up bravely around his head.

'No, Mr Wilson, you don't.' Fran smiled and advanced. 'We're friends of Dan—' she hesitated, realising she didn't know Dan's surname.

'Dan from Heronsbourne?' Joe shook her hand, smiling delightedly. 'How is he? Haven't seen him for ages.'

Libby came forward to shake hands, then looked at Fran for guidance.

'Actually, Mr Wilson, Dan thought you wouldn't mind if we asked you some questions.' Fran's tone was gentle.

'Of course not, dear. What was your name again? Do sit down.'

They introduced themselves.

'Now then.' Joe beamed at them. 'I suppose it's about that Jackie, again, is it?'

Chapter Thirty-three

Wind taken completely from their sails, Fran and Libby could only gape.

Joe cackled. 'There, surprised you, didn't I?'

'You did, rather.' Libby giggled, and Fran frowned at her.

'Oh that's all right, dear,' Joe said to Fran. 'It is funny. Well, not for the poor girl of course. But tell me, what's your interest? Couldn't make out what that Sutcliffe woman wanted.'

'Marjorie Sutcliffe?' asked Fran. 'Did she come to see you?'

'Oh, yes.' Joe grinned wickedly. 'Talked to me as though I was daft. So I played up to her, didn't I? Didn't get nothing out of me.'

Fran and Libby both laughed.

'Actually,' said Libby, 'we ought to tell you why we're here.'

'That's the idea, gal,' said Joe, sounding like Hetty.

Between them, they explained, more or less, why they had come.

'And the police don't seem to know how Jackie managed to rent your lovely cottage either,' Libby finished up. 'So, as we know a lot of people in Heronsbourne, we thought we'd ask. But it looks as though you've already been asked.'

'Yes, dear. But that Sutcliffe woman – never trusted her for a minute. And the other one . . .' He looked thoughtful. 'Couldn't make him out at all.'

'Who was it?' asked Libby.

'No idea, gal.' Joe looked up. 'Big bloke. Said he was from the solicitors. 'Course, he wasn't. He thought I was daft, too.' He cackled again, loudly. 'Here, shall we have some tea?' He got up and pressed a bell on the wall. 'This is something like, this is. Service all the way.'

'It's a lovely room,' said Fran, looking round.

'Young Dan and Emily got me in here. Em comes by now and then.'

There was a brief knock on the door, and a pretty young woman with a lot of dark, curly hair peered in.

'Tea for three, Joe?' she asked.

'Yes please, Sandy.' He beamed at her and she disappeared. 'Five-star service, it is.'

'I can see that,' said Libby. 'Are you happy here?'

'Happy as Larry, gal. People to talk to when I want, all me meals cooked, sheets changed by someone else. And no struggling with them darned bottle tops.'

'So this man – what exactly did he want?' asked Fran.

'Wanted to know who'd set young Jackie up in my house. Said it was something to do with the agreement or something. So I just said my solicitors did it all. Same as I said to the Sutcliffe woman. Truth is, I never did know much. My solicitors really did do it all, and paid the rent into my account an' all.'

'You never knew Jackie, then?' said Libby.

'Never even knew her name.' Joe shook his head. 'As I said, solicitors did it all.'

Another brief knock heralded Sandy pushing a trolley loaded with a teapot, cups, milk, a sugar bowl and a three-tiered cake stand. She grinned at Libby and Fran.

'We spoil him,' she said, and hurried out of the room.

'See? Five-star service,' said Joe again and cackled.

'Now, why do you trust us?' asked Fran, as Libby poured tea.

Joe cocked his head on one side. 'Know who you are, of course.'

'But you asked us . . .' said Libby.

'Wanted to make sure.' He took a cup and winked over the rim. 'Young Em, it was. She rang.'

Libby and Fran both sighed.

'Should have known,' said Fran.

'This bloke,' said Libby. 'What solicitors did he say he came from?'

'He didn't. I think he thought I'd reckon he came from mine, so I asked him direct. "From Asquiths?" I said. "Mr Gorman didn't tell me." 'Course, he couldn't really say anything to that, so he waffled. Very smart bloke, he was.'

'And what exactly did Marjorie Sutcliffe want?' asked Fran.

'What I knew about this Jackie. As I said, I just told her I didn't know nothing, the solicitors did it all. Money came in regular, that's all I worried about.'

Joe slurped his tea and took a cake. 'Help yourselves,' he said. 'Tell you what,' he said, after a moment's eating. 'You go and ask Mr Gorman at Asquiths. Police should have gone already, shouldn't they?'

'That's what we thought,' said Libby. 'You sure you don't mind?'

'Gor love you, 'course not. I want to know, too. 'Specially if she was up to no good.'

Libby leant back on the sofa and stretched out her legs. 'We don't think she was actually a criminal,' she said.

'But there's a question of blackmail,' said Fran.

Joe pulled a face. 'Nasty, that is.'

'It is.'

Joe put down his cup. 'Listen, I'll give Asquiths a ring right away, and you can go and see them when you like.'

'Where are they?' asked Libby, feeling too comfortable to move.

'Here in Nethergate. Up the top of the town.'

'Near the station?' asked Fran.

'That's it. You from round here?' Joe screwed up his gnome-like face in query.

'Harbour Street,' said Fran. 'My husband's got a gallery, and we live just along from there.'

'I know it!' said Joe delightedly. 'I'll have to pop in when I go for me walk!'

230

'Oh, do!' said Fran smiling back.

'What about you, gal?' Joe turned to Libby.

'Steeple Martin,' said Libby. 'Not quite within walking distance, but I could always come and pick you up. You'd get on well with my mother-in-law.'

Joe cackled again and went to the chest of drawers, where Libby noticed for the first time there was a phone and a notepad.

'We don't want to tire him out,' said Fran, putting her cup back on the trolley.

Libby grinned. 'He's thoroughly enjoying himself. I like Joe.'

Fran grinned back. 'So do I.'

Joe spoke into the phone for a few minutes, then turned back. 'Got driving licences with you?'

'Yes,' they both said.

'Right,' he said. 'That's you all set.' He sat back in his armchair. 'Now, you've got to promise me you'll tell me all about it.' He frowned. 'Don't like the idea of my little cottage being mixed up in murder.'

'How long had you been there?' asked Libby.

'Going on sixty years. My and my missus moved in when we got married.' He looked wistful for a minute. 'And I remember you taking that cat.' He nodded at Fran.

'Dan said you did. He lives with me now. You can see him if you come and visit.'

Joe nodded. 'Sad old business that was.'

They both agreed, then Fran stood up. 'We'd better get on,' she said. 'Leave you in peace.'

'Come again,' said Joe, getting up again. 'Lovely to have new company. And I'll be down to visit.'

'Well,' said Libby, as they walked back to the car, 'that was instructive and very pleasant.'

'It was,' agreed Fran. 'When are we going to Asquiths?'

'I was thinking about that,' said Libby. 'I think we ought to tell Ian first. After all, it's news he needs to hear.'

'He might stop us going, though,' said Fran.

'We could tell him literally on the doorstep. Say we've got an appointment.'

'All right,' Fran nodded, as Libby unlocked the car. 'Now?'

'Might as well,' said Libby.

Libby drove to the top of the town, parked in the station car park, and realised that neither of them knew where Asquiths actually was.

'Let's go in and ask in the café,' suggested Fran.

Sheila smiled in recognition as they came in.

'More questions?' she asked. 'Only Debbie's not here today.'

'No – we wanted to ask you if you knew where a firm of solicitors were: Asquiths? We were told it was at the top of the town,' said Libby.

'So it is.' Sheila nodded. 'Hang on while I take this coffee over.'

'At least she's friendly now,' said Libby, as Sheila bustled over to a table in the window and delivered two coffees.

'Now,' she said, as she came back wiping her hands on her apron, 'Asquiths. Couple of them come in here lunchtimes, actually.' She led them back to the door and pointed. 'See that little road running down along the railway line? Just at the bottom there. Big white house. Not far.'

'Thanks, Sheila,' said Fran. 'We'll be back for a sandwich in a bit.'

'Will we?' whispered Libby, as they walked away.

'We'll need lunch by then,' said Fran. 'And she's a very good source of information.'

'Ooh, you're so hard!' mocked Libby.

The road was indeed short, and at the bottom, just as it turned itself into a cul-de-sac, stood a large, double-fronted white Georgian house. On the wall beside the big doors was a brass plate announcing itself as Asquiths and, in stone above the portico, Nethercombe House.

They exchanged surprised glances.

'Named after the town, or the other way round?' whispered Libby.

Fran pressed the old-fashioned ceramic bell, and now one half of the door swung open.

'Good morning,' said Fran, to the slightly droopy youth who lounged against the door jamb. 'Mr Joseph Wilson arranged for us to see a Mr Gorman.'

The youth straightened up. 'Names?' he asked in a bored voice.

'Sarjeant and Wolfe,' said Libby.

The youth nodded and waved a listless arm towards the interior. Taking this as an invitation, they went in. The youth passed them and began to climb the wide staircase.

'I assume we follow,' said Fran, just loudly enough to be heard. The youth paid no attention, but stopped in front of a door at the top.

'People to see you, Mr Gorman,' he said, after barely opening the door.

'Names, Trevor?' issued a rather gritty voice from inside.

'Mrs . . .' began Trevor, and hesitated.

'Mrs Wolfe and Mrs Sarjeant,' said Fran, pushing past him.

'With a "J",' added Libby.

A short man with a straining waistcoat and a surprised expression stood up from behind a rather grand partner's desk.

'Er – good morning, ladies!' he said. 'Won't you sit down?'

They sat in the two red velvet-upholstered chairs in front of the desk, while Mr Gorman resumed his own seat, and leant forward, earnestly clasping his hands in front of him.

'Now, Mr Wilson said you were looking into something on behalf of the police?'

Libby opened her mouth and shut it again.

'There is some confusion about how Jackie Stapleton came to rent Mr Wilson's property in Pedlar's Row, Heronsbourne,' said Fran, perfectly self-possessed.

'Oh.' Mr Gorman still looked surprised. 'There's really no mystery about it. I assumed the police would have already looked into it.'

'They haven't been to see you?' asked Fran.

'Well, no.' Mr Gorman shook his head. 'The tenancy ceased,

obviously, with Miss Stapleton's death. We are waiting to see what Mr Wilson wishes to do with the property, but under the circumstances, we assumed the police would still be – er – occupying the cottage.'

'What about Miss Stapleton's . . . principal, so to speak?' asked Libby, finally finding her voice.

'You mean, how her rent was paid?' Gorman smiled. 'No mystery about that, either. There was a trust fund. Quite legal. She came in to sign all the documents when she first rented the property.'

'A *trust* fund?' Libby was astonished.

'Do you know when it was established?' asked Fran.

'Not off the top of my head,' said Gorman. 'We weren't the lady's solicitors, so we hold no documents other than those relating to the property.'

'Would you be prepared to allow the police to see them?' asked Fran, continuing to astonish Libby.

'Of course.' Gorman stood up, giving his waistcoat a tug. 'Would you like to take them with you?'

'An officer will come and collect them, if you don't mind,' said Fran. Gorman sat down again.

'So there's nothing else you can tell us?' asked Libby finally.

'I'm afraid not,' said Gorman, then hesitated.

'Yes?' prompted Fran.

'Nothing to do with Miss Stapleton, exactly, I'm afraid.' Gorman gave them a deprecating smile. 'It was more . . . I wondered if *you* could help *me*?'

Fran and Libby looked at each other in surprise.

'If we can,' said Fran.

'I'm sure you're aware of a pressure group in Heronsbourne?'

'Save the Marshes?' said Libby.

'Indeed.' Gorman nodded, looking troubled. 'And, incidentally, to save the ruined church—'

'St Cuthbert's,' said Fran.

'And a – er – yew tree, I believe?'

234

'Yes,' said Libby with a smile.

Gorman leant forward over the desk again. 'Originally we were instructed to act for the group. But I'm afraid they were – um – less than businesslike. They wanted us to prevent development of the area. As I'm sure you are aware, there are procedures for these things, and the lady we dealt with was just not prepared to do things properly. We had to decline to act, I'm afraid. We have subsequently been told that another suit has been prepared, properly, by some other residents.' He stopped and stared at his desk. 'Our problem is, this lady was prepared to go to rather extreme lengths. In fact, we understood that Miss Stapleton had been a member of this group but had left, or been asked to leave. She came to us about it.' He looked up. We – myself and my partner – had begun to worry if her death . . . well, not to put too fine a point on it, had something to do with the group?'

Chapter Thirty-four

'Are you talking about Marjorie Sutcliffe?' asked Libby, after a moment.

A faint flush rose on Gorman's rather chubby cheeks.

'It's all right, Mr Gorman,' said Fran. 'As you surmised, we and the police are aware of the group.'

'And we happen to know the people who have launched the new suit. I gather it looks as if there will be little objection,' said Libby.

'Quite right.' Gorman looked relieved. 'We had initially informed Mrs Sutcliffe of this, but she was – shall we say – unnaturally determined.' He lowered his voice. 'Actually, I rather think it was she who asked Miss Stapleton to leave.' He nodded. 'And I believe she's lost a lot of support since then.'

'It seems so,' said Fran. 'Can you tell me exactly what extreme measures she was prepared to use?'

The flush rose to Gorman's cheeks again. 'I'm afraid . . .' he began.

'Never mind, Mr Gorman,' said Libby. 'The police do know about the group and Mrs Sutcliffe, but we'll pass this information on, if you don't mind.'

'Please do.' Gorman looked relieved. 'I hope I've been some help.'

Fran stood up, and Libby scrambled to her feet. 'You've been most helpful, Mr Gorman,' she said. 'We'll inform DCI Connell, and I'm sure an officer will call on you shortly.'

Gorman escorted them to the door and called for Trevor.

'I keep trying to train him,' he sighed, 'but I fear his ambitions do not lie in this direction.'

'By the way,' said Libby, as they waited for Trevor to trudge up the stairs, 'this is a beautiful house.'

'Isn't it?' Gorman became enthusiastic. 'Built by one of the original benefactors of the town, you know. There's a leaflet in reception, if you . . .'

'I'd love to,' said Libby, and shook hands. 'I'll pick one up on the way out.'

'Well,' said Libby, as they began to walk back to Hal and Sal's Place, 'that was interesting.'

'Certainly was.' Fran stopped. 'I think we ought to call Ian before we do anything else. We didn't call him before we went, after all, did we?'

'No.' Libby looked at her friend seriously. 'I think you're right. You or me?'

'I'll do it,' said Fran, fishing out her mobile. 'And on his work number.' She found the number and pressed the screen. 'Yes, Ian – it's me. No – listen. We've got something important to tell you.'

Libby listened while Fran repeated the results of their visits to Joe Wilson and Mr Gorman at Asquiths.

'And I told him you'd send an officer to pick up the documents,' she finished up. 'I didn't think we ought to take them.'

There was an obvious silence from Ian, while Fran raised her eyebrows at Libby. Then came a burst of sound that even Libby could hear. Fran winced.

'Yes, all right. We'll be in the café. No, Hal and Sal's Place by the station, where Jackie worked.' She put the phone away.

'Was he very mad?' asked Libby, as Fran began to march ahead.

'You could hear him, couldn't you? Yes, he was, but luckily, not with us.'

'DI Winters?' hazarded Libby.

'Yes – although he didn't actually say his name. He's sending DS Stone right away and she wants to meet us.'

'In the café,' said Libby, nodding. 'I heard.'

When they arrived at the café it was fuller than it had been earlier, but Sheila showed them to a small table tucked away almost round the corner of the counter.

'Oh, that's good,' said Libby. 'Someone's coming to meet us.'

Sheila raised an eyebrow but didn't ask. 'What can I get you?' she asked instead.

They ordered sandwiches and coffee.

'I wonder what's going to happen?' mused Libby. 'I have the feeling we'll be right out of it now.'

Fran nodded. 'He's got what he wanted from us at last.' She grinned slyly. 'As long as he tells us all about it!'

They were just finishing their sandwiches when the door opened and a young woman with a mass of curly chestnut hair, unsuccessfully tamed with an assortment of combs, entered. She looked round the café, but before Fran or Libby could attract her attention, Sheila had taken her by the arm and drawn her towards the small table.

'Mrs Wolfe and Mrs Sarjeant?' she asked, with a smile of thanks to Sheila.

'Yes.' Libby indicated the third chair they had squeezed in. 'DS Stone?'

'Yes.' She sat down with a sigh and tried to push an errant comb back into place. 'But please, call me Claire. You're friends of DCI Connell's, aren't you?'

'Yes, so please call me Fran,' said Fran.

'And Libby,' said Libby. 'And please tell us what's going on.'

Claire took a deep breath, then looked over her shoulder. 'Do you think I could have some coffee?'

Sheila, who had been keeping a beady eye on their table, responded immediately to Fran's mouthed request.

'Now.' Claire looked from one to the other. 'First of all, where have I got to go to pick up these documents?'

'Just across the road,' said Libby. 'We'll show you when you leave.'

'Right.' Claire smiled up at Sheila as a large mug was put in front of her.

'I hope you don't mind straightforward white coffee,' said Libby, *sotto voce*. 'Sheila doesn't go in for anything else.'

'I'm used to station coffee,' said Claire, taking a grateful sip. 'Anything else is a bonus.' She put the mug down. 'Is this how you get information out of people? By becoming friends with them?'

Fran smiled and Libby laughed.

'More or less,' said Fran. 'Or Libby does, anyway.'

Claire sighed and rubbed a hand over her rosy, slightly freckled face. 'I'm not at all sure what's been going on. The DCI has been passing me odd pieces of info that I know the DI wouldn't take any notice of. They're all important – at least I think they are – but . . . well. So he got this phone call from you a bit earlier, and I was hauled off the job I was doing and told to come straight here.'

'What were you doing?' asked Libby. 'Was it to do with this case?'

'Yes.' Claire looked awkward. 'I can't—'

'No, no,' said Fran hastily. 'Don't tell us. Will you be able to go back to it?'

'I don't know.' She frowned. 'Ian – DCI Connell – said you would tell me what had happened this morning and what I had to pick up.'

'We will, and call him Ian if you like. We always do.'

'Thank you,' said Claire, and Libby reflected that she was the second person that morning who had blushed.

Once again, Fran launched into a description of the morning's activities. At one point, Claire evinced extreme surprise and opened her mouth to interrupt, but shut it again, and mimed 'carry on.' She was quiet for a long time when Fran finished. Eventually, twirling her coffee mug between her fingers, she shook her head.

'Well, I don't know what I'm supposed to say to all that,' she said at last. She looked from one to the other of her table companions. 'What do you think?'

'What we think doesn't matter,' said Libby. 'Presumably Ian knows what he's going to do.'

'Yes.' Claire sighed again. 'It's all going to get very uncomfortable.'

'To say the least,' said Fran. 'Now, do you want us to go over anything you need to say to Mr Gorman?'

'Yes, please.' Claire took her standard issue tablet out of her shoulder bag. 'You know, I'd really rather stick to my old black notebook, but this is the way forward. Easier to share info, apparently.' She suddenly grinned. 'Makes me sound like a dinosaur, doesn't it?'

'Join the club,' sighed Libby.

Between them, they went over the entire conversation with Gorman, adding in the information Joe Wilson had given them, while Claire took notes. At the end, Claire sat back and, looking round, signalled to Sheila.

'More coffee?' she asked Fran and Libby.

Sheila took the order and left the three of them looking at one another.

'How much do you know about this case?' Claire asked eventually. 'I gather from Ian it's a fair amount.'

Fran nodded.

'It is,' said Libby. 'Simply because people talk to me – well, us – and we get involved. And we came up with a few nuggets that Ian didn't know. He said it was because he was office-bound and DI Winters was the SIO.'

Claire nodded slowly. 'So I guess I won't be letting any cats out of the bag if I discuss it with you?'

'No, but if you feel uncomfortable . . .' said Libby.

Sheila appeared with three more coffees and swept up the used mugs.

'Do you come here often?' asked Claire, watching her retreating back.

'No, we only came here a week or so ago because Jackie worked here,' said Fran.

Claire smiled at them both. 'And made friends.'

'I suppose so.' Libby smiled back.

'You know Rachel Trent, don't you?'

'Yes. She comes by for a cup of tea now and than,' said Libby.

Claire nodded. 'She's a friend of mine. So, you see, I know quite a lot about you.'

'Now you can see the worst,' said Fran.

'Oh, I wouldn't say that,' said Claire

While they finished their coffee, they chatted about mutual acquaintances in the force, and those individuals involved in the case who Claire had interviewed after information received from Libby and Fran. Then Claire stood up and stretched her back.

'I'd better get on with this Gorman,' she said. 'Will you show me the way?'

They both escorted her to the door and shook her hands.

'Oh, I'll see you again soon, I'm sure,' she said. 'Thanks for all your help.'

They watched her cross the road and start down towards Nethercombe House.

'What do we think of that, then?' asked Libby, as they collected their belongings and went to the counter to pay.

'All right?' asked Sheila, promptly appearing. 'Nice-looking girl.'

'She is,' said Libby. 'A detective sergeant.'

Sheila nodded wisely. 'Thought as much. Young Debbie'll be mad to miss her!'

Libby and Fran returned to Libby's car.

'Do we need a post-mortem?' asked Fran. 'I assume you do?'

'Yes please,' said Libby, turning into the street. 'But no more coffee. I'm awash.'

Miraculously, there was a space almost opposite Coastguard Cottage on Harbour Street. Fran opened the door to let Libby in, while she went along to the gallery to let Guy know she was home.

'What do we think, then?' asked Libby from the window seat with Balzac.

Fran looked up from lighting the fire. 'I'm sure you're going to tell me.'

'I think Claire's older than yer average DS, don't you?'

'What?' Fran laughed.

'Must be almost the same age as the victim. Or Hannah Barton. Very pretty.'

'Average age for a DS, I'd have thought.' Fran sat back on her heels. 'What's all this about?'

'It occurred to me that Ian's been talking about her a lot.'

'Oh, come on! Because she's been his contact with Winters's team.'

'Hmm,' said Libby, stroking Balzac's ears. 'You've been quite useful, pal,' she told him. 'Breaking the ice for us.'

Fran smiled at her cat. 'And apart from Claire?' she said. 'What, if anything, are we going to do now, or do we think, as we said earlier, we're right out of it?'

'Well, now,' said Libby. 'I think I'd quite like to talk to Marjorie Sutcliffe again. What about you?'

Chapter Thirty-five

'Why particularly?' asked Fran. 'Because of what Gorman said?'

'Yes. She was not only a bit of a pain in the village, but now it seems in the legal world as well.'

'Only in that Asquiths declined to act for her.'

'But it's odd. This attachment to St Cuthbert's and the yew.'

'But absolutely nothing to do with Jackie,' said Fran, getting up from her knees and collapsing into an armchair.

'I know that. But everything she's done seems to have lost her support, which is odd. You'd think she'd realise. She's thrown out two members, Alice and Jackie, for no reason other than prejudice, lost several others including a vicar, and now doesn't seem to have any legal backing either.'

'Although,' said Fran, 'it looks as if the marsh will be saved anyway, thanks to this other legal challenge.'

'Yes. I wonder who's the solicitor behind that?' Libby gazed at Balzac's sleek black head. 'Who do we know?'

'Grimshaw's? Robert Grimshaw?'

'Oh, yes! He's local.' Libby looked up. 'I could ask him.'

'Wouldn't it be better to ask John and Sue? Or even Alice Gedding? Although I don't know why you want to know.'

'No.' Libby grinned at her friend. 'Neither do I. But I do want to know why, despite the fact that Marjorie must know there's another case going on about the marsh, she's still so involved with her own.'

'What does it matter?' asked Fran. 'As I said, it's nothing to do with Jackie. She wasn't killed on the marsh, was she?'

'No, I know. It just intrigues me. She intrigues me. She's such an odd woman.'

'An unpleasant woman, I thought,' said Fran.

'You don't fancy taking a walk round there again, then?' Libby looked hopefully at Fran's discouraging expression. 'No, I can see you don't. Well, I think I will. I'll call John and Sue and see if I can park on their drive tomorrow morning.'

Fran's expression now became positively disapproving.

'Nothing's going to happen to me in the full light of day, is it? Marjorie's hardly likely to attack me. And maybe John or Sue will come exploring with me.'

'I hope one or both of them will,' said Fran, 'but I don't see why you want to go. The woman's obviously, well – not quite normal. You might find she starts pestering you.'

'I'm just intrigued.' Libby looked accusingly at Fran. 'After all, you went on your own.'

'Oh, all right.' Fran sighed. 'You're sure this isn't just because we're going to have to back off?'

Libby made a face. 'Probably. And I do hope Ian puts us in the picture soon.'

'He might not have time,' said Fran. 'I imagine if he's got to haul DI Winters over the coals it's going to stir up a considerable kerfuffle in the ranks, which he'll have to deal with.'

'Mmm.' Libby played idly with Balzac's ears. 'I wonder why he did it?'

'Did what? Didn't follow procedure?'

'And ignored obvious lines of inquiry. Not just to score off Ian, surely?'

'With hindsight, it looks as if he was trying to actually derail the investigation. Send it in the wrong direction.' Fran gazed into the fire. 'But why?'

'Because he's the murderer?' said Libby, looking excited.

Fran laughed. 'I don't think so. But perhaps . . .' she paused. 'Perhaps he *knows* the murderer. Perhaps he's involved in some scam or other . . .'

'Sounds plausible,' said Libby. 'I wonder if we'll ever know? The force might try to hush it up.'

'I would think so, if they could. Wouldn't do public confidence much good.'

'No. And can you just imagine the gutter press?' Libby gave a theatrical shudder. 'Doesn't bear thinking about.'

'It doesn't. And let's just pray *our* names don't get out there this time.'

Libby was just loading the dishwasher after dinner later that evening when she heard Ben answer the door.

'Lib.' He came to the kitchen door, frowning. 'Rachel Trent's here.'

Libby's heart missed a beat. That was exactly what it felt like. 'R–Rachel Trent?'

Ben nodded.

Libby closed the dishwasher door and followed Ben back into the sitting room.

'Rachel!' she said, forcing a smile. 'Haven't seen you for ages.'

'Libby.' Rachel's own smile was tired.

'Sit down.' Ben waved her to the armchair by the fire. 'Would you like something to drink? Coffee? Tea? Something stronger?'

'Oh, I'd love a cup of tea!' said Rachel, subsiding gratefully into the chair. Sidney glared at her, but Rachel had known him too long to be offended.

'So what's the problem?' asked Libby when Ben had disappeared back into the kitchen.

Rachel stared into the fire for a moment.

'You saw Claire this morning, didn't you?'

'Yes. She said you were friends?'

'We are. She worked for some time up in Dartford, but came down here when there was vacancy for a DS. Not ideal.' She sighed.

245

Libby frowned. 'Why?'

'Personal reasons,' said Rachel. 'Still, that's not why I'm here.'

Ben came in with Rachel's tea. 'Shall I go?' he asked.

'No,' said Rachel, and smiled at him. 'I've just been asked to give you a brief outline of what's going on.'

'Really?' Libby's eyebrows rose. 'Who by?'

'The DCI, of course.' Rachel sipped her tea. 'He said – his words – you'd be eaten up with curiosity, so we'd better tell you at least part of it before you dived in again.'

Ben laughed. 'Just about right.'

'That's very kind of him – I think,' said Libby. 'Go on then. We rather gathered, after we'd seen Claire, that he was going to – um – have words with DI Winters.'

'Explode a bomb underneath him would be more accurate,' said Rachel. 'I was there.' She shut her eyes. 'I've never seen anything like it. I thought Ian – sorry, the DCI – was going to have a heart attack.'

'Did DI Winters get a word in?' asked Ben.

'He didn't bother.' Rachel sighed. 'He's claiming a right to silence until he's spoken to a lawyer and his official representative.'

'I can understand that,' said Libby. 'We gathered that he'd been deliberately sending the investigation off track. Is that right?'

Rachel nodded. 'Apparently so. Each aspect of it now has to be torn apart and re-investigated. The workload will be horrendous.'

'And will you lose any suspects?' asked Ben.

'I would imagine so,' said Rachel, sighing and stretching out her legs. 'And some will be trying to make claims against the police. They *will* do it, despite the fact that nothing comes of it.' She shook her head. 'The *damage* it will do!'

'So this was why Ian kept encouraging Fran and me to poke our noses in?' said Libby. 'We'd guessed as much.'

'Yes. And poor Claire was right in the middle.'

'We thought she was rather nice,' said Libby.

'She is.' Rachel sat up. 'And now I'd better go. Ian says he'll be in touch soon, and please don't get into any trouble.'

246

Libby grinned. 'And am I to tell Fran?'

'Yes please. I think he's going to be a bit busy for a few days. Have you still got my number?'

'Yes, in my phone. Shall I put Claire's in there too?'

'Not just yet,' said Rachel, busying herself with her shoulder bag. She stood up. 'Thanks for the tea, Ben. I'll see you both soon.'

'And are you going to stay out of it?' asked Ben, after Rachel had gone.

'Yes. Fran and I had already decided that after we'd seen Gorman and Claire earlier. I am, however, going to go and have a look at the marsh again. I want to see Marjorie Sutcliffe and find out why she's so devoted to it. And before you say anything, that's nothing whatsoever to do with Jackie. I want to have a look at that ruined church, too.'

'But everyone knows you've been involved in the investigation. Won't you still be exposing yourself to   well, to put it mildly – abuse?'

'I don't think so,' said Libby, mentally crossing her fingers. 'I'm going to ask John and Sue to go with me.'

'Make sure you do,' warned Ben. 'And now I think we can have a celebratory drink.'

'Celebratory?'

'Your successful part in Ian's exposé. Whisky?'

On Friday morning, Libby called Fran to tell her what Rachel had said.

'And are you still going to go foraging on the Marsh?' asked Fran.

'Yes – I'm going to call John and Sue right now. Sure you don't want to come?'

'No, thank you. I've had enough of marshes – and golf courses, come to that.'

Sue answered almost as soon as Libby had dialled.

'Oh, I'm sorry, Libby, we're just off to do our weekly shop,' she said. 'We'll be free this afternoon?'

'No, don't worry,' said Libby. 'I'll jus pop down and have a little wander round. May I park on your drive?'

'Of course. Just leave us room to get back in!'

February was treating the world to an almost spring-like day. When Libby arrived in Heronsbourne, she decided, for once, to heed the warnings of her nearest and dearest, and pulled in to the car park next to The Red Lion.

'I'm not stopping, George,' she called as she pushed open the door. 'Just going exploring on the marsh. I'll pop in for a coffee on the way back.'

George appeared with rolled-up shirtsleeves and a wet cloth.

'You still investigating?' he asked.

'No, we're off the case!' said Libby. 'I just wanted a look at the church and the yew. I'm very puzzled as to why yew trees aren't a protected species.'

'Take care, then,' said George. 'You leaving the car here?'

'No, on John and Sue's drive.' Libby waved a hand. 'See you later.'

It was very quiet when she got out of the car at Hobsons. There was a muted, far-off sound of sheep, and the ever-present background orchestra of birdsong, but no human sound at all. She set off across the tussocked ground in the general direction of the church, which she could see on the horizon to her right. She followed what could have been a sheep track, or a rabbit track, for all she knew, and attracted the attention of a couple of lambs, who stared curiously until recalled to their mother's side by anxious bleating.

The track joined a more defined path as she neared the church. She now saw it had a notice board, which she hadn't spotted on her previous visit, attached to what could once have been a fence. The yew stood sentinel beside it, a brooding, dark-green presence. Libby went right up to within a few feet of the fence. The church was really no more than a collection of old stones, although she could see the odd piece of carving here and there.

'What are you doing here?'

The harsh voice made her jump.

'Oh, Mrs Sutcliffe! It's you.' Libby turned, forcing a smile to her face. 'I wanted to come and see the church. And particularly the yew.'

'Why?' Marjorie Sutcliffe, dressed exactly as she had been before, moved a step closer.

'Why shouldn't I?' asked Libby. 'You want to save it, don't you?'

'You'd best keep away.' Marjorie moved even closer. Libby moved further backwards.

'You can't keep it all to yourself,' she said, turning to wave towards the church. 'Or the tree.'

It was the last thing Libby said.

Chapter Thirty-six

Libby found herself lying on her back with Marjorie Sutcliffe bending over her. She tried to manoeuvre herself up onto one elbow, only to find herself pinned down by two strong hands.

'Interfering bitch!' Marjorie's voice, harsh and breathy, sounded above her. She was looking borderline horrified, Libby thought confusedly, then became aware of something else. Someone was shouting, and suddenly, Marjorie was flailing helplessly on the ground beside her.

'Bloody hell,' said George. 'Can you get up, Lib? I daren't let go of this one.'

Libby tried to sit up and failed. Her head was pounding and her vision didn't seem to be quite right. 'No,' she managed to squeak. 'Police.'

'Done.' George was now kneeling on Marjorie's back. 'Called while I was running over.' He took a deep breath. 'Good job you told me where you were going. You all right?'

'No.' Libby closed her eyes. 'Don't feel . . .'

Another voice cut in, shouting. 'George? Everything OK?'

'No!' George shouted back. 'Over here!'

Libby sighed and lost focus.

When she next became aware of her surroundings, she was being propped up against another body.

'It's all right, Libby. It's Gary – Gary Turner. Remember?'

'Gary – yes,' Libby croaked. 'How . . . what? George . . .'

'Yes,' said George. 'I'm here. Don't talk, love.'

Libby's head, though still pounding, was clearing a little. She was still lying, supported by Gary, next to St Cuthbert's yew, and George was sitting next to her, his arms clamped round a subdued Marjorie Sutcliffe. In the distance a police siren was sounding.

'Mustn't drive across the marsh,' Libby muttered, and received a glare from Marjorie. She glared back. 'Why did you hit me?' she asked. There was no reply.

Suddenly, there were more people. Libby registered uniforms, and then DS Claire Stone, looking pale and strained.

'Libby!' she said, kneeling down. 'Are you OK? No – silly question.' She sighed, and felt for Libby's pulse.

Libby grunted a chuckle. 'I'm not dead yet, Claire.'

Claire chuckled back. '

'Ambulance is on its way.'

'Oh – not hospital!' Libby tried to struggle upright, but was prevented by the combined efforts of Gary and Claire.

'Just let them check you over,' said Claire, and turned away to where Marjorie was now on her feet between two uniformed officers.

The paramedics arrived and duly checked Libby over, while Gary and George were questioned by Claire. Libby, feeling considerably better, was assured that there was no lasting damage, not even a concussion, as far as could be seen, though she would need to watch for any symptoms. She managed to stand up, felt appallingly sick for a moment, and took in the rest of her surroundings properly for the first time. Claire returned to her side.

'They're going to put you on a stretcher in the ambulance, just to get you off the marsh,' she said. 'They can't get a wheelchair across. George says to take you to the pub. All right with you? We'll come and talk to you there.'

Libby nodded and decided not to. 'OK,' she said.

The ambulance ride was short but bumpy. She was taken, on the stretcher, in through George's back door.

'Best this way,' said one of the paramedics. 'Lot of people out the front.'

'Oh, dear,' groaned Libby. 'Poor George.'

'Not a bit of it,' said the other paramedic. 'Do his takings a world of good.'

'Oh, great,' said Libby, with a weak smile. 'I think he saved my life.'

She was delivered into the small room at the back of the bar, where George was waiting for her.

'Fine thing to happen on a bright Saturday morning,' he said, grinning.

'Thank you, George,' said Libby, and found herself weeping.

'Hey, now, none of that.' George took her from the arms of the paramedics and put her in the only armchair. 'Can she have a brandy?'

'Just a small one,' said the paramedics in unison, and smiled.

They left and George handed her a brandy goblet. 'Less chance of spilling it out of that,' he said.

Libby wiped her eyes on her cuff. 'Thank you, George,' she said again. 'You saved my life. What happened?'

'Sure you're up for the gory details?'

'Yes.' Libby straightened up. 'Why did that woman hit me? And how come you were there?'

'Well, see,' said George, making himself comfortable on a stool, 'after you'd gone, I went out front to check the cellar doors. We'd had a delivery earlier, and I always go and check afterwards. And I saw the Sutcliffe woman starting down the path towards the marsh. Only she was going sort of cross-country.' He frowned. 'Don't know what made me think – anyway, I decided to follow her.' He shrugged. 'And I'd just got sight of you both, when . . .' He gave her a sheepish smile. 'I couldn't believe it. So I just ran.' He patted his rounded publican's belly. 'Managed to pull her off. Well, you were awake then, weren't you? The young Gary came pounding up. He'd been going down to the flats.'

252

'What for?'

'He's a birdwatcher, young Gary. What do they call them – twitchers? So he comes rushing up to help. Good lad, he is.'

'I must thank him, too,' said Libby.

'Oh, he'll be in soon.' George laughed. 'Like half the bloody village! By the way, do you want me to ring your Ben? Or that Fran?'

'Not yet.' Libby cringed. That was a pleasure she'd happily defer.

There was a knock on the door, and Claire put her head round.

'Up to talking to me, Libby?'

'Of course.' Libby settled herself more comfortably and finished off her brandy.

'I'll just be behind the bar,' said George, sliding off his stool.

'Right,' said Claire, taking his place. 'Can you take me through what happened this morning?'

Libby conscientiously went through everything she'd done since arriving at The Red Lion.

'Why were you here?' asked Claire.

'Fran and I were off the Jackie Stapleton case, but I'd got intrigued about the church and the yew. If there'd still been a petition I'd have signed it, but there's simply a legal challenge going on now. Sutcliffe's Save the Marshes group appears to have dissolved, by all accounts.' She made a face. 'Although Sutcliffe seems to have appointed herself the custodian.'

'Yes.' Claire glanced down at her tablet. 'Did she say anything to you?'

'Called me an interfering bitch.' Libby smiled. 'Not the first time I've been called that.'

'Nothing else?'

'No. I was a bit surprised, because I told her I was just interested in the church and the yew. Particularly the yew. I don't understand why they aren't protected by law.'

'No.' Claire continued to stare at her tablet before sighing and straightening up. 'When was the last time you saw Marjorie Sutcliffe?'

'Couple of weeks ago on the marsh. She wasn't threatening then. Just a bit – odd.'

'Right. Now how about getting you home?'

'My car's still parked in my friends' driveway.'

'Well, you're hardly going to drive yourself home, are you? We'll organise a lift.' She stood up. 'Stay here for a bit.'

George reappeared almost as soon as Claire had gone. 'There's a lot of people out there asking about you,' he said. 'Your mates John and Sue are a bit concerned.'

'Should I see them?' asked Libby. 'Only my car's still at theirs.'

'Can do. I'd see young Gary first, though.'

'Oh, yes please.' Libby smiled.

'And another wee brandy?'

Libby smiled even wider. 'Yes, please.'

She was wondering what had happened to both Gary and the brandy, when the door to the bar opened. Gary came in first, followed, almost inevitably, Libby thought, by Ian.

Ignoring him, Libby held out her hand to Gary.

'Thank you so much, Gary,' she said. 'Thank goodness you were there.'

He took her hand and gave it a squeeze. 'Oh, I didn't really do anything,' he said. 'It was George who was the hero. Glad to see you looking better.' He relinquished her hand and stood aside. 'And now this gentleman wants to speak to you.'

'Yes,' said Libby. 'I thought he might.'

Gary left and Ian sat down on the stool, regarding her gravely.

'Before you start,' said Libby nervously, 'I didn't do anything.'

'I know you didn't,' said Ian with a sigh. 'But you do manage to get yourself into some dangerous spots, don't you?'

'But what was dangerous about going for a walk on the marsh to see an ancient monument?'

'On the face of it, nothing.' Ian leant forward and took the hand Gary had given up. 'But, in an odd sort of way, you've done us a favour.'

'Eh?'

'I'll tell you more when I can,' he said, 'but having Marjorie Sutcliffe in custody is a bonus.'

'I wish it hadn't been at the expense of my head,' said Libby.

'So do I.' To her surprise, Ian leant forward and kissed her cheek. 'Now, I'm not going to say another word, because in a minute your irate partner is going to walk through that door to take you home.'

'Oh, no.' Libby put her head in her hands.

Ian laughed and opened the bar door. 'He's not really mad.'

Libby looked up, just as Ben's comforting arms wrapped round her. 'Not now, I'm not,' he said in a gruff voice.

'I'll leave you to it,' said Ian. 'But I might need to come and see you later, if that's all right?'

They both agreed, and then they were alone.

'Honestly, Ben, it wasn't my fault,' said Libby, feeling unexpectedly tearful again.

'I know. At least four people have explained that to me.' He kissed her. 'And George prevented you from being hurt even more. We must give him a medal.'

'We must. Do you know any more about what happened out there?'

Ben helped her to her feet. 'No, except there was quite a police presence. I expect Ian will tell us.'

'Does Fran know?'

'Of course she does. I had to persuade not to come dashing over.'

Libby gave another shaky smile. 'Can we go out the back door? I don't feel up to facing the mob.'

'Let me tell George.' Ben opened the door to the bar, and muttered to the publican. 'Come on then, invalid.'

Libby dozed most of the way home, and after a rather tentative shower, put her feet up on the sofa and tried to eat a lovingly prepared sandwich. She carried on dozing, coming to the surface several times when various phones signalled either friends, relatives, police, or, maddeningly, reporters, wishing to speak to her. Ben fielded them all, but allowed Adam in at about five o'clock, just in time to share a cup of tea. By this time, Libby was feeling more herself, and demanding to answer phone calls.

When Adam, assured that his mother wasn't going to leave them just yet, had departed to get ready for his evening shift at The Pink Geranium, Ben sat down opposite the sofa with his own mug of tea.

'You look serious.' Libby swung her legs to the floor and sat up. 'What's up?'

'No easy way to say it,' said Ben, 'but Ian's asked me to tell you before he comes round later.'

'Tell me what? Come on, Ben,' Libby said, as he hesitated. 'Tell me the worst.'

'You know you said something about Marjorie being protective?'

'Yes – of the church and the yew. Everybody we talked to said that. But she became rather odd about it. She'd thrown people out, like Alice and Jackie, and people were leaving her group. Mr Gorman said he'd told her to be careful when we saw him yesterday. Was it only yesterday?'

'Yes, it was, but listen, Lib.' Ben put his mug down on the hearth. 'The police decided to have a look round the ruin and the tree while they were there, and she got quite violent apparently.' He looked down at the floor, and then up again. 'And they found something, Lib.'

'What?' asked Libby, already knowing what he was going to say.

'A body.'

Chapter Thirty-seven

'Marjorie killed somebody?' Libby whispered. 'Who?'

'I don't think they knew when Ian told me,' said Ben, coming to sit next to her on the sofa. 'But it was obvious Marjorie knew, even if she hadn't killed him.'

'It was a "him", then? Not another girl?'

'A man, yes. And Ian said she was protecting someone.'

Libby stared into her mug. 'Can I phone Fran?'

Ben sighed. 'I suppose so. But neither of you can do anything. I'd wait until you've seen Ian.'

Libby reluctantly agreed, but fidgeted so much that, in the end, Ben practically forced her to ring her friend.

After expressing horror about the attack and cursing the loss of her own prophetic powers, Fran asked what Libby wanted to do.

'Well, as Ben said, there really isn't anything we can do. I just wondered if we could work out who it might be, somehow.'

'Not much point, surely?' said Fran. 'The police will know soon enough. Perhaps Marjorie will tell them.'

'And who she was protecting? Oh, damn! I wish we'd got a bit closer.'

'Cheated of your big denouement?' Fran sounded amused. 'Just be thankful it wasn't more dramatic.'

After a few more inconclusive guesses, Fran ended the call, saying Sophie had just turned up with a takeaway curry. A little later, Adam arrived with a takeaway from The Pink Geranium, 'courtesy of the boss,' as he said. To her surprise, Libby found she had quite an appetite.

It was after nine o'clock when Ian arrived. He looked tired and stressed.

'Scotch?' offered Ben.

Ian nodded and gave him a weary smile. 'How are you feeling?' he asked Libby.

'Much better, thank you. How are you?' She swung her feet to the ground and leant forward, peering at him.

'Tired.' He loosened his collar. 'I got dropped off, so Edward's coming to collect me. Hope you don't mind?'

Libby shook her head, as Ben delivered Ian's scotch.

'So – the body. I suppose you and Fran have been wondering who it was?' Ian took a large sip of his drink.

'We all have,' said Ben.

Ian paused. 'Vincent Halliday,' he said.

Ben swore and Libby gasped.

'*Halliday*?' repeated Libby.

'Indeed. Buried, somewhat superficially, just the other side of the yew tree. Sutcliffe first swore she didn't know, then admitted she knew it was there, but not who it was.'

'How long had it been there?' asked Libby.

'First guess, but awaiting confirmation, around three weeks.'

'So after Jackie's murder.' Libby frowned. 'So was he the murderer and this was revenge, or did he know who the murderer was?'

'Sadly, a corpse has no way of telling us that,' said Ian, 'and Sutcliffe is being remarkably tight-lipped about it. So at the moment we're reliant on guesswork.'

'Will she talk eventually?' asked Ben.

'I hope so. Meanwhile, it's back to the drawing board.' He smiled at Libby. 'Come on, what's your theory?'

'Give me a minute,' she said. 'Ben – am I allowed a scotch now?'

Ben looked at Ian, who shrugged. 'Only one,' he said and went back to the kitchen.

'Well, there's the obvious link to Jackie,' said Libby. 'What about that trust fund that was supposedly paying her rent?'

'Ah, yes. One of the more obvious links DI Winters ignored.' Ian scowled into his scotch. 'Apparently a perfectly legal fund set up by a solicitor in – wait for it – Felling.'

'Felling? Is that significant?'

'The solicitor in question was an old friend of, believe it or not, Nick Nash.'

Nick Nash was the victim in the last case. Libby almost spilt her newly acquired scotch.

'Which implies that Halliday was also part of that group. So were Fran and I right in thinking that Jackie was one of those "disappearing" girls? What about Sarah Elliot's friend, Jill Stevens?'

'One of the things our overstretched officers have had to do today is interview Sarah. She confirmed that the photograph of Jackie could well be her old friend. She said she was rather surprised no one had been to see her before now.'

'DI Winters again,' said Libby.

'It would appear so.'

'And Sutcliffe didn't admit to knowing Nash?' said Ben.

'But we're pretty sure she did.' Ian finished his scotch and Ben silently took his glass and went to fetch a refill.

'So.' Libby was thoughtful. 'Halliday knew Jackie from twenty years ago – or so – back in St Aldeberge. Did he recognise her when she turned up here?'

'It rather looks as though he did. He found her the cottage in Pedlar's Row and kept paying her rent, via this spurious trust fund. We know he was the person she was most linked with at the golf club. Perhaps she thought she could manipulate him into making sure the golf club turned itself into a party venue.'

'Which didn't work. She'd have been mad,' said Libby.

'And threatened to unmask him there and then,' said Ben.

'That's what it looks like,' said Ian. 'On the face of it, someone else recognised both of them and decided to make sure neither of them talked.'

They all pondered this scenario for a minute.

'What if,' said Libby slowly, 'Halliday knew this other person and threatened blackmail in his turn, perhaps guessing – or knowing – that he or she had murdered Jackie?'

'Given the time between Jackie's murder and the presumed time of Halliday's death, it's a distinct possibility,' said Ian.

'So who?' asked Ben. 'And what about the business of the dodgy leasehold deals, or whatever they were, on the three new houses? Have they got anything to do with it?'

'Never looked into on Winters's watch,' said Ian. 'We wouldn't have known anything about it if it hadn't been for you and Colin and Gerry. Your friend Dotty and her husband were offered the freehold for a very reasonable price sometime after they'd moved in, but we're still going through the paperwork on the other two houses.'

'And was that all down to Halliday, too?' asked Libby.

Ian smiled. 'It was. Again, as far as we can tell – it's taking a long time to unravel – the other two houses were sold cheaply. Oh, not obviously, and maybe it was only the Hughes's. Paul Hughes was apparently into some dodgy dealing in London, and it could be that Halliday was mixed up in it.'

'Didn't someone mention something about that before?' said Libby

'Yes,' said Ian, 'but we've been blundering in the dark for a lot of this time thanks to Winters consistently pointing us in the wrong direction. Of course, he knew which way I wanted to go, and sadly Claire was there to give him the inside track.'

'Claire?' gasped Libby. Ben grunted in disgust.

'Oh, not willingly or knowingly. She just had to do what her boss wanted. It wasn't until I hauled her in and asked her point blank that she admitted being unhappy about the course the investigation was taking. And again, he knew exactly what was going on behind the scenes. People were reporting your activities to him, which he rather stupidly disregarded. Incidentally,' Ian smiled at Libby, 'we got confirmation of Halliday being part of the St Aldeberge set-up by going to see your friend Connie Barstowe.' He laughed. 'She was not impressed by being interrupted in her Saturday night TV viewing, by all accounts.'

'Golly!' Libby was wide-eyed. 'And all this in one day!'

'In one afternoon and evening, actually,' said Ian. 'Although we were already investigating Winters and his misdirections. But once Sutcliffe attacked you, everything stepped up a gear. At first, we even thought Winters might have killed Halliday himself.'

'Wow,' said Ben. 'And you've been kept out of the action!' he said to Libby.

'After this morning, I'm quite glad of that,' said Libby. 'But, given what you've confirmed so far, with the shenanigans over the houses and all, what about the deeply suspicious Mr Peterson?'

'Who?' said Ben.

'The ex-vicar who lives next door to Dotty,' explained Libby. 'I've been worried about him from the start.'

'We know you have, Lib,' said Ian with a smile, 'and after that report from one of Lewis's guests, we looked into him. And yes, he actually is the ex-minister from the House of The Sacred Flame in the States. A naturalised American, who'd been in charge there for – oh, some ten years at least. All above board. We checked everything.'

'Oh,' said Libby, deflated.

'Why? What were you worried about?' asked Ben.

'I thought he might have been the Reverend Turner in disguise.'

'He'd be mad to come back here, surely?' said Ben.

'I know. It just seemed too good to miss.' Libby sighed. 'But it must be someone from that time, mustn't it?'

'Again, on the face of it, it would seem so,' said Ian. 'But don't forget, Winters himself is now in the frame. We're currently looking into his background to see if he has any links to that time.'

'Of course,' said Ben, looking thoughtful, 'it could be nothing to do with that. It could be someone else – from the golf club, perhaps – who was involved in shady property deals, the building company, or the cheap houses, who had a relationship with Jackie that got out of hand. And Halliday knew.'

'I know.' Ian sighed. 'And although everyone there was investigated, it was very superficial. We've now started going back over everything Winters did.'

'Good grief,' said Libby. 'I don't envy you.'

'I don't envy my hordes of officers who are now having to work overtime with a vengeance,' said Ian. 'This is not going to reflect well on the force.'

'No.' Libby and Ben looked at him in sympathy.

There was a tentative knock on the door.

'Edward,' said Ian, standing up. 'No, I'll go. I must try and get some sleep before going back in.'

Edward put his head to say hello, and, after giving Libby a kiss and shaking Ben's hand, Ian took his leave.

'What's the time?' said Libby when the door had closed. 'I must call Fran.'

'Nearly ten,' said Ben. 'Bit late.'

'I'll send a text,' said Libby, and did so.

Almost immediately, her phone rang.

'What's happened?' asked Fran.

As accurately as she could, Libby reported the results of Ian's renewed investigations.

'So it looks,' she said, 'as though we were helpful, and right a lot of the time. But what a waste!'

'Of time and resources,' said Fran. 'And the problem Ian has now, is that all those already questioned will be on their guard.'

'Oh, yes! I didn't think of that. Got any ideas, then?'

'Give me a chance! I shall have to digest it all. I'll ring you in the morning. Are you well enough to go to Hetty's?'

'Of course I am! I've had a Harry meal tonight and a scotch. Fighting fit tomorrow.'

'At least it'll keep you out of mischief,' said Fran, a sentiment shared, Libby knew, by Ben, Ian, and most of her friends.

Chapter Thirty-eight

By the time Libby and Ben arrived at The Manor on Sunday, all the usual suspects had arrived, and all, as Libby had expected, knew what had happened the day before.

'Goes to show what happens gettin' mixed up in murders,' said Flo, sniffing disapprovingly.

'Ian said he'd never have got this far without Libby and Fran,' said Edward, tentatively. He rarely offered an opinion in company.

'Quite right,' grunted Hetty from the Aga.

Libby looked at her in surprise.

'Did yer get anywhere with that home?' asked Lenny, lifting his nose out of his wine glass.

'Oh – yes! Nightingale House – no, it wasn't a care home after all. It was flats,' said Libby. 'Another dead end.'

'So to speak,' said Peter. 'Harry'll be along in a bit. He's opened today for a few bookings, but only a few. He says not to wait.'

In fact, they had barely started on the roast beef when Harry arrived, still in his whites.

'Catch me up, then, mates,' he said sitting down and starting to load his plate with vegetables. 'You better today, flower?'

'Yes, thanks, Harry. It was a lovely meal last night.'

'Thought you was bashed up yesterday,' said Flo.

'Hand-delivered, Flo,' said Ben with a grin.

'We do takeaways, Flo,' said Harry. 'Even to you.'

'Veggie muck,' said Flo, with another disapproving sniff.

'Tell me all about it, then,' Harry went on. 'What have I missed?'

'Not much,' said Ben, sending a warning glare across the table, while Peter gave his beloved a dig in the ribs. The conversation turned elsewhere.

Later, as Ben, Libby and Edward walked down the drive with Peter and Harry, Harry said: 'I gather I was being warned to shut up back there? What was so terrible?'

'Just a lot of it is definitely not in the public domain,' said Libby, 'and Flo would have had a field day.'

'So are you going to enlighten me over the traditional Sunday afternoon alcohol?' asked Harry, as Peter opened their front door.

'Of course.' Libby smiled at him, settled into her usual sagging chintz armchair and began her story.

'So was my spying on the golf club blokes any use?' asked Harry at the end.

'Yes, it was.' Libby smiled reflectively. 'Scared one of them to bits.'

'Really?' Harry looked pleased.

'He realised he'd been overheard by a friend of the police.'

'Did he give anything away?'

Libby thought about it. 'We-ell—'

'You said he didn't,' said Ben.

'No.' Libby frowned. 'But . . .'

'Oh, here she goes,' said Peter. 'Stop it, you old trout. You're Off The Case, remember?'

'Sorry.' Libby grinned. 'I'll stop now.'

But nobody could stop Libby thinking.

Overnight, the thoughts engendered by Harry's question percolated in Libby's brain. Nothing more had been heard from Ian since Saturday night, and despite scouring the media, online, on television, and in print, nothing seemed to have got out about the Heronsbourne murders. On Monday morning, Libby decided to go down and see Lewis and Edie.

'What are you up to now?' asked Ben in a defeated fashion.

'Just going to ask Lewis a question or two. I'll be quite safe, don't worry.'

'Shall I come with you?'

Surprised, Libby laughed. 'To protect me from the Osbourne-Walkers? No, darling, I'll be fine. And I'm quite recovered now.'

Her car, having been retrieved and brought back by the police, had to be turned round and, naturally, have the seat and mirror adjusted, Libby being somewhat shorter than the average police officer.

She could not repress a slight shudder as she drove past The Red Lion, but despite February having reverted to its normal grey and dismal self, she felt reasonably optimistic as she approached the turning for Creekmarsh. To her surprise, Lewis was waiting for her outside the kitchen door.

He grinned as she got out of the car.

'Ben called,' he said. 'We've all got to keep an eye on you since your misadventures on Saturday.'

'Oh, you've heard about that?' said Libby.

''Course we have. Police have been all over the place. Not just on your account, apparently.'

'No. Fran and I are off the case and they're investigating more aspects . . .'

'Like another body?' said Lewis. 'Come on. Mum's already made the tea.'

Edie enfolded Libby in a bear hug.

'You got to take care of yourself, lovie,' she said. 'I've told you before.'

'I know, I know.' Libby kissed her cheek. 'Can't get into trouble here though, can I?'

'What did you want to talk to me about?' Lewis asked, when they were all sitting at the kitchen table with large mugs of builder's tea, Edie's speciality, in front of them.

'That chap you introduced me to,' said Libby.

'Martin?' Lewis's eyebrows rose. 'What about him?'

'Edie.' Libby turned to look across the table. 'Why did you say "watch him"?'

Edie held her gaze for a moment, before dropping her eyes.

'Mum?' Lewis said sharply. 'What did you mean?'

Edie looked up. 'Sorry, love,' she said. 'That family's never been no good.'

Mouths open, Lewis and Libby exchanged bemused looks.

'His dad,' she went on, 'was one o' the biggest crooks in the East End. Fingers in all sorts o' pies.'

'But he was captain of the golf club!' said Lewis.

'Reckon he bought his way in,' said Edie. 'And a bit funny the boy followin' on, isn't it?'

'You didn't know anything specific about him, then?' said Libby.

'No.' Edie's eyes slid sideways. 'Shifty bloke, though.'

'Oh.' Libby sighed and gave Lewis a rueful smile. 'I thought I'd got something there.'

'You said you were off the case.'

'We are. It was just . . . oh, I don't know. I can't leave well alone, I suppose.'

'Who are the police looking at, then?' asked Edie.

'I don't actually know,' confessed Libby. 'They're re-interviewing a lot of people, I think.'

'It was because Harry overheard Martin and Doug Saville talking that you wanted to speak to him, wasn't it?' Lewis sat back and surveyed her. 'Putting two and two together?'

'Yes.'

'And that was when you heard about the treasurer taking Jackie to the golf club?'

'Yes.'

'And now he's dead. It is him, isn't it?'

'Yes. Vince Halliday.'

'So it wasn't him that killed her.'

'Can't imagine so. That would mean there were two killers.'

'What else have they found out?'

'I can't tell you that,' said Libby. 'I don't know much, anyway.'

'So basically,' said Lewis, 'it's someone who knew them both and had the opportunity in both cases.'

'And the motive,' said Libby. 'I just wondered if the golf club committee had a motive.'

'No one would kill Jackie just for making a fuss about the club,' said Lewis. 'It was someone who knew her before.'

'And Vince did,' said Libby. 'Whoops! Shouldn't have said that.'

'So someone who knew them *both* before.' Lewis frowned.

'Exactly. Any ideas?'

'Was it something to do with all that business about the girls who disappeared? And that bloke who was murdered before?'

'Yes. If you mean Nick Nash. Oh, Lord! I shouldn't be saying that.'

'I won't tell!' Lewis grinned. 'But it means someone recognised them both.'

'Yes, we'd got that far, thanks!'

Edie laughed. 'Keep going, gal! You'll get there.'

'I don't think I will, Edie, but thank you.' Libby stood up. 'Thanks for the tea. I'll go and have a little walk down by Dotty's house to clear my head and then go home.'

Libby drove back towards the golf course and turned down the track leading to Dotty's house. As she parked, Dotty appeared at her doorway.

'Coming in for a cuppa?' she called.

'No, thanks, Dotty. I'm going to take a walk down by the sea.' Libby walked over to her. 'Just one thing, though. Have the police asked you about your freehold? You know – when you bought it?'

Dotty immediately became serious. 'Yes, they have.' She moved nearer to Libby and lowered her voice. 'There was something funny about it, apparently. We're all legal, though, luckily, but I'm not sure about Sally and Paul next door. She looked over her shoulder. 'Sally's already left – gone back to London, I expect – and Paul's hardly been seen. Police have been in there.' She shook her head. 'Do you know what it's about?'

'Only that I heard there was something odd about their lease from Colin and Gerry – you know.'

'Oh, yes. Nice boys, they seem.'

Libby suppressed a grin at this description, which she would pass on at the earliest opportunity. 'What about your other neighbour?'

'Haven't seen him at all,' said Dotty. 'Not that we see much of him at the best of times.'

'Oh, well, good luck,' said Libby. 'I'll pop in on my way back.'

'You do that,' said Dotty, giving her a pat on the shoulder.

Libby walked on towards the sea. She couldn't see over on to the golf course, and reflected how concealed this path was. And how easy it could have been for someone to come down here to meet Jackie. Especially at night. She sighed. The most obvious suspect, in the light of all the recent investigations, would have been Vince Halliday, but now he was dead, who could it have been? She realised she had been pinning her hopes on Martin Harris, but there was no evidence, apart from his desire to keep the golf club both open and free from suspicion. But . . .

She suddenly stopped dead. Harris knew Vince. He – apparently – came from a criminal background. Could he have known both Vince and Jackie back in St Aldeberge? He was the right age.

Her heart thumping, she turned round to retrace her steps, feeling a little shaky.

'Good afternoon,' said a voice.

Chapter Thirty-nine

The man in front of her was tall and grey-haired, with a small beard.

'Good afternoon,' muttered Libby and went to pass him. He moved swiftly into her path.

'Mrs Sarjeant, I presume?' The voice was smooth, cultured. 'I believe we have friends in common.'

'We – we have?' her breathing was coming faster, now. 'I don't think we've met?'

'No, I don't think we have.'

Libby tried once again to pass him. 'Excuse me,' she said, from a very dry mouth, 'my friends are expecting me.'

'Ah, yes. They'll be in a very good position to say the last time they saw you was walking towards the sea.' He was smiling at her now.

'The last—' Libby swallowed, suddenly very frightened.

'Marjorie Sutcliffe didn't make a very good job, of it, did she?'

Now he had hold of her arms, and she felt oddly weak.

'Who are you?' she whispered.

'I wondered when you'd ask.' He swung her round and captured her arms behind her. 'Come, my dear. This won't take long.'

He was walking her back towards the sea. She stumbled and he pulled her roughly to her feet.

Think, Libby, she told herself. *What can you do?* Stopping suddenly, she kicked out viciously behind her. Her foot connected with thin air and he laughed.

'No, my dear, that won't work. I think you have to accept that your nasty inquisitive little ways have come to an end.'

They were almost at the beach now. Libby prayed to a God she didn't believe in that someone would be taking an afternoon stroll.

And someone, God or not, heard her.

'Mr Peterson!' called the voice. 'We were looking for you.'

'It was your friend Lewis, actually,' said DS Rachel Trent as they sat in Dotty and Eddy's living room. Libby was still shaking, and Dotty had wrapped a big pink throw round her shoulders, while Eddy was busy making tea. 'He called us and told us where you were going. He said he was worried, although he didn't actually know why.'

'So then they called us,' said Dotty, nodding at Rachel, and we said where you'd gone.'

'H-he said it would be th-the last time,' Libby managed.

'Well, it wasn't, was it?' Rachel smiled. 'And aren't you glad that your earlier suspicions were right all along?'

'He was Turner!' said Libby.

'He was indeed,' said Rachel and, to Dotty, 'I'm sure Libby will tell you all about it soon.'

Eddy handed Libby a mug of tea, which she had to hold very carefully in order not to spill it.

'Now, when you've drunk your tea,' said Rachel, 'we'll run you home and someone will drive your car back for you.'

'Again!' said Libby, with a shaky laugh.

'Just don't make a habit of it,' said Rachel.

Libby was unprepared for her reception committee. Not only was Ben waiting outside number seventeen, but so were Harry, Peter, Hetty, Colin, Gerry, and Adam.

They all crowded round as Rachel ushered her out of the police car.

'I think she needs to be on her own for a bit,' said Rachel, smiling as Ben enfolded Libby in a gentle hug.

'We just wanted to see that she was all right,' said Harry. 'Hello, Rachel! Haven't seen you for ages.'

'Oh, you'll see a bit more of me, soon,' said Rachel as Ben, Hetty, and Adam went inside. 'I'm sure Ben will let you know when she's receiving. Why don't you all go to the pub?'

'Good idea,' said Harry. 'Come along, gang.'

Rachel went in to number seventeen.

'Are you going to tell us what happened?' asked Adam, from his place on the floor by his mother's feet.

'Libby will tell you, and I'm sure DCI Connell will fill in the gaps later on.' Rachel turned to Libby. 'Sure you're all right? Don't hesitate to call the doctor if you feel at all unwell.'

'It's only shock,' said Libby. 'Honestly, Rachel. I'm fine.'

After Rachel had left, her family sat looking at Libby with expressions varying from worry and concern to, oddly, pride.

'It was the Reverend Turner,' she said. 'And I don't know anything else.'

'Why did he attack you?' asked Adam. 'Not that I know much of what's been going on . . .'

'I think he thought I'd worked everything out. I had, some of it, but we'd ruled him out. Him as Godfrey Peterson, anyway.'

Hetty and Adam looked even more puzzled.

'We'll explain another time,' said Ben. 'Mum, will you be all right getting home?'

'I'll walk with her,' said Adam, scrambling to his feet. 'Then I'll go and find the others. Bet they're in the pub.'

'I'll come to the pub, instead,' said Hetty. 'Not going to be left out.'

Ben let them out, then went to sit next to Libby.

'Can you tell me exactly what happened?'

Libby leant against him, and began her story with her visit to Lewis and Edie.

'Apparently, Lewis didn't know why he was worried, he just was.'

'I expect he was remembering last time you went for a walk on your own – what, two days ago?' Ben grinned at her. 'Can't keep out of trouble, can you?'

'But it wasn't my fault! I hadn't even spoken to anyone except Dotty. There's a cloud hanging over me,' Libby finished up gloomily.

'I suppose Dotty didn't tell Peterson where you were?'

'Shouldn't have thought so. Oh, don't!' Libby put her head in her hands. 'Don't tell me I've to suspect them!'

'I doubt it, or Rachel wouldn't have taken you back there, would she?'

'No. Thank goodness for that.' Libby sat up straight. 'So how did he know? Watching out for me with his binoculars?'

'Did he kill Jackie?' asked Ben. 'If so, I bet that's what he did.'

'We don't know, do we?' Libby looked at Ben wide-eyed. 'We don't know anything.'

'Ian will tell us,' said Ben comfortingly. 'Meanwhile, you are going to go to bed for an hour or so. And Harry will have to provide us with another Harry meal later.'

When Libby was allowed downstairs, she immediately called Fran, who had been told not to call by both Guy and Rachel. Fran was uncharacteristically tearful.

'I'm fine,' said Libby. 'The trouble is, we still don't know anything. Not even if Turner/Peterson is the killer.'

'Oh, surely, he must be,' said Fran, sniffing bravely. 'He was going to kill you.' She shuddered audibly.

'Don't!'

They were both quiet.

'Well,' said Libby eventually, 'Ian will tell us. Rachel seemed to think he'll pop by tonight.'

'I doubt if he'll be able to tell you much by then,' said Fran. 'He won't have had time.'

And so it proved.

272

'We haven't got very far,' said Ian, when he arrived just after nine-thirty looking even more tired and harassed than he had before. Ben handed him a scotch.

'We thought as much,' said Libby. 'But have you discovered if Peterson was the killer?'

Ian sighed. 'Oh, yes. For a start we found Jackie's phone in his house. Remember we hadn't found one?'

'No laptop?'

'She'd hardly have had that with her on New Year's Eve,' said Ian.

'Someone took that from the house?'

'We're guessing Halliday,' said Ian.

'Did he kill Halliday too?' asked Ben.

'We think so, but we're having to pull everything apart now.' He sighed even more heavily. 'It looks as if Winters was more involved than we thought, so we're plugging away at him, and Sutcliffe, of course.'

'And the other members of the golf club?'

'They were already being questioned again, but it doesn't look as though any of them were involved.' He smiled at Libby. 'We heard about your suspicions of Martin Harris, but he was guilty of nothing but turning a blind eye to Halliday's manipulating of the sale of the two new houses.'

'So there was something dodgy there,' said Libby.

'There was, and we'd already, thanks to you, uncovered that. The same solicitors who dreamt up Jackie's trust fund were responsible there.'

'Do you think you'll get to the bottom of it all?' asked Libby. 'Are you allowed to question them?'

'Oh, yes. Winters, Sutcliffe, and Peterson are all in custody on a variety of charges. Up before magistrates in the next few days. Hopefully we'll have more evidence, and a good bit more of the story, by then.' He finished his scotch. 'I am now going to go home to bed. I'll let you know when I can tell you more.'

★

273

In fact, it wasn't until the following Monday that Ian sent a text to both Libby and Fran. Both had been following the news assiduously, but very little had been said, other than that arrests had been made.

'What did it say?' asked Ben.

'If we'd like to meet him in The Red Lion he can tell us a bit more. He feels George needs to know too.'

'And your friends over there, and Lewis and Edie?' said Ben.

'I'll text him,' said Libby.

In the end, the entire Steeple Martin contingent, as well as all those involved in Heronsbourne, gathered in The Red Lion that night, and George had stuck up a 'Private Party' notice on the door.

'The others can always go down the road to The Fox,' he said to Libby with a grin.

Ian, on a stool by the bar, faced his audience.

'Now,' he said. 'Some of you here will be used to me giving explanations, others won't. Well, let me tell you – I'm not supposed to.'

There was a ripple of laughter.

'This time, however, it's even more serious, as I'm already in hot water.'

There was an audible rumble of distress at this.

'But to start at the beginning, the police were called in when Jackie Stapleton's body was found on the golf course. I don't propose to go through the entire police procedure as it was almost fatally flawed, so I shall go back to the motives in the case.'

'That vicar?' said somebody.

'Yes, that vicar. Do you want me to start there?'

There was a chorus of assent, and Fran and Libby exchanged glances.

'Last November we investigated the murder of a man called Nick Nash from St Aldeberge. He had been involved some twenty years before with the Reverend Turner in some very unpleasant child abuse cases. Both he and Turner had disappeared abroad, but Nash came back. We never traced Turner, who, we have now learnt, went to America and founded a small church called the House of the

Sacred Flame. He decided to come back – why, we have yet to learn – under the name of Godfrey Peterson.'

There were more rustlings among the audience.

'It now appears that Vincent Halliday had also been a member of that infamous St Aldeberge club.' Ian smiled at Patti. 'Sorry, Patti.'

All eyes turned Patti-wards.

'He was persuaded to sell one of the new houses to Turner, on pain of his history being revealed. We believe there was a certain amount of cross-pollination –' Ian noticed frowns among his audience – 'as in that each could reveal a lot about the other.

'And then, Turner joined the Save the Marshes group and saw Jackie. And recognised her, just as she recognised him.'

'I was right,' whispered Libby.

'In the meantime, Jackie, who had been one of the girls involved in the original St Aldeberge business, had met and recognised Vincent Halliday while she was living and working in Nethergate. She, in turn, blackmailed him, first to take her to the golf club events, and then, somehow – we haven't quite got to the bottom of this – to organise her tenancy of Mr Wilson's cottage in Pedlar's Row.'

This provoked more response.

'Was he payin' her rent?' called one voice.

'Yes, he was. So there Jackie was, a double threat. And because of her refusal to stay out of anything that was going on in the area, a loose cannon. We believe, although he hasn't admitted it, that she went to see Turner and threatened him. And on New Year's Eve, as his neighbours did,' with a nod to Dotty and Eddy, 'he watched the fireworks on the beach from his balcony. And spotted Jackie.'

'And went down to the beach by the path,' said Libby.

'No doubt he will tell us, in time.'

'What about the Halliday bloke. He kill him too?' asked Eddy.

'We think, on evidence supplied by DI Winters, whom he told, Halliday knew or guessed that Turner had killed Jackie, and threatened him. Somehow, Marjorie Sutcliffe was inveigled into helping bury the body by the yew tree. She had developed quite a crush on the Reverend when he joined her group, so was probably easy to manipulate.'

'Always said she was mad,' muttered someone.

'And she, of course, was so determined to protect her reverend and her yew, that she attacked Libby, here.'

Nods and smiles in Libby's direction.

'What about this policeman, then?' asked Edie.

More agreement.

'I'm going to ask for guesses,' said Ian with a grin.

'Keep quiet,' said Ben to Libby and Fran. 'Let them work it out.'

And of course, someone did.

'Was he part of that St Aldeberge set-up, too?' said John.

'He was indeed,' said Ian, amid a positive shout of approval.

'So he weren't even really lookin' into it?' asked someone.

'Not really,' said Ian. 'And now I'll tell you why I'm in trouble.'

There was immediate quiet.

'In the past, as I'm sure some of you know, I've been assisted in investigations by Libby Sarjeant and Fran Wolfe.'

All eyes now turned their way.

'This time I asked them to investigate the aspects of the case I felt had been ignored by DI Winters. And went against all the rules.' He paused and took a drink. 'So now, I'm under investigation too.'

This time, the roar was of indignation.

'Thank you,' said Ian when the noise died down. 'But although in the end we have apprehended the killer, and others, we do have to abide by the rules, and I have to take my medicine. But,' he stood up and took a breath, 'I'm glad we did it, and I felt you, who have been at the centre of the whole thing, deserved to know the truth. So, thank you for your help and your understanding, ladies and gentlemen.'

There was a spontaneous outbreak of applause and cheering at the end of this remarkable speech. Libby wiped her eyes and Fran sniffed into a tissue.

Ian managed to make his way towards them, beckoning, as he did so, to someone over by the door. Rachel Trent and Claire Stone sidled up somewhat sheepishly.

'That was very brave,' said Libby, giving him a kiss on the cheek.

'And are you really under investigation?' asked Fran.

'Oh, yes.' He pulled a face. 'These two shouldn't be here at all.'

'But we're on the side of right,' said Rachel with a grin. 'We're standing up for him.'

'So's everybody else,' said Claire, 'especially all the officers on my team, who are furious.'

'With Winters?' said Guy.

Claire nodded.

'You've managed to keep it out of the press so far?' said Edward.

'Only a matter of time,' said Ian. 'Never mind. I could do with a good long rest.'

He spent the rest of the evening refusing drinks and supplying his own support team with more.

George came over to Libby towards closing time.

'Well, me old china,' he said, 'can't say it wasn't interesting.'

'That's one word for it,' she said with a smile. 'And thank you, George. You were a great help. And you saved my life.'

'Nah. She wouldn't have killed you.' George gave her a quick hug. 'Now don't be a stranger – you hear?'

'Well, said Ian, standing up and surveying the Steeple Martin regulars, 'I'm off to my virtuous couch. Thank you, Edward, for driving.'

There was a chorus of protest.

'No, I must. I'm up before the Chief Super in the morning.' Ian kissed both Libby and Fran. 'Thanks, everybody. I might see you on Wednesday, I might not.'

'Come on, then,' said Ben into the little silence that had fallen following Ian and Edward's departure. 'We might as well go too.'

Their own departure was somewhat lengthened by the number

of goodbyes there were to say. When they at last emerged into the car park, Libby shivered.

'Not sure how soon I'll feel like coming back,' she said.

'All depends on how soon someone commits another murder,' said Harry. 'What?' he said innocently, at the predictable outcry.

'Watch out it isn't yours,' said Peter.

Acknowledgements

This book was written during the worst year I, and most of the planet, have experienced. It would never have been written without the encouragement and support of a particular group of writer friends: Sophie Weston, Joanna Maitland, Liz Fielding, Sarah Mallory, Louise Allen, and Janet Gover. Thank you all for keeping me going. Thanks also to my family, Leo, Phillipa, Miles, and Louise, who looked after me in the best possible way, and again, without whom there would have been no book. And of course, to the NHS.

Thanks also go to the estate of the late Dame Ngaio Marsh, which allowed me to use 'The House of the Sacred Flame', the name of a similar institution in her novel *Death in Ecstasy*.

More traditional acknowledgements, thanks to Miles and my friend Margaret Waller for the original idea, my agent, Kate Nash, Toby Jones at Headline for his patience, and my indefatigable editor Greg Rees.

And finally, as always, my apologies to police forces everywhere.